Distant Friends

Distant Friends

stories by
Greg Johnson

Ontario Review Press / Princeton

Most of these stories have previously appeared, often in a slightly altered form,
in the following journals: "Crazy Ladies" and "El Paso" in *Southern Humanities
Review*; "Leavings" and "The Burning" in *Kansas Quarterly*; "Passion Play" in
Greensboro Review; "Grieving" in *Windsor Review*; "The Metamorphosis" and "Dis-
tant Friends" in *Ontario Review*; "Wintering" in *Virginia Quarterly Review*;
"Wildfires" in *Cimarron Review*. "Crazy Ladies" was reprinted in *Prize Stories
1986: The O. Henry Awards* and "The Metamorphosis" in *The Ways We Live Now:
Contemporary Short Fiction from Ontario Review*.

Lyrics from "Free Again" copyright © 1966 by Emanuel Music Corp. Used by
permission.

Cover photo by David Akiba

Publication of this book was made possible in part by a grant from the National
Endowment for the Arts.

Library of Congress Cataloging-in-Publication Data

Johnson, Greg.
        Distant friends : stories / by Greg Johnson.
        Contents: Crazy ladies—Leavings—El Paso—A summer romance—
The burning—Passion play—Grieving—The metamorphosis—
Wintering—Wildfires—Distant friends.
        I. Title.
PS3560.03775D5   1990   813'.54—dc20   90-7384
        ISBN 0-86538-071-6

Typesetting by Backes Graphic Productions
Printed by Princeton University Press

ONTARIO REVIEW PRESS
in association with Persea Books

Distributed by George Braziller, Inc.
60 Madison Ave., New York, NY 10010

—*for* BOB SCHOFIELD

CONTENTS

Distant Friends

Crazy Ladies

E VERY SOUTHERN TOWN had one, and ours was no exception. One year, my sister and I had an after-school routine that included watching the Mouseketeers on TV, holding court in the neighborhood treehouse we'd built, along with several other kids, in a vacant lot down the street, and finally, as dusk began and we knew our mother would soon be calling us to supper, visiting the big ramshackle house where the crazy lady lived. Often she'd be eating her own supper of tuna fish and bean salad, sitting silently across from her bachelor son, John Ray, who was about the same age as our parents. Becky would slither along through the hydrangea bushes, then scrunch down so I could stand on her shoulders and get my eyes and forehead— just barely—over the sill of the Longworths' dining-room window. After a few minutes I'd get down and serve as a footstool for Becky. More often than not we dissolved into a laughter so uncontrollable that we had to race back through the bushes, snapping branches as we went, and then dart around the corner of the house to avoid being caught by John Ray, who sometimes heard us and would jump up from the table, then come fuming out the back door. He never did catch us, and to my knowledge was never quick enough even to discover who we were. Naturally his mother didn't know, and didn't care. But there came a time—that summer afternoon, the year Becky was thirteen and I was eleven—when the crazy lady took her obscene revenge.

For me, that entire summer was puzzling. Our father, the town druggist, had begun keeping unusual hours. We could no longer count on his kindly, slump-shouldered presence at the dinner table, and when he did join us there was a crackling energy in him, a playfulness toward Becky and me that he'd never shown when we were younger. And while our father, a balding and slightly overweight man in his forties, had taken on this sudden, nervous gaiety, our mother underwent an alarming change of her own. Her normally delicate features, framed by fine, wavy auburn hair, had paled to the point of haggardness. There was a new brusqueness in her manner—she scrubbed the house with a grim ferocity, she made loud clattering noises when she worked in the kitchen—and also a certain inattention toward her children, a tendency to focus elsewhere when she talked to us, or to fall into sudden reveries. This bothered me more than it did Becky, for it seemed that even she was changing. In the fall she'd be starting junior high, and she'd begun calling me "Little Brother" (with a slight wrinkling of her nose) and spending long hours alone in her bedroom. All through childhood we'd been inseparable, and Becky had always been called a tomboy by the neighborhood kids, even by our parents; but now she'd started curling her hair and painting her stubby nails, gingerly paging through movie magazines while they dried. What was wrong with everyone? I wanted to ask—but when you're eleven, of course, you can't translate your puzzlement into words. For a long while I stayed bewildered, feeling that the others had received a new set of instructions on how to live, but had forgotten to pass them along to me.

One humid afternoon in August, the telephone rang; from the living room, we could hear our mother snatch up the kitchen extension.

"What?" she said loudly, irritated. "Slow down, Mother, I can't make out—"

At that point she called to us to turn down the TV; from my place on the floor I reached quickly and switched the volume completely off, earning a little groan from Becky. She sat cross-legged on the couch with a towel wrapped tightly around her

head, like a turban. We'd been watching *American Bandstand*.
"*You* turn it up," I said, with the same defiant smirk she'd
begun using on me.
"Hush," Becky whispered, leaning forward. "I think something's wrong with Grandma."
We sat quietly, listening. Our mother's voice had become
shrill, incredulous.
"Why did you let her in?" she cried. "You know she's not
supposed to—"
A long silence. Whenever our mother was interrupted, Becky
and I exchanged a puzzled look.
"Listen, just call John Ray down at the bank. The operator,
Mother—she'll give you the number. Oh, I know you're nerv-
ous, but— Yes, you can if you try. Call John Ray, then go back
in the living room and be nice to her. Give her something to
eat. Or some coffee."
Silently, Becky mouthed the words to me: *the crazy lady.*
I nodded, straining to hear our mother's voice. She sounded
weary.
"All right, I'll call Bert," she said, sighing. "We'll get there as
soon as we can."
When she stopped talking, Becky and I raced into the kitchen.
"What is it, Mama?" Becky asked, excited. "Is it—"
"It's Mrs. Longworth," Mother said. Absent-mindedly, she
fiddled with my shirt collar, then looked over at Becky. "She's
gotten out of the house again, and somehow ended up in your
grandmother's living room." Briefly, she laughed. She shook
her head. "Anyway, I've got to call your father. We'll meet him
over there."
But what had the crazy lady done? we asked. *Why was Grandma
so frightened? Why were we all going over there?* Mother ignored
our questions. Calmly she dialed the pharmacy, setting her jaw
as though preparing to do something distasteful.
Within five minutes we were in the car, making the two-mile
drive to Grandma Howell's. Dad was already there when we
arrived, but he hadn't gone inside.
"Well, what's going on?" Mother asked him. She sounded
angry, as if Dad were to blame for all this.
He looked sheepish, apprehensive. He always perspired heav-

ily, and I noticed the film covering his balding forehead, the large damp circles at his armpits. He wore the pale blue, regulation shirt, with *Denson Pharmacy—Bert Denson, Mgr.* stitched above the pocket, but he'd removed his little black bow tie and opened his collar.

"I just got here," Dad said, helplessly. "I was waiting for you."

Mother made a little *tsk*ing noise, then turned in her precise, determined way and climbed the small grassy hill up to Grandma's porch. Dad followed, looking depressed, and Becky and I scampered alongside, performing our typical duet of questions. *Do you know what's wrong?* Becky asked him. *Why did you wait for us?* I asked. *Is Mother mad at you?* Becky asked. *Are you scared of the crazy lady?* I asked. *Scared to go inside?*

I asked this, of course, because *I* was scared.

Dad only had time to say, uneasily, that Grandma's St. Augustine was getting high again, and I'd have to mow it next Saturday. It was just his way of stalling; he'd begun evading a lot of our questions lately.

The front door was already open, and as we mounted the porch steps I could see Grandma Howell's dim outline from just inside the screen. Then the screen opened and I heard her say, vaguely, "Why, it's Kathy and Bert, and the kids . . ." From inside the room I heard a high, twittering sound, like the cries of a bird.

In the summertime Grandma Howell kept all the shades drawn in her living room; she had an attic fan, and the room was always wonderfully cool. It was furnished modestly, decorated with colorful doilies Grandma knitted for the backs of chairs and the sofa, and with dozens of little knickknacks—gifts from her grandchildren, mostly—set along the mantel of the small fireplace and cluttering the little, spindly-leg tables, and with several uninspired, studiously executed paintings (still lifes, mostly) done by my grandfather, who had died several years before I was born. A typical grandmother's house, I suppose, and through the years it had represented to us kids a sanctuary, a place of quiet wonder and privilege, where we were fed ginger cookies and Kool-Aid, and where Grandma regaled us with stories of her childhood down in Mobile, where her family had been among the most prominent citizens, or of her courtship by that rapscallion, Jacob Howell, who'd brought her northward (that is, to our town—which skirted the northern edge of Alabama) and kept her there. Grandma liked to roll her china-blue eyes, picturing herself as a victim of kidnapping or worse; through the years she refined and elaborated her act to rouse both herself and us to helpless laughter, ending the story by insisting tongue-in-cheek that she'd met, and adjusted to, a fate worse than death. (Grandfather Howell was a postal clerk, later the postmaster, and by all accounts a gentle, kind, rather whimsical figure in the town; it was always clear that Grandma had adored him.) Now, at sixty-one, she looked twenty years younger, the blue eyes still clear as dawn, her figure neat, trim, and erect, her only grandmotherly affectation being the silvery blue hair she wore in a tidy bun. On that day I decided she'd always seemed brave, too, even valorous in her quiet, bustling self-sufficiency, for that afternoon I saw in her eyes for the first time a look of unmitigated fear.

"Yes, come in, come in," she said, still in that vague, airy way, trying to pretend that our visit was a surprise. Then she turned back to the room's dim interior—her head moving stiffly, I thought, as if her neck ached—and said in a polite, tense, hostessy voice: "Why look, Mrs. Longworth, it's my daughter and her family. We were just talking about them."

Grandma Howell nodded, as though agreeing with herself, or encouraging Mrs. Longworth's agreement. The twittering birdlike sound came again.

By now we were all inside, standing awkwardly near the screen. Slowly, our eyes adjusted. On the opposite side of the room, and in the far corner of Grandma's dainty, pale-blue sofa, sat Mrs. Longworth: a tiny, white-haired woman in a pink dress, a brilliant green shawl, and soiled white sneakers, one of whose laces had come untied. The five of us stared, not feeling our rudeness, I suppose, because for the moment Mrs. Longworth seemed unaware of our presence. She kept brushing wispy strands of the bone-white hair from her forehead, though it immediately fell back again; and she would pat her knees briskly with open palms, as if coaxing some invisible child to her lap. It was the first time I had encountered the crazy lady up close, and my wide-eyed scrutiny confirmed certain rumors that had circulated in the town for years—that she wore boys' sneakers, for instance, along with white athletic socks; that her tongue often protruded from her mouth, like a communicant's (as it did now, quivering with a sort of nervous expectancy); and that, most distasteful of all, the woman was unbelievably dirty. Even from across the dimmed room I detected a rank, animal odor, and there was a dark smear—it looked like grease—along one of her fragile cheekbones. The palms and even the backs of her hands were filthy, the tiny nails crusted with grime. Like me, the rest of my family had been stunned into silence at the very sight of her; it was only when her tongue popped back inside her mouth, and she cocked her head to begin that eerie, high-pitched trilling once again, that my mother jerked awake and abruptly stepped forward.

"Mrs. Longworth?" she said loudly, trying to compete with the woman's shrill birdsong. "We haven't met before, but I'm—"

She gave it up. Mrs. Longworth's head moved delicately as she trilled, cocking from side to side as if adjudging the intricate nuances of her melody—which was no melody at all, of course, but only a high, sweet, patternless frenzy of singing. (For it was clear that Mrs. Longworth thought she was singing; her face and eyes, which she still had not turned to us, had the vapid, self-satisfied look of the amateur performer.) She would stop when she was ready to stop. My mother stepped back, then drew Grandma closer. They began a whispered conference.

"How did she get in?" my mother said hoarsely. "Why did you—"

"It happened so fast," Grandma interrupted. Her face had puckered, in an uncharacteristic look of chagrin. "I was outside, watering the shrubs, and suddenly there she was, standing in the grass. Right away I knew who she was, but she looked so— so frail and helpless, just standing there. Then she asked for a glass of iced tea. She asked in a real sweet way, and it was so hot out, and she didn't *act* crazy. But once we got inside . . ."

Grandma's voice trailed away. I saw that her hands were shaking.

"You *know* what happened the last time she got loose," Mother said. She was almost hissing. "Wandered down to the courthouse and started screeching all kinds of things, crazy things, and then started taking off her clothes! In broad daylight! It took four men to restrain her before John Ray finally got there."

Becky whispered, excitedly, "But doesn't he keep her locked up? At school the girls all say—"

"Yes, yes," Mother said impatiently, with a little shushing motion of her hand. "But she manages to get out, somehow. I've never understood why John Ray can't hire someone to stay with her in the daytime, or else have her committed. My Lord," she said, whirling back upon Grandma, "just imagine what could have happened. People like her can get violent, you know."

"Ssh. Kathy, please," Grandma said anxiously. She glanced back at the crazy lady, who had continued trilling to herself, though more softly now. "She isn't like that, really. I don't think she'd hurt anyone. In fact, if you'd heard what she told me—"

"Mother, the woman's crazy!" my mother whispered, hard put to keep her voice down. "You can't pay any attention to what she says."

"What was it?" Becky asked, and though I was afraid to say anything, I seconded her question by vigorously nodding my head.

"Hush up," Mother said, giving a light, warning slap to Becky's shoulder blade, "or I'll send you both outside."

Now my father spoke up. "Listen, Kathy," he said, "we ought to just call John Ray down at the bank. He'll come get her, and that'll be that."

"I've a mind to call the police," Mother said, and I looked at her curiously. She had sounded hurt.

"She hasn't done anything," Dad said gently. "And anyway, it's none of our business."

Grandma pressed her hands together, as if to stop their shaking. "Oh, if you'd heard what she told me, once I brought her inside. I gave her the iced tea, and a little saucer of butter cookies, and for a while she sat there on the sofa, with me right beside her, and she just talked in the sweetest way. Said she was just out for a walk this afternoon, but hadn't realized how hot it was. She said the tea was delicious, and asked what kind I bought. Hers always turned cloudy, she said. And I'd started thinking to myself, This woman isn't crazy at all. She dresses peculiar, yes, and she should bathe more often, but people have just been spreading ugly gossip all these years, exaggerating everything. Anyway, I gave her more tea, and tried to be nice to her. She kept looking around the room, saying how pretty it was. She noticed Jacob's pictures, and couldn't believe he'd done such beautiful work. She asked if I still missed him, like she missed Mr. Longworth, and if I ever got lonesome, or frightened. . . . And it was then that she changed, so suddenly that I couldn't believe my ears. She started talking about John Ray, and saying the most horrible things, but all in that same sweet voice, as if she was just talking about the weather. Oh, Kathy, she said John Ray wanted—wanted to kill her, that he was going to take her into the attic and chop her into little pieces. She said he beats her, and sometimes won't let her eat for days on end, but by then she'd started using her husband's name—you know, mixing up the names. One minute she'd be saying Carl, the next she was back to John Ray. And pretty soon she was just spouting gibberish, and she'd started that crazy singing of hers. She said did I want to hear a song, and that's when I came to phone you. I didn't know what to do—I didn't—"

Tears had filled her eyes. Mother reached out, taking both her hands. "Never mind, you were just being kind to her," she said. "Bert's right, of course—we'll just call John Ray, and that'll be that."

Grandma couldn't speak, but her blue eyes had fixed on my mother's with a frightened, guilty look. It was then that Mrs. Longworth's eerie trilling stopped, and we heard, from the sofa: "Bert's right, of course, we'll just call John Ray. And that'll be that." The voice was sly, insinuating—it had the mocking, faintly malicious tone of a mynah bird.

I looked at Dad. His face had reddened, his mouth had fallen partway open.

"Would you like some more tea?" Grandma asked, in a sweet overdone voice. She inclined her head, graciously, though it was clear that she couldn't bring herself to take another step toward Mrs. Longworth. But the crazy lady didn't seem to mind.

She cocked her head, and at the very moment I feared she would resume her weird singing, she said in a casual, matter-of-fact way, "No thanks, Paulina. I like the tea, but it isn't sweet enough." And she smiled, rather balefully; her teeth looked small and greenish.

Grandma began, "I could add more sugar—"

"Do you have Kool-Aid?" Mrs. Longworth asked. "That's my favorite drink, but my son won't let me have it."

"Yes, I think so," Grandma said, uncertainly. "I'll go and look."

"Red, please," Mrs. Longworth said. "Red's the best."

Grandma hurried back to the kitchen, leaving the rest of us to stare awkwardly at the old woman, while she looked frankly back at us. She had a childlike directness, but her eyes glittered, too, with the wry omniscience of the aged. Particularly when she looked down at Becky and me, her glance seemed full of mischief, as though she were exercising her right to a second childhood. And there was something in her glance that I could only feel as love, born of some intuitive sympathy. Young as I was, I remember sharing Grandma's thought: This woman isn't crazy at all.

For the moment, her attention had fixed on Becky. She held out a dirty, clawlike hand, as though to draw my sister closer by some invisible string.

"You're a pretty girl," she said, in the tone one uses for very young children. "Such pretty hair, and those cute freckles. . . . I used to have freckles, when I was young. *I* was a pretty girl."

She shook her head, as though hard put to say how pretty. "And I had nice dresses, cotton and gingham, all trimmed in lace. I'll bet you like pretty dresses. Your little nose is turned up, just like mine was."

Becky looked spellbound; her face had paled. "Thank you— thank you very much—" she stammered.

"Would you like to have some of the dresses I wore?" the old woman asked. "They're up in the attic, in a special trunk. We'll steal the key from John Ray. The dresses are safe, no bloodstains and none of them ripped. You could wear them to church, or when the young men come calling." She raised one finger of the still-outstretched hand. "But you'd have to bring them back. You couldn't steal them. We'll sneak them back late one night, when John Ray's asleep."

Becky tried to smile. I could see how scared she was, and I stood there hoping Mrs. Longworth wouldn't turn to me. Somehow I felt safer, being a boy.

"I—I don't know— It's real nice of you—" Becky couldn't put her words together.

"And you still have pretty clothes," my mother said suddenly, stepping forward. "That's a lovely shawl, Mrs. Longworth."

The crazy lady glanced down; she pulled the shawl tighter around her shoulders, as though she'd suddenly felt a chill.

"I had a cashmere shawl, pale gray," she said, "that my husband gave me. It was before John Ray was even born. Mr. Longworth went up to Memphis, and afterward he showered me with presents. An opal ring, too. And a set of hair combs. I was a pretty woman, you know. I still wear shawls, but it's not the same. This one's green."

She spoke in a circular, monotonous rhythm, as though reminiscing to herself; as though she'd spoken these words a thousand times. It was a kind of singsong. I thought again of her birdlike trilling.

"Well, it's very pretty," Mother said.

"It's *too* green," the crazy lady said, "but I think it hurts John Ray's eyes. He has weak eyes, you know. When he goes blind, I won't have to wear it."

Grandma came in from the kitchen, carrying a tray with six glasses and a large pitcher of Kool-Aid.

"It's raspberry, Mrs. Longworth," she said as she put the tray on the coffee table. Her hands still shook, and the glasses clattered together. "I hope you like it."

She poured a glass and held it out; Mrs. Longworth grasped it quickly, then took several long gulps. She closed her eyes in bliss. "Oooh!" she cried. "Isn't that good!"

Grandma maintained her brave smile. "Kathy, would you and Bert like—"

"No, Mother. We can't stay long, and Bert has a phone call to make. Don't you, Bert?"

"Yes—right," Dad said awkwardly.

"How about you kids?" Grandma said. She was trying gamely to make all of this appear normal; then, perhaps, it would somehow *be* normal. That was always Grandma's way. But, much as I loved her, I was afraid to join in anything the crazy lady was doing. Like Becky, I stiffly shook my head.

Mrs. Longworth emptied her glass, then held it out to Grandma. "More, please," she said. While Grandma poured, she said (again in that matter-of-fact way): "You might not believe it, but I don't get good Kool-Aid like this. John Ray says it rots my teeth and my brain. I can drink water, or coffee without sugar." She made a face. "And if I don't drink it, John Ray gets mad. Now Carl, he never got mad. But my son is going to cut me with a long knife one of these days, and hide the pieces in the attic, all in separate trunks. When it starts to smell, he'll throw the trunks in the river."

She took the second glass of Kool-Aid that Grandma shakily handed her. Then she sighed, loudly, as if the details of her gruesome demise had become rather tiresome. "My son works in a bank," she said, "and his teeth are big and strong. So he can have sugar. If I try to sneak some, he pinches my arms, or hits me with a newspaper. That hurts, because he rolls it up first and makes me watch. The pinches hurt, too, but not always. He works in a bank, and so he knows all about locks and trunks and vaults. He has a map, so he can find the river when he needs it. I should be able to have red Kool-Aid, and to sing. I used to sing for Carl, and sometimes I sang to John Ray when he was a baby. Now, he's tired of taking care of me. He says, Don't I have a life to live? Don't I?" Again she spoke like a mynah bird, pitching her voice very low. "That's what he says, and that's why he wants to cut me into pieces, and why I have all these bruises on my arms. You want to see them? It's not fair, because my singing is pretty. Carl said I had a prettier voice than Jenny Lind, and he heard her in person when he was a boy. He's dead, though. You want to hear me sing?"

She stopped abruptly, her eyes widened. She waited.

"Would you like some more Kool-Aid?" Grandma asked, helplessly.

"Bert, you and Jamie go back into the kitchen. We'll wait out here with Mrs. Longworth." My mother gestured to her ear, as if holding an invisible telephone.

Dad said, "Come on, sport," and I joined him gladly. I glimpsed Becky's look of envy and longing as we escaped into the dining room, and finally back into Grandma's tiny kitchen.

"What's wrong with her? Why does she say those things?" I asked breathlessly, while Dad fiddled with the slender phone directory. I tugged at his arm, like a much smaller child; my heart was racing. I wore only a T-shirt and short pants, and I remember shifting my weight back and forth, my bare feet unpleasantly chilled by the kitchen linoleum.

"Just simmer down, son," he said, tousling my hair in an absent-minded way. Frowning, he moved his eyes down a column of small print. "Ah, here it is. First National." And he began to dial.

I didn't understand it, but I was on the verge of tears—angry tears. When Dad finished talking with John Ray, his eyes stopped to read the little chalkboard hanging by the phone. "I can't believe it," he said, shaking his head. "It's still there."

Grudgingly, I followed his gaze to the chalkboard, and for the hundredth time read its message, in that antique, elaborate hand: *Paulie, Don't forget Gouda cheese for dinner tonight. I'll be hungry at six o'clock sharp. (Ha ha) Jacob.* If Grandma was out when my grandfather came home for lunch, he would leave her a note on the chalkboard. But he hadn't lived to eat that Gouda cheese—he was stricken at four that afternoon, and died a short while later—and Grandma had insisted that his last message would never be erased. Mother disapproved, saying it was morbid, and more than once I'd seen Grandma's eyes fill with tears as they skimmed across the words yet another time. But she could be stubborn, and the message stayed.

"You'd know it was still there," I said, sniffling, "if you ever came with us to visit Grandma. But you're always gone."

The resentment in my voice surprised us both. My father's clear brown eyes flashed in an instant from anger, to guilt, to sorrow. He shook his head; the gesture had become familiar lately, almost a tic.

"Well, Jamie," he said slowly, licking his lips. "I guess it's time we had a little talk."

And for five or ten minutes he did talk, not quite looking at me, his voice filled with a melancholy dreaminess. He told me how complicated the grown-up world was, and how men and women sometimes hurt each other without wanting to; how they sometimes fell "out of love," without being able to control what was happening. He knew it must sound crazy, but he hoped that someday I would understand. Things were always changing, he said softly, and that was the hardest thing in the world for people to accept. Even my mother hadn't accepted it, not yet; but he hoped that she would, eventually. He hoped she wouldn't make it even harder for all of us.

The speech was commonplace enough, though startling to my young ears. As he spoke I kept thinking of Mrs. Longworth, and how she'd talked of her husband who had died, and how everything changed after that. I felt the cold, sickish beating of my heart inside my slender ribcage.

"But will Mother turn crazy, like Mrs. Longworth?" I asked, imagining myself, in a moment of terrified wonder, turning mean like John Ray. "Is it always the ladies who go crazy?"

Dad looked stymied; nor did I know myself what the question meant. I wouldn't even recall it until decades later, visiting my sister Becky in the hospital, where she was recuperating from a barbiturate overdose after the disappearance of her third husband. It would come back to me, in a boy's timid, faraway voice, like the echo of some terrible prophecy, a family curse. After a moment, though, my father reacted as though I'd said something amusing. Again, he tousled my hair; he smiled wearily.

"No, son," he said gently. "It's not always the ladies. You shouldn't let Mrs. Longworth get to you."

"But she said—"

"She's a crazy old lady, Jamie. She has nothing to do with us —don't pay any attention to what she says."

Hands stuffed in my pockets, one foot rubbing the toe of the other, I stood looking up at him. There were questions I wanted to ask, but I couldn't put them into words; and I somehow knew that he didn't have the answers.

"Now," Dad said, with a false heartiness, "why don't we—"

It was then that the kitchen door swung open, and there was my mother; she looked back and forth between Dad and me, as though she didn't recognize us.

"Honey? What is it?" Dad said, panicked.

"We—we couldn't stop her," Mother began, wildly. "She took off the shawl, then started unbuttoning her dress, that filthy dress—"

Dad crossed to her; he gripped her firmly by the upper arms. "Calm down, Kathy. Now tell me what happened."

My mother was trembling. She said, haltingly, "Mrs. Longworth, she—she said she would show us, prove to us how cruel John Ray was. Before we could say anything, she started undressing. She undid the dress, then slipped it down to her waist. We—we just stared at her. We couldn't believe it. There were bruises, Bert, all over her arms and chest. Big purplish bruises, and welts. . . . And she said, *John Ray did this*, in that little singing voice of hers—"

Dad had already released her arms. He went to the phone and dialed again. For a moment my mother's eyes locked onto mine. I'd never seen her lose her composure before, yet for some reason I was filled with a remarkable calm. From that moment forward, everything was changed between us.

"Oh God," she whispered, grief-stricken. "How I wish Becky hadn't seen."

Dad hung up the phone, then led us back into the living room; he kept one arm draped lightly around Mother's shoulder. John Ray had arrived, and sat on the sofa beside Mrs. Longworth. Her dress and shawl were in place, so it was hard for me to envision the scene my mother had described. Mrs. Longworth sat staring blankly forward, as if her mind had wandered to some distant place. John Ray held one of her hands, and sat talking amiably to Grandma. He was a big-chested man, almost entirely bald, and had teeth that were enormous, white, and perfectly straight. He smiled constantly. He was telling Grandma about all the times his mother had been "naughty," wandering into a department store, or a funeral parlor, or a private home. He hoped she hadn't been too much trouble. He hoped we understood that she meant no harm; that for years she hadn't had the slightest idea what she was doing or saying.

A small, terrible smile had frozen onto Grandma's face. She stood near the front door, her arm around Becky, who looked pale and dazed.

"She—she wasn't any trouble," my mother gasped.

"Oh no, none at all," said Grandma.

There were a few moments of silence, during which the five of us stared at the Longworths, John Ray giving back his imperturbable smile and Mrs. Longworth seeming lost in the corridors of her madness, her mouth slightly ajar, her hand resting limply inside her son's. I tried to picture John Ray beating her, or shouting his threats of a gruesome death. I decided it could not be true.

When the police arrived, neither John Ray nor his mother protested. The officer spoke to Mrs. Longworth by name, and returned a few pleasantries to the smiling John Ray. As he followed them out the door, the officer gave a knowing, barely perceptible look to my father, who nodded in acknowledgment, then turned his attention back to us.

"Well," he said, jovially, "why don't we all go out for an ice-cream sundae?"

Beyond that, I can't remember clearly. I don't believe that anyone, including myself, ever talked about the incident again; there was a tacit assumption between Becky and me that we would not resume our spying on the Longworths, but they continued to be tormented by other kids we knew. I remember feeling, for years afterward, that life had become disappointingly routine. Evidently the police hadn't charged John Ray: he was still working at First National by the time I left home for college. Nor had anything untoward happened to Mrs. Longworth: one night, about three years after wandering into our lives, she died peacefully in her sleep. It was whispered around town that John Ray was wild with grief.

By then, the tensions between my parents had all but vanished; my father's unexplained absences had stopped, my mother no longer seemed angry or depressed. Grandma stayed absorbed in her garden, her knitting, her memories. Becky had plunged headlong into her adolescent social career, and with great effort had attained her obsessive goal: popularity. It seemed that I alone had changed. Violence had failed to erupt, and I became uneasy, tense, and vaguely suspicious. If I could have foreseen what would happen to my sister, I would not have been surprised. Like her, I left the South as soon as I was old enough, relocating in a big, overpopulated city where violence is commonplace. Although I often worry about Becky, and Mother, and even Grandma, I know there is no reason to feel guilty, just as there is no logic to the dream I've had, recurrently, for more than twenty years: a dream in which I open a door to find the three of them perched on a sofa, cocking their heads from side to side, trilling their songs of madness and despair.

Leavings

O N CLAIRE'S FIRST MORNING back in Georgia, she found
a feather lying in the bottom drawer of the squat, smallish
chest—a "chifforobe," her aunt Lillian called it—where Mack
had stored all his things, and at first she didn't react. Slowly
she twirled the feather between her fingers, noting its undi-
minished sheen of pale silver, shading to white at the edges,
and the stem shiny and hard as a thumbnail. A pigeon feather,
preserved for all these years. Sleep-muddled, or perhaps a little
dazed from yesterday's journey—the long flight, the jolting car
trip with Lillian into this lush, dim, unforgettable countryside,
the rather embarrassed reunion with Lillian herself—she merely
gazed at the feather with her mint-green eyes, moved as if to
replace it in the drawer, then abruptly walked to the made-up
bed and dropped the feather inside her purse. She stood there,
neatly dressed, a trim and competent-looking woman of thirty-
six, bathed in the golden, nearly palpable sunlight pouring in
at the white-curtained windows: stood waiting, as if curious
about the reaction that did not come.

   Though it was scarcely eight o'clock, Lillian had their breakfast
already laid. "Did you sleep well?" she said airily when Claire
entered the room, but of course she did not wait for a reply.
She had the brisk, single-minded energy often found in elderly
women of the rural South, her voice a singsong, her movements

insouciant and quick. She arranged the platters of eggs, sausage, toast; she poured grapefruit juice from a pitcher. Claire, standing quietly behind her chair, wanted to begin: "I found a pigeon feather in Mack's drawer. When we were children . . ." But she pictured the furrowed, discouraging stare Lillian had given her last night when, waiting in baggage claim for her luggage, she'd rasped out, "Oh Lillian I'm so sorry." There had been a sickish pause, then that inscrutable wordless look. And then Lillian had asked if she'd had a pleasant journey.

Now Claire said, "Quite well, thank you. This certainly looks delicious."

Lillian sighed. "It's not up to snuff," she said, "but I've been on the phone with that man about the sale. I told him we could have it Sunday, now that you're here to help."

Claire sat, keeping her eyes lowered as she fiddled with her napkin. Lillian's matter-of-fact voice jarred her nerves, though she told herself that her aunt's pragmatism was a healthy sign in an old woman who had lost her lifelong companion and only child, and who was about to be uprooted. Even as a girl she had noted Lillian's air of invincibility, the impression she gave of relentless forward motion. To Claire herself clung a reputation for level-headedness, containment, and for long stretches of her life it seemed she had no nerves. Yet now they jangled. She sat quietly as Lillian, absorbed in buttering her toast, talked of the sale, the professional auctioneer who would drive over from Macon, the work that was in store for herself and Claire during the next few days; more than a decade had passed since their last visit, yet Lillian chatted as though they shared breakfast every morning. It had surprised Claire, at first glance, how little her aunt had changed: still the florid face, set with eyes unexpectedly hard and blue, framed by thinning whitish hair; still the mottled, quivering flesh of her upper arms, exposed by a short-sleeved housedress. She was capable, domineering, superficial, vulnerable, and doomed, Claire thought, knowing that the superficiality was deliberate, Lillian's way of deflecting any move toward intimacy or candor.

Now her aunt glanced at her, with a half-guilty look. "I do thank you, Claire," she said softly, "for taking the trouble to come down."

"I'm glad to help, of course," Claire said. "My only hesitation was—"

"It'll sure relieve my mind, putting all this behind me," Lillian cut in. She was pouring herself another cup of coffee. Claire, her senses sharpened, knew the "all this" meant more than the sale of the nursery and house where Lillian had lived for thirty years, and more than the coming days of upheaval and backbreaking work. Suddenly Claire thought of the pigeon feather—its marvelous plainness, its delicacy. Impulsively she said, "Lillian, I found a feather upstairs that Mack had saved since we were children. One summer he kept a pigeon coop, I'm sure you remember it, and we—" but she broke off, for again Lillian had given her that leveled steely gaze.

"Claire, don't even bother," she said. "I won't ever forgive that boy."

Yet he was not a boy, as Claire had understood many years ago. It was the summer her mother died: she was fourteen, Mack a couple of years older. Though Claire and her mother had always lived in town, and had not seen much of Lillian and Mack, she'd known from the day her mother entered the hospital that she'd end up "out on the farm." That was how her mother referred to Lillian's place, though it was a nursery rather than a farm. "I know your mother never liked me"—these had been Lillian's first words to Claire as they drove home from the funeral. "My own sister, yet," she'd sighed. "I guess it's because I moved out here, became a country girl," and she'd given her quick laugh. Even then Claire had known that Lillian's never having married Mack's father, whoever he was, was the real reason her mother had remained cool toward Lillian through the years. Claire's mother, though good-hearted in her way, had been above all respectable: she'd married a local attorney, had become a regular churchgoer, and after being widowed at an early age had raised her daughter quietly in her small clapboard house near the edge of town. Her sister Lillian, out there in the countryside among all that unchecked greenery, all those cultivated, sickly-bright flowers, was something of an embarrassment.

As for that peculiar son of hers, that Mack: he was not even to be acknowledged.

Yet Claire, once she had settled in and sensed Lillian's attention straying back to the nursery and her current male companion, had been pleased when Mack had taken her under his wing,
as though she were the little sister he'd always wanted. From
the first she'd sensed how lonely his life had been until now—the
nearest farm was half an hour's walk—and she'd passively, if
rather coolly, accepted his affectionate enthusiasm, listened to
his eager monologues, and tried her best to overlook his rather
clumsy, unprepossessing manners and appearance. In later
years she'd often marvelled at how unlike they'd been—Mack
so garrulous, open, artless; Claire so watchful, composed, and
withdrawn. Yet that summer he'd devoted himself to her, and
she'd never felt the lack of other company. He took her on
lengthy tours of the hothouses, naming each flower or seedling
and detailing the care it required; he took her roaming through
Lillian's hilly, verdant acreage ("a gift from some man," Claire's
mother had snapped, when Claire had innocently inquired),
with its bewildering array of kudzu, vines, and mosses, its tower-
ing elms and magnolias; and he let her join in the various "projects" that Mack always had in hand. Out behind the main hot-
house, he had his own small garden, neatly tended rows of
peas, squash, string beans. In an old potting shed he kept and
cared for a mongrel bitch and her three puppies, having found
them all abandoned one day on the oiled road leading into town.
He'd made the dogs comfortable with straw and old blankets,
and each evening made a game with Claire of sneaking out food
from the supper table, usually adding a "dessert" of stale bread
crumbled and mixed with milk. (Lillian, who was tight with her
money and unsentimental about animals, grudgingly allowed
him to keep the dogs when she finally discovered them: even
four years later, when Claire went off to college, all the dogs
were well and thriving under Mack's care.) And there had been,
late that summer, the pigeon coop Mack had built, with Lillian's
reluctant approval, on an edge of the property farthest away
from the nursery.

"Those ugly, smelly old things!" Lillian had cried, when he
brought the half-dozen birds in from town. "You keep that coop
out of my sight, Mack, and out of my customers' sight, too.
That's a good way to scare off business!"

Mack had looked at Claire, and they'd both giggled. They were always giggling together, like much smaller children; though in a way, as Claire sensed at about this time, neither of them had ever been a child.

One day, after the pigeon coop had been in place for several weeks, Claire came home from school to find Mack peering anxiously inside.

"What are you doing, Mack? Is something wrong...?"

The coop was an enormous, complex structure for so few birds: made of two-by-fours and chicken wire, it was seven by nine feet, six feet high, complete with four "windows"—also covered with wire—and both a front and back door. Mack, shirtless and dressed in overalls, was gazing up at one of the pigeons; it was perched quietly near the feeding trays, its eyes closed, set apart from the other five who strutted noisily about the cage.

"He's sick," Mack said, not glancing aside. His hands clasped the side of the coop, fingers curling through the wire holes.

"Are you sure?" Claire asked. She came up beside him, squinting inside. It seemed to her that the bird was simply resting.

"That bird's gonna die," Mack said hoarsely.

Claire glanced at him, alarmed by something in his voice she had detected before, but had not really thought about. It was a childlike, gurgling sound from the back of his throat, the sound of defeat or of a grief beyond tears. Mack was a tall, sturdy, dark-haired boy, and handsome in his way—muscular arms and shoulders, a long well-molded face, green eyes that were thickly lashed. Some people, even his mother, insisted that he was "slow," and it was true he'd quit school long ago, but Claire had never heard him say a foolish thing; he knew about animals and plants, and could work well with his hands. The misapprehension of others probably arose from his childlike moodiness— he was exuberant and gay one minute, and might seem to be choking back tears the next—or from his quick, eager grin, or from the general absence in Mack of cunning, malice, or any sense of the future. It did seem an assumption, somehow, that he would never leave this place, that his days would always be divided between his rambling, boyish pursuits and his being "a help to his mother." Until that day at the pigeon coop, Claire had never questioned any of this. Mack was rare, special, and he loved her; at school she was like the other kids (though perhaps somewhat shyer, more "citified" than most), but at home she was Mack's partner, his playmate, his "perfect friend." For, out of the blue, he had called her that one day, reaching out to touch a whitish-blond strand of her hair.

Now he had begun crying, as Claire watched in horror. He still had not looked at her. In the way he stood there, grasping the chicken wire as though it were a prison wall, gazing through tears at a sickened bird that now seemed—for she still possessed, back then, the ability to see with Mack's eyes—so much more than a bird, and making that pathetic, heartrending noise at the back of his throat: in his posture and grief Claire saw not the momentary fit of a child, but a man's abiding, incommunicable sorrow, sharpened by frustration or longing, wordless and even soundless but for the unashamed gurgling in his throat that was the sound of someone trying to wake from a nightmare, she would later think, grasping for a metaphor; or the sound of a drowning man.

That day she'd had no metaphors, only a sudden coldness in her heart. Stepping back from him, she'd said cautiously: "I've got some homework to do, Mack. I'm sorry about your bird. . . ." It was that moment, the moment she'd said *your bird*, from which she dated her treachery, her becoming part of the great world Mack would never acknowledge or understand. He hadn't answered her, and she'd hurried away from him and the coop, but it turned out that Mack either hadn't grasped what she'd said or hadn't cared. For only a few days later he came into her bedroom, shyly, holding two of the dead bird's feathers in his calloused palm. "Let's always keep them, all right?" he said, holding one out to Claire. "Keep them for as long as we live . . . ?" Claire had taken the feather, intrigued; had twirled it in her fingers. The idea charmed her, and she'd smiled back into her cousin's anxious, shining eyes.

"All right," she said.

Late on Friday afternoon the telephone rang, startling Claire. She and Lillian had been working since dawn, packing boxes, supervising the men who had come for the nursery stock, and after lunch Claire had come into the living room—she couldn't remember why—and had collapsed upon the sofa. Five minutes, she'd thought drowsily. When Lillian appeared at the door to announce that Claire's husband was on the line, she added a censorious smirk. "It's past six o'clock, you know."

Dazed, Claire hurried from the sofa to the oak telephone stand in the hall. She fought past cardboard boxes, grocery bags filled with trash.

"Hello? Jeffrey? What are you—"

"Claire, it's only me," her husband said drily. "I called to see how things were going."

"What? I just woke up—"

"You were sleeping? In the middle of the day?"

"Yes, I took a nap," Claire said, glancing around. She could sense Lillian's presence somewhere behind her, monitoring every word. Or had she picked up an extension?

"But you never take naps," Jeffrey said. Already his voice was peevish. She pictured him on the bar stool, in his typical after-work posture: sleeves rolled up his big arms, fleshy face shadowed by the day's growth of beard, his left hand curled around a double martini. An air of exasperation, defeat. When he returned home, Claire was usually fresh from her bath, scented, and had begun preparing dinner: her talk, her busy movements often revived him.

"I was tired," Claire said. "We've been working since early this morning."

"What about Lillian?" he asked.

"Oh, she's fine. She's holding up better than I am, I think." If Lillian were on the extension, Claire thought, she'd grasp Claire's meaning. Though Jeffrey, of course, did not.

"I told you, Claire. I told you the whole trip was a bad idea, that too much time had passed—"

"I wanted to come back, Jeff."

"And anyway, it's obvious she doesn't need you."

"She *does*, Jeffrey. And it's not just that. I want to be here."

"Claire, I don't—"

"I used to live here, remember? It's all being dismantled now, and I can't just ignore it."

Jeffrey paused, stymied. She heard the clink of ice cubes, a thousand miles away, as he gulped the martini down. She wondered how many it would take, with Jeff alone in the house. She knew she ought to be there, too; but she'd become selfish about the past, wanted to meet its demands for a brief while. If she wanted to tend to Jeffrey later, she could.

"Jason called," her husband said. "I didn't know if I could give him the number down there."

"Of course you could!" Claire cried, irritated. Most irritating was her husband's torpor, the deadly calm of his voice. Jason was their twelve-year-old, off at boarding school and very unhappy, very lonely, and it had recently occurred to Claire that Jeff had begun to use him, trying to heap guilt upon Claire to balance his own guilt. At thirty-eight he was a fairly successful insurance lawyer, but had been getting the impression that the firm no longer believed in him, would keep him on the routine cases; the result had been an increase in his drinking and an unexpected aptitude for malice. For a while Claire tried to assuage his guilt, denying his idea that he'd "failed" her and Jason, insisting that their diminished sex life was only a temporary result of stress; but like the drinking, the guilt had gotten beyond them. When he turned it outward upon her, and then upon Jason, she had lost sympathy. In recent weeks they'd begun discussing divorce, though not seriously. The divorce was as vague in Claire's mind as the European vacation they'd been promising themselves for years, or as the memories of her life before Jeffrey, memories which had turned out so manageable, so disappointingly tame.

"I was going to call him anyway, later tonight," Claire said coldly. "I'd better go now."

"But when are you coming home?" her husband asked.

"When I finish all this," Claire snapped. "I don't *know*."

"But—"

She put down the phone. Exasperated, she ran her fingers back through the short, plainly cut whitish hair that gave Claire her look of severe competence. Mostly she was annoyed with herself for having napped, when there was so much work to be done. She went back to the kitchen, where Lillian was packing dishes into an enormous wooden crate.

"Why don't you rest for a while, Lillian? Let me do that."
Grunting, the old woman lifted her arms for more dishes.
She didn't look around.

"No time for restin'," she muttered.

Claire fell in beside her, and the two women worked steadily
through the evening. Now that Lillian had begun this project,
she had a grim determination to finish, and it displeased Claire
to understand that she'd inherited the trait. Since arriving she'd
been forced to visualize again the two poles represented by her
mother and aunt—her mother's genuine, sanctimonious affection that even now, so many years after her death, gave Claire
a thrill of loathing, and Lillian's permissive carelessness in which
Claire, at fourteen, had felt acutely the lack of specific warmth—
and to see, in fact, more of Lillian in herself than she'd ever
imagined. The poise, the oblivious strength, the impression of
coldness—Lillian presented these to the face of her upheaval,
just as Claire had moved so calmly, in recent months, through
the gradual dissolution of her marriage. Despite many opportunities, and a few specific hints from Claire, Lillian had been
unwilling to discuss Mack's suicide except as a set of facts, and
as it represented a natural turning point for her. Mack had borrowed a neighbor's shotgun, she said; he hadn't left a note, and
had been considerate enough to go far back into the woods. Lillian had considered selling the place for years, so now seemed
the appropriate time. It was then Claire had mentioned that she
might be getting a divorce soon, might leave everything behind
and move away from Philadelphia, maybe even back South, but
Lillian had shrugged as if this were only the natural course of
things.

When they'd finished packing in the kitchen, having sorted
out the few items Lillian wanted to keep for her small apartment
in town, Claire suddenly asked her aunt if she might keep the
feather she'd found in Mack's drawer. Lillian, who had begun to
tire in spite of herself, turned slowly from the set of wine glasses
she'd been marking for the sale. Sourly, she smiled at Claire.

"What would you want that for?" she asked. "A filthy thing
like that?"

Her aunt's smile, so ghastly and incongruous, paralyzed
Claire.

"It's just a feather," Lillian said contemptuously. "Something he plucked off a dirty pigeon, twenty years ago. I thought you had more sense."

"I—I just wanted it," Claire stammered. "I put it in my purse, but if you want it back—"

"Hell, I don't want it. Everything that boy left is going in the sale, I told you that. Clothes, tools, that old album full of worthless stamps—everything. I ain't taking nothing of Mack's along, when I move to town."

Claire's anger came quickly, as it had when she'd spoken to Jeffrey on the phone. She despised his self-pity, and now she despised her aunt's pretended callousness. Which was, she thought, another form of self-pity.

She said, in a steely voice, "Then you don't mind if I keep the feather."

Lillian shrugged, the ugly smile playing again at her mouth, then turned with the box of wine glasses toward the dining-room door.

"I don't care what you do," she said airily.

I don't care what you do. The phrase had always been a signature of Lillian's, her way of sidestepping emotions or awkward moments she couldn't handle, and had revealed an attitude that Claire, even as a girl, had cautiously admired. She liked the bravado, the hint of dangerous freedom. During the years she spent with Lillian and Mack it often occurred to her that she knew of no one like her aunt: women she encountered from nearby farms, her girlfriends' mothers, even her own dead mother seemed to her imagination pathetic figures trapped inside narrowed, sour lives, an atmosphere of constriction and fruitless care. Yet there was something in her aunt, too, that chilled her. She felt it most during her last weeks before college, when she would overhear Lillian remarking on the phone, "Now that Claire's leaving . . . ," or complaining that there was no one to do Claire's Saturday chores at the nursery. "I'd hoped that Mack could take over," she said to Claire one day, sighing. "But that boy gets more and more useless as time goes by. . . ."

Much as Claire hated hearing this, she knew it was true. Mack had continued his eccentric, childish pursuits, though he was past twenty; he'd grown careless about watering the plants, or doing repairs to the sheds or fences. On Saturdays, Lillian's busiest time, when it was Claire's job to keep track of the money and Mack's to load the customers' purchases into their trunks or pickups, he would usually have wandered away before noon, and that evening they'd find him on the back porch, whittling crude little statues out of a piece of rotted fencepost, or playing stray tuneless melodies on a toy guitar he'd gotten one Christmas as a child. Lillian would breeze right by, contemptuous, as though he weren't worth scolding. Sometimes Claire would stop to talk, but Mack couldn't pretend interest in her activities at school, and Claire was bothered by the way his eyes had sunk inward, as if through exhaustion or excessive dreaming, and by his snarled hair and dirt-encrusted nails. Claire had become a blond, tanned, popular teenager, particularly since the local kids knew her mother had left behind some "money"—the word spoken in a hushed monotone—and that she was among them only for a time. Very few of her friends even knew about Mack, and anyone she brought home probably assumed he was a hired hand; Claire noticed that her friends didn't really see him, even though he might be sitting at the kitchen table as they passed through to Claire's bedroom, and Claire saw no point in introductions, explanations, complicated attempts to describe the person Mack was. She wasn't ashamed of him; she simply knew that he couldn't take part in the mainstream of her life. When they were alone she talked to him, gaily, or asked him idle questions, as though they were children enclosed forever in a paradise of flowers and sloping green hills, children whose bond no meddlesome adult or passage of time could sever. Yet even these occasions grew less frequent, since Claire was in fact a bright, self-reliant teenager and Mack a prematurely aging man, morose and whimsical and doomed. It was on a Sunday evening, about three weeks before she left for Vanderbilt, that Claire understood how relieved she was to escape this place. She and Mack were sitting on the back porch, around sunset, and he had turned to her with his dark, doleful eyes to ask quietly: "Claire, why does everything have to die?"

Her first impulse had been to laugh, as one laughs at the
ingenuous query of a child. Yet the moment passed, and Mack
sat waiting tensely, almost severely, staring at Claire's mouth.
That was a habit of his—he stared at your mouth after asking
a question.

Claire bit her lip. She gave a strained smile.

"Well, Mack..."

She'd been thinking about a boy, Jake Summers, who had
taken her to the senior dance and had "liked" her all this year
but who didn't seem sufficiently upset, Claire thought, about
her going off to college. When she'd teased him about this he'd
said, using an odd phrase, that for a long time he'd known it
was an "established fact." That's what Claire's mother had saved
up her money for, wasn't it? Claire had smiled at Jake, uneasily;
had nodded. Out on the back porch, that mild August evening,
she summoned back the same uneasy smile for her cousin with
the bruised-looking eyes and the darkness in his veins. Behind
them, in the kitchen, Lillian was clanking dishes together as she
got their supper. How she longed to escape these people! She
answered Mack by saying evenly, as though she were reading
the words off a blackboard, that death was part of God's plan;
and for the first time in her life despised herself.

Yet the moment passed, and Claire's mind quickly filled with
other cares. In those last, hurried, dreamlike weeks, she had
been almost too busy to notice Mack. There was the constant sorting of her clothes, her indecision over what to take, what to leave
behind; there were shopping trips to town, for additional clothes;
there was a visit to the bank accompanied by an unusually solemn Lillian, where the money Claire's mother left had been
accumulating all these years. There were forms to fill out, sent
by the University. There were stationery, supplies, and the occasional odd item to buy—a reading lamp, a waste basket. There
were long stretches of time passed at her bedroom window,
hours of excited or languid daydreaming, harmless fantasies
about her roommate, her teachers, her first college boyfriend.
In all this pressure and elation, this breathless forward-looking,
Mack had almost no part: he was at the periphery of her life
and even of her vision, a shadow appearing at the far end of

the hall, startling her, or a slump-shouldered figure trudging through a distant field, darkening the corner of her eye for an instant as she bounded out the kitchen door. Yet when they did come together—at mealtimes, usually—Mack behaved as if nothing were different, evidently feeling no sense of loss or betrayal. So Claire told herself, and smiled brightly at him over Lillian's blackberry cobbler, and listened to him talk about a lame squirrel he'd found the other morning, his dark-ringed eyes hectic in their sockets, his beautifully molded mouth with its decaying teeth and his strong, soiled fingers moving jerkily as he talked, wanting to communicate the entire experience to Claire. "And it wasn't but three days ago," he said shyly, pleased with himself, "and this morning he was hoppin' around outside that box, playin' in the hay. His coat's come around, too. All nice and shiny." Claire smiled, and asked every question she could think to ask, as if compensating for all Mack's future projects for which there would be no one to show any interest. She comforted herself, at least, by thinking that he hadn't asked again about death. The question meant nothing, she told herself; it was the idle query of a child.

And so the time came for leaving. Mack and even Lillian had gotten dressed up—this touched Claire—and they helped her load the two big suitcases into Lillian's old Plymouth, then drove her into town where she would catch the bus for Nashville. Lillian, as Claire might have predicted, was awkward at good-byes, and had roughly brushed her niece's cheek as she muttered something about coming back to visit. Then, stepping back, she said in an overloud voice: "Why, she won't be gone for long—tell that to Mack, Claire honey, cheer him up a bit! She'll be here a month at Christmas, then all next summer, and once she's had enough of schoolin' she'll be back for good. Ain't that so, Claire?" And Lillian, betraying herself, threw back her head and laughed, something Claire had never seen her do in her life.

Claire turned slowly to Mack. Uncomfortable in his musty dark suit, and the starched cotton shirt with no tie, he stood shifting his weight from one foot to the other. In the morning sun outside the depot, his face looked more shadowed than ever, as if a little oblong cloud had perched just above him. He'd cut himself shaving, Claire saw. She reached out to touch him and, not exactly meaning to, brushed the tiny scratch at his jawline. Alarmed, she drew back her hand. "Goodbye, Mack," she said quickly, embarrassed, and tiptoed up to kiss his other cheek. It occurred to her that she'd never come this close to him before. He smelled of the outdoors, of the long, sweet grasses carpeting the hills, of the pleasantly rotten dampness of black soil. His eyes were clear as rainwater, but they filled. "Gonna write me every day?" he said hoarsely. By now she sensed the anxiety in him, a voltage she suddenly imagined could send his black-suited limbs flapping like a scarecrow's. She touched his shoulder. "It's all right, Mack, don't worry. I'll write all the time, and I'll be home for visits. Just like your Mama said." Lillian had stood aside during all this, pretending interest in the activity inside the depot, but Claire watched as Mack shot his mother a quick, resentful look, of the kind she'd never seen from him. Her heart gave a queer leap, then just as quickly sank. "And I'll call you, too," she added lamely. "On the telephone."

Wiping his eyes, Mack stepped back. He'd straightened his shoulders, assuming an air of dignity that tore at Claire's heart. Suddenly she felt, as she hadn't in years, that he was central to her life—her childhood playmate, her unassuming teacher, her silent, bruised-looking friend. Yet it was not true, as she supposed even then, that she would return to him, or that they would evolve into anything beyond what already seemed a twilit, vaguely haunted past. Though she did come back for several visits during her college years, and wrote bright, simply phrased letters to Mack whenever she could, it was her new interests that absorbed her: a year-long passion to become an archaeologist, which evolved out of her crush on an art-history professor; in her sophomore and junior years, her apartment and roommates and exhausting summer job with a fashion merchandising firm (Claire had majored in business, finally, and never returned to Georgia for the summer because of her need, as she put it in a letter to Lillian, to get "real-life experience"); and, finally, her relationship and impulsive marriage, near the end of her senior year, to a handsome pre-law major from Philadelphia, who whisked her off so quickly to a book-filled, stylishly ratty apart-

ment, less than a mile from Penn, that she wasn't even able to
attend her own graduation. There had been cards, phone calls,
small gifts exchanged between her and Mack; there had been
one or two visits after her marriage, during which she talked
easily with both Lillian and Mack, warning herself against even
the most justifiable condescension. She had moved beyond
them, of course. Happily married, pregnant, with no particular
ambitions for herself beyond leading a life both intelligent and
sensual, she had the emotion toward them one has toward old
black-and-white photographs, suddenly encountered after many
years: a sense of amazement or even dismay, but little more. By
the time Jason had become an energetic toddler, Claire always
had an excuse for not visiting; and gradually Lillian stopped
asking her. They'd been out of contact for several years when
Claire received the telegram about Mack—which had been brief
and tersely worded, even for a telegram.

Though she couldn't have predicted all this when she was
eighteen, and boarding that whinnying Trailways bus, it might
not have surprised her. Sitting at the tinted window, she felt
already detached from them as they stood out in the sunlight,
both squinting as they passed their gaze along, unsure which
window was hers. Several times they both waved, vaguely, and
she waved in return, but she was never certain that they saw
her. The bus was so high up, so impersonal. It wasn't until it
had left the depot, and was already on the interstate heading
north, that Claire let her gaze stray from the window and looked
down to see the small but unmistakable bloodstain on her fore-
finger. Her first reaction had been to wipe at it, horrified, or to
hurry back to the restroom and scour her hands. But she hated
herself for this, and in a moment her heart quieted. She'd always
been a sensible girl, and she simply waited, leaning back her
head and enjoying the scenery, until the bus made its first stop
and it was time for Claire to wash her hands for lunch.

"Claire, there's something that don't seem quite right," Lillian
said.

They were standing in the near-empty living room: the sale
was over. The auctioneer, an unsmiling potbellied man in his

fifties, had set up business on Lillian's back porch, having brought a card table, an ancient filigreed cash register, and a couple of slack-mouthed assistants. These younger men, in their early twenties, had kept disappearing into the house and returning with more of Lillian's goods, and each time something was brought out the auctioneer would turn to the gathered spectators and exclaim—not very convincingly, Claire thought—over its beauty or value. While Lillian and Claire waited at some distance, under the shade of an old pecan tree, people had arrived and formed a semicircle around the porch, a few having brought lawn chairs and jugs of lemonade. The day was hot, cloudless. From under the tree the two women watched in silence, dazed by the incessant work of the past few days and feeling detached from the sale itself now that their own work had suddenly ended. It surprised Claire that almost everything went quickly—one by one the auctioneer cried "Sold!" over the washing machine, Lillian's china cabinet with the beveled glass panels, Mack's small, squarish bureau. Each item looked so diminished, Claire thought, so pathetic as it was brought out of the dark kitchen into the glaring noontime sun. With a folded newspaper, Lillian stood fanning herself. She did not seem to mind that most of the buyers were people she'd known for years, town neighbors and longstanding customers of the nursery. She'd only commented that the auctioneer's two assistants looked "pretty shiftless" to her, and she remarked, sighing, that maybe she should have kept her good china, in case she ever had company in town. Then she'd laughed, shortly. Claire hadn't replied.

When the auction was over and the small crowd had dispersed, the auctioneer handed Lillian her share of the cash and within ten minutes had driven off in a late-model paneled truck, the two assistants following in a badly rusted van with dark-tinted windows. Absently, the two women moved inside and began wandering through the empty rooms, noting the paltry leavings of the sale, remarking that in Lillian's new apartment the few items marked "Not for Sale" would not look so tiny and insubstantial as in these overlarge rooms. In the kitchen there were still the breakfast table and four chairs; in the dining room a small mahogany hutch; in the living room a wine-colored love seat, an old fringed rug, a few chairs and lamps. It was here that Lillian stopped cold, frowning as she passed her gaze slowly around the room.

"What do you mean?" Claire asked. "Is something still here that you wanted sold?"

"No," Lillian said. "I don't know, but there's something not quite right."

Claire crossed the room to stand beside her aunt. "It's just that everything's gone," she said gently. "The room looks so big, so barren. . . ."

"No," her aunt repeated. A note of asperity had entered her voice, as if she resented having to speak to Claire at all. In these last days Claire had treated her with tact, even with deference, not presuming to ask anything further about Mack: though it was a fact—and one she resented, mildly—that she'd begun to think obsessively of him. She'd had to content herself with imagining (idly, as if she were creating a story that might never have happened) a slow transformation in her cousin through the years: a gradual dawning of his consciousness as time passed, facing a vision of himself as one of those lame animals caught somewhere in the obscurity of these hills, where no kind stranger would ever happen along; or suffering an equally slow encroachment of the darkness, a constriction and a narrowing, until the neat depthless circle of black inside a gun's barrel had concentrated all the reality Mack would ever know. These were identical answers, Claire thought. Any supposition of hers arrived at the same unknowable—and undeniable—conclusion. So there was no reason to bother Lillian, who doubtless had torments of her own, and Claire had simply helped her with the work as if she were a servant, obedient and quiet, joining in idle conversation when Lillian seemed to want it, privately counting the days until the auction. Their only argument had centered on that, in fact, because Claire had informed her aunt that she intended to leave that very night, when the cleaning and packing and the auction itself would be over. Lillian had claimed to need help with the move into town, but Claire pointed out that the movers would arrive on Monday morning, that there would be precious little to unpack, and in any case the landlord at Lillian's new apartment house could help her if any problems arose. Claire really should fly back at once: she was separating from her husband, she told Lillian frankly, and needed to find an apartment of her own.

Now she waited patiently as her aunt continued to survey the room. "I don't know," she was muttering, "I can't understand it, but there's something—" and then, abruptly, she stamped her foot. "Claire, look over in that corner—why, it's the television set."

"What? Do you mean—"

"Gone," said Lillian. "Stolen."

Alarmed, Claire stared at the empty corner where the color television set had rested on a small end table. The table, dusty and nicked, was still there.

"But there must have been a mistake," Claire said. "The auctioneer must have thought—"

Lillian clapped her hands, then walked to the front door and opened it. She peered outside, as if expecting to find the culprits waiting on the porch to be discovered. "Told you they were shiftless, didn't I?" she said, glancing back to Claire. Her eyes gleamed with satisfaction. "While we were all out back, those boys were taking things out the front door—setting them in that old van, I'll bet. Stealing me blind!"

"Oh Lillian, I don't think—"

Her aunt shook her finger, as if Claire had been complicitous in the theft. "Now listen, that TV had one of them red tags on it, big as life. *Not for sale.* You put it on yourself, didn't you? Eh?"

"Yes," Claire said quietly.

"And you didn't see them bring it out back, did you? There wasn't any television set put up at the auction, was there?"

"No," Claire said.

"That's right," said Lillian, slamming the door. "No tellin' what they got away with."

Helplessly Claire followed her aunt back through the other rooms, able only to shake her head when Lillian pointed inside the hutch where a valuable figurine had stood, a gift from some long-ago admirer; examining the shelf, Claire could see a small clean circle in the dust. In the kitchen there were service pieces missing. "Only silverplate," Lillian said, pointing to an empty cabinet beneath the sink, "but still." More than anything Claire was paralyzed by her aunt's manner—unsurprised, grimly jovial, as if the discovery of each theft helped confirm a theory she'd been trying for countless years to prove. She was a big, strong, willful woman in a brightly flowered dress, her white hair drawn back carelessly in a bun, the back of her neck damp with perspiration: following, Claire felt silent and insubstantial as a ghost. Lillian's manner reminded her of her husband's on those nights when he drank straight through dinner and into the night—the cynicism, the rancor, the wayward energy that seemed to arise out of helplessness itself but was no less prodigious for that. Claire's own energies were controlled, efficient, lacking in much emotion; she was a born manager, cool and diplomatic. She thought to herself, clearly, that she did not understand these other people. She allowed Lillian to lead her upstairs, thinking *By this time tomorrow I'll be home*, but Lillian had stopped at her bedroom door. She said something intended, probably, as "Hah!" but that came out diminished, as if the sound had strangled in her throat.

Claire came forward, then briefly closed her eyes. The room had been torn apart—drawers flung out of the bureau, their contents strewn along the floor; the mattress had been lifted partway off the bed, then dropped; some boxes and suitcases in Lillian's closet had been ransacked. She and Claire moved slowly into the room. At last the old woman seemed chastened, but Claire could not comfort her: she could barely contain her own sense of outrage. As a child she had played with Mack in this room, getting into Lillian's makeup and jewelry, giggling; once she'd even dressed Mack in one of his mother's loudly printed dresses, had squealed with laughter as Mack stood there snickering and blushing. Suddenly it came to Claire how many lovers of her aunt must have stayed in this room, slept in that very bed. Neither Claire nor her aunt were particularly sentimental, but nonetheless they stood there a long time. Claire's heart pounded. Her fists were clenched at her sides.

Lillian said, finally, "My, my . . ."

"They'll be easy to catch," Claire said, severely. "We should call the police right away. They couldn't have expected to get away with this."

Lillian was walking around the room, lifting items and then

dropping them, shaking her head. "Why bother?..." she said vaguely.

"But you have the man's number," Claire said. "It must have been one of those boys he brought with him, I doubt the auctioneer himself had anything to do with it. If you'll just call him—"

"No," Lillian said, sharply. "Let them have it. Let them do what they want with everything, with *me*...." To Claire's horror, her aunt had begun to whimper. She stood by the night table and suddenly held up an object—a white straw purse. "Look, they even emptied this, not even a kleenex left...." Lillian turned the opened purse upside down; nothing came out.

With a startled cry, Claire turned and ran out of her aunt's bedroom and down the hall to her own room. Her heart beat wildly, like a maddened bird inside her chest. She thought, *This isn't me, this isn't happening*— At the doorway she saw that the small, scantily furnished room had not been ransacked; perhaps they had spared her.... But entering she saw it, fallen to the floor beside her bed, her own small navy handbag with the white trim. Before she bent over, numbly, to pick it up, she could already see that the clasp had been opened. She lifted the purse; without looking inside, she turned it upside down over the bed. Nothing happened. Then she rooted inside with her fingers, almost ripping the satin lining, but in their rush they had taken everything, her wallet and lipstick and keys, her small address book and her packet of traveling tissue, and even the small worthless feather it had taken her twenty years to lose.

Weakly she thought, *Mack*..., but it was too late for that. She dropped her purse on the bed, she left the room and tried to console her aunt. Lillian had already recovered, but Claire offered to phone the auctioneer. When she called, the man told her gruffly that those "sorry fellers" had disappeared: he'd hired them just last week, he was sorry if they took advantage but he couldn't be responsible, it was hard to get any decent help these days.... As the man spoke, Claire listened numbly. When he stopped talking she simply hung up, not knowing what else to do.

They decided not to call the police. There was no point, really; they were already exhausted, and the chances were slim that the police would recover their property. So they cleaned up the house, made themselves a light supper, and Claire had her suitcase—the thieves hadn't touched it—packed and ready by six o'clock. Claire told her aunt, in a sensible voice, that after all her purse had contained nothing that couldn't easily be replaced; there had been less than fifty dollars in her wallet and she would cancel the credit cards; the airline ticket, thank God, was tucked safely inside a compartment in her suitcase. Probably the thieves had dumped the contents of both purses into a box, hurrying, not troubling to examine what they were stealing. But there was no point in chasing after them, Claire said, let them have whatever they wanted. . . . Lillian hadn't replied. The matter was settled. On the way to the airport the two women talked idly, as people do when they know they will never meet again, and on the plane Claire felt a miraculous calm overtaking her, as if by returning home unburdened, empty-handed, she had become innocent once again.

El Paso

E VERY AUGUST, between the ages of ten and fourteen, I boarded a train in east Texas, that land of humid summers and dew-hung pines, and traveled to the western city of El Paso, where my aunt, uncle, and three cousins had moved in the late 1950s, seeking relief from my cousin Roger's severe case of asthma. This 700-mile journey linked a pair of worlds so dissimilar, so unlikely to exist on the same planet, much less in the same state, that each summer I felt that I couldn't return: that the hazy skies of the pine-covered hills surrounding our town, and my parents' modest house of white stucco, and my parents themselves, slump-shouldered but cheerful at the station, must cease to exist the moment the train roared away toward the west. This fantasy rose out of a childish belief, occasionally resurrected in adulthood, that nothing did exist outside the temporary focus of my own perception, my own longings—though I couldn't, of course, know this at the time. I felt only that a magical change had occurred, that reality had shifted in a way that seemed sudden, thrilling, and irrevocable, and that I might never get home again.

Nor was I bothered by this idea. An only child, I felt constricted and resentful during the long months of June and July, trapped in a dwindling neighborhood sorely lacking in children, and in a house whose routine was peaceful but tedious, ruled by the departures of my father to his factory job, by my mother's visits to the grocery store and the post office. The humid afternoons seemed interminable; my parents never quarreled despite money problems, my father's fondness for Jack Daniels and cutthroat poker, or their own inevitable boredom. In short, nothing ever happened. This seemed the singular, wildly unjust fate of my childhood years, and my annual escape to El Paso—ah, how I rolled the exotic syllables over my tongue, *El Paso!*—seemed an unattainable fantasy when I daydreamed alone in our wooded back yard on a June evening, closing my eyes to summon the cool, dry air, the gargantuan mountains with their snowy peaks, the miraculous absence of trees.

In truth, these boyish fancies, abetted by the romance of the train ride itself, gave way soon enough to the routines of my aunt's household. Busy as she was, Aunt Carolyn managed to keep track of her three sons and myself, seeming vaguely uneasy that the four of us were left to our own devices, more or less, during most of the day. Carolyn worked with my Uncle Hugh in his large accounting firm downtown, and though Hugh left before seven in the morning, Carolyn was still home when my cousins and I woke around eight-thirty or nine, straggling into the kitchen in cut-offs, shirtless, our hair uncombed. Carolyn moved about briskly, already dressed for the office—she favored pleated skirts in white or navy, and lots of Mexican jewelry—but taking the time to help get our cereal bowls on the table, give the maid her instructions for the workday and for the evening meal, and in general to monitor our plans for the long hours of her absence. This routine varied little, I think, during the four consecutive summers I visited El Paso. Only during that last summer, when I was fourteen and my three cousins were seventeen, thirteen, and twelve, did my aunt reduce her hours at the accounting office by half (she still left around nine but would return at one or two in the afternoon, looking pale and demoralized), and at that same time she began to lose patience with the latest, and youngest, in a long string of Mexican maids who came across the border from Juarez—this one a cheerful, gap-toothed, painfully awkward seventeen-year-old named Yolanda.

Whatever the reason, Aunt Carolyn had little patience with Yolanda. At breakfast, which for Carolyn was a significant, regimented affair, a time for discussing the day ahead, Yolanda tended to bumble, spilling milk as she tilted the carton toward our cereal bowls (she held the carton too high, as I and my middle cousin, Roger, tried repeatedly to show her; but eventually we started bringing paper towels with us to the table, prepared for these inevitable spills), or dropping the *pan y mantequilla* she prepared for us—all the Spanish phrases I learned during those summers related to food—and dropping it, always, buttered-side down. Carolyn, who could get our breakfast together twice as quickly and without mishap, nonetheless seemed determined that Yolanda would learn. "*No, no, aqui*," Carolyn would repeat, exasperated, as again Yolanda laid the spoons to the left of the cereal bowls, knives to the right. The two women seemed to my young eyes a marvel of opposites—Carolyn blond, fortyish, angular and quick, Yolanda with matted dark hair reaching nearly to her shoulders, young and plump, her awkwardness the result of a slower, more deliberate pace, and undoubtedly of her confusion within the roominess and splendor of my aunt's house (a sprawling ranch-style whose panelled family room alone seemed larger than my own relatively shabby home, back in that unimaginable place, east Texas). Yet they communicated quite well, though Yolanda spoke not a word of English. My aunt, always quick-minded and efficient, had mastered an impressive-sounding "pidgin Spanish," as she called it, which enabled her to converse with her maids about the household, the cooking, and even—in a rare, relaxed moment—to exchange "women's talk," which in Yolanda's case, I knew, focused on her mother, now residing back in the interior of Mexico, who had also been one of Carolyn's maids. Her name was Dolores—a squat, abrupt-mannered woman I had not really liked, but who had prepared the most wonderful enchiladas imaginable—and Carolyn had been very disappointed the previous summer when Dolores had quit, pleading the need to return to her family but promising to send her oldest daughter as a replacement. So here, in August of 1966, was the young, perplexed, and hopeless Yolanda, presenting my aunt—for the first time, it seemed—with a situation she could not handle.

"Why don't you just fire her?" asked Ted, my oldest cousin. Though Yolanda hovered around us as we ate her burnt toast and bitter coffee, of course she could not understand. "Just because Dolores quit, it doesn't mean we have to keep supporting the whole family."

Somehow, I had never liked Ted. At seventeen, he was remote from my younger cousins and me; he was athletic, handsome, and had a clipped, knowing air that often seemed heartless. Part of my dislike, I'm certain, arose from Ted's having successfully crossed the tremulous bridge of adolescence that I was now approaching, and having made the crossing with such panache. Scorning our childish cut-offs, he wore khakis and starched, button-down shirts; he'd won bowling and golf trophies, and possessed a much fawned-over 1957 Chevrolet; and most important he had a girlfriend, with whom he'd begun spending long hours, that summer, alone in his bedroom, evidently with Carolyn's consent. (Our Uncle Hugh was absent so much, it can fairly be said that Carolyn ran the household.)

Sighing, Carolyn brushed toast crumbs off her white pleated skirt. She lit up a Kent, and took one of her long, slow draws that I'd always found, for some reason, quite thrilling. It was early morning, but already her bony, attractive face looked tired.

"I don't know," she said. "I suppose I should."

"I wish we could get Luisa back," said Roger, to whom I was closest both in age and temperament. "She was great."

Carolyn widened her eyes at him, in mock exasperation. "She *stole* from us, Roger. She stole *money* from your father's wallet."

Roger shrugged. "I liked her," he said, then lifted his cereal bowl to finish off the milk.

"Roger, stop that," Carolyn said, swatting at him, and as a joke he extended his two little fingers outward as he drank from the bowl.

My aunt shook her head, her lip curled.

"You just liked Luisa because she was pretty," said Henry, my youngest cousin and, though just twelve, the most cynical. "You said she looked like a movie star."

"She did," I put in. "Sophia Loren, she looked like her."

"She looked *better* than her," said Roger.

Ted stretched his arms, bored. "She wore too much makeup,"

he said, "and she was dishonest. Look, Mom, I've got to go."
He stood, bent his lanky six feet over to kiss Carolyn, and left.
He had on his golfing clothes. One thing I appreciated about
Ted was that he was always leaving for somewhere.

It was then, I believe, that something amazing happened.
Though Carolyn had been in a familiar mood—a teasing mood,
roguish and talkative, treating us as rather shady but likable
characters—it now seemed that she'd left us altogether. Yolanda
had stopped just behind her shoulder to ask her something, and
Carolyn had risen quickly, her hand trembling so that the ash
from her cigarette fell to the glass-topped table. "¡Yo no sé!" she
shouted at Yolanda. "¡Yo no sé!" And then she hurried from the
room, bursting into tears. We heard her out in the foyer, rummaging through her purse for her keys, and then she was gone.

Yolanda had cringed back against the refrigerator, and now
she too hurried away, toward the tiny maid's quarters sand-
wiched between the kitchen and the laundry room. I looked
back and forth between my two cousins.

"What happened?" I asked. "What did Yolanda say?"

Roger shrugged. He was buttering a piece of toast. "I couldn't
understand."

"Yes, you could," said Henry, in the tone of disgust he often
used toward Roger. Though Henry was the youngest, he'd always been the best at Spanish; he'd been only four or five when
the family moved to El Paso. "She asked Mom what she wanted
her to make for dinner," Henry said, a little smugly.

"That's all?" I asked, surprised that neither of my cousins
seemed upset by what had happened.

Henry got up, scratching his bare, flat belly. "That's all," he
said. "Later, you guys. I'm going out to the pool."

"Later," Roger and I told him, speaking at the same moment.

Several years would pass before I would understand that the
glamour of my "summer family," as I liked to consider them,
related simply to money. In truth my mother and her sister,
Carolyn, weren't so different: both were efficient, sharp-witted,
and had a good head for business, and though Carolyn was
more emotional, more unpredictable, there were stories in the

family about my mother's temper, too, most notably the tale of her incapacitating a neighborhood bully, at the age of eight, with a croquet mallet nearly as large as herself. By the time I was fourteen, though, Mother appeared to have settled into a drab, grim domesticity, using her agile mind to organize grocery coupons or to ferret out the best possible school clothes for me, at a price within her budget. I do not remember her uttering a word of complaint, or anger. Occasionally she would clank pots and pans together so loudly I could hear her from the living room, over the blaring TV, or she would slam cabinet doors much harder than necessary, but I never said anything, nor would my father look up from his paper, his cheap cigar, his after-work tumbler of Jack Daniels. Even the colors of my home life seemed drab—the nondescript gray of the kitchen walls, waterstained near the ceiling; the khaki color of my father's factory uniform; the smudged deep-olive of the trees outside our windows. I felt these colors as both dull and oppressive; they served only to strengthen my youthful drive toward fantasy, toward discovering exotic boldness and glamour and style in the quite ordinary, even banal signposts of affluence.

The contrast of color, however, seemed to give these signposts the universal benison of nature. In El Paso the blue sky was pale and crisp, the mountains were a speckled brown, capped with lacy edges of snow along the peaks; even the houses and streets glimmered whitely in the sun, seeming weightless in the dry air; and some of the yards were filled not with grass but with jagged white pebbles, creating an effect I found especially drama-tic. In the mornings, after breakfast, Roger and I would often go walking through the wide, winding streets of the neighbor-hood, a suburb composed of sprawling houses set far back from the road, each with a large water cooler perched on the roof, each with a Mexican maid framed in the kitchen window or watering spiny-looking bushes in front of the house. Almost all the houses had, in the back yards, swimming pools filled with glinting turquoise water, and my cousins and I usually spent the largest portion of each day near our own pool. Henry, espe-cially, spent endless hours floating on his red-and-white striped air mattress, reading comic books and listening to local radio

shows, eating the big helpings of chocolate ice cream Yolanda
would bring him from the kitchen. Often the three of us would
sneak a beer from the refrigerator or break out our stash of
cigarettes, usually waiting until Yolanda went to her room for
a nap, since we never knew if she might decide to tell Carolyn,
as Dolores had often done. (Smoking was one of Carolyn's strict-
est taboos, though she smoked two packs a day herself.) Occasionally Ted would come out to the pool in the late afternoon,
with his girlfriend, fresh from the golf course or the bowling
alley. He would chide us for not doing anything "constructive"
with our time, and Henry would say something like "Get off
my case," or "Spare me, killer," and then Ted and Sheila would
disappear back inside the house. It was on such an afternoon,
a few days after the breakfast incident, that Carolyn came home
early and had another argument with Yolanda.

"There they go again," said Roger, sitting on the edge of the
pool with his feet in the water.

"What's the matter?" I said, cocking my ear to the kitchen's
sliding glass door, which someone had left partway open. I could
hear Carolyn's shrill voice, punctuated by Yolanda's indecipher-
able torrents of Spanish.

"Oh, that stupid Yolanda," Henry said, floating belly upward
in the pool. He'd gotten so dark that Ted had begun to tease
him about it and call him "Hernandez"—a nickname Henry
hated. "She was supposed to defrost the meat for tacos," Henry
said, "and of course she forgot."

"But what's Yolanda saying?" I asked.

"Who knows," said Roger. "Just a bunch of excuses, probably."

"I told Mom already," Henry said, floating along gracefully.
I saw the reflections of fluffy white clouds in his dark glasses.
"I told her, next time let's get a *white* maid. Even if it costs more."

"You should talk, Hernandez," said Roger, in weak imitation
of Ted.

"Brother, you're a dead man," Henry said calmly.

I'd kept my eyes trained on the glass doorway, where Aunt
Carolyn now appeared. "Hey, you boys, how many times have
I told you to keep these doors *closed*!" she yelled out. For as long

as I could remember, Carolyn had been worried about scorpions entering the house, or snakes; such occurrences were not rare in El Paso, even in the best neighborhoods.

"Yolanda did it," Henry called out, in a sly voice. "The last time she went inside."

"Yeah," Roger shouted, "after bringing Hernandez his fifth bowl of ice cream for the day."

Carolyn paused for a moment, her lip curled. "I've told you, Henry, to make your own snacks during the day, and let Yolanda do her job. No wonder she forgets things, if she's waiting on you guys all the time."

Henry floated, not glancing aside. He lifted one hand in a little wave toward his mother.

Carolyn pulled the door shut, and I sank back inside my deck chair, hoping the incident was over. That evening, though, Carolyn didn't come to the dinner table, nor had Uncle Hugh returned from the office. On my way back to the bedroom to change, I'd noticed that Carolyn's door was closed, and from inside I heard muffled sobbing. I hurried past, shamefaced. At the dinner table, Yolanda served ham and eggs to Ted and Sheila, and to Roger, Henry, and me. It seemed a strange gathering, all kids and no adults, though Ted assumed an adult role, of course, trying to impress his girlfriend (or so I thought) by making belittling remarks to us. Right after dinner, though, he disappeared with Sheila into his own room, and again the three of us were alone.

"Hey, what's going on?" I said finally.

Roger and Henry had the TV on; both of them shrugged, looking bored.

"Who knows," Henry said. "Dad's working late at the office."

"But what about—"

Just then, we heard the front door opening. It was Uncle Hugh, and by the time he reached us in the living room, we heard Carolyn's shrill voice growing louder from the hall—the same voice she'd used on Yolanda that afternoon. I noticed a brief flicker of annoyance in Hugh's eyes, but then he came into the room and began speaking in his hearty way, as though nothing were wrong. He asked about our day, and he asked me

(as he did almost every evening) if I were enjoying my visit to
El Paso. He was always extremely polite to me, yet there was
something about Hugh that struck me, even then, as remote
and somehow forbidding. At that moment, for instance, Carolyn
had reached the doorway and stood there, panting, having asked
him some shrill, ringing question. She looked haggard: her blond
hair mussed, as though she'd been lying down, her face puffy
and drained of color. Her eyes were swollen as though from
crying and she wore only a nightgown (though it wasn't yet
nine o'clock) and had nothing on her feet. Yet Hugh, still in his
business suit, handsome and fresh-looking, simply ignored her.
He asked about the program we were watching, and talked
about a documentary he wanted to see later that evening—a
program about the American Indians, I think it was. For years
he'd been interested in Indian lore and artifacts, and on his rare
weekends away from the office would pack us into a rented van
and take us out into the desert to hunt for arrowheads or shards
of pottery. He liked to talk about the history of the area, the
colorful legends of the Southwest, the geological formations.
Once, I remember, an idle query of mine about the city's name,
El Paso, had brought a disquisition on its earliest settlement in
the 1820s, its series of names—Magoffinsville, Franklin, "El Paso
del Norte"—and its symbolic importance as a gateway, the passage toward a new life. Hugh loved to talk about the El Paso of
a hundred years ago—the clusters of adobe buildings, the excitement of a new settlement forming in the shadow of Mount
Franklin, the continual influx of travelers across the Old Over-
land Trail. Hugh had been a city boy, raised in Dallas; he could
become romantic and wistful when discussing these distant
events, and I noticed how this contrasted to his friendly but
rigidly controlled demeanor in the house—his ability to ignore
a shrieking, disheveled Carolyn, for instance, and speak calmly
about a television documentary.

The contrast did seem chilling. For all his geniality, Uncle
Hugh was ranged in my imagination with Ted and Henry—like
them he was lean, dark, muscular—as against the fair-haired,
emotional Carolyn and Roger, whom I resembled. So there was a
hesitant catch in my voice as I answered his polite inquiries about

my day; I kept looking from him back to Carolyn, whose eyes had fixed on her husband with a mingling of rage and incredulity. Both Roger and Henry were staring at the television, as though dazed by the cool flickering brightness of the screen.

"Will you *listen* to me? Will you *answer* me?" Carolyn screeched at her husband, in a ragged, desperate voice. Yet it seemed that no one else heard.

Hugh draped his jacket over a chair, tousled Roger's hair—my cousin did not look up—and went into the kitchen where Yolanda worked noisily, opening and shutting cabinets, clanking dishes together.

At the same moment Carolyn turned, half stumbling, and went back down the hall, slamming the bedroom door. Later, I knew, Hugh would join her in the bedroom, and there would be no shouting, no arguing; Uncle Hugh never argued. Nor did Roger or Henry say anything. When I mentioned, just before bed, how upset Carolyn had been earlier in the evening, Henry just said, "Don't worry about it, Steven," and threw a pillow at my head. He laughed, and then Roger laughed. The next morning Carolyn met us in the breakfast room, dressed smartly for work. She instructed Yolanda and joked with us boys in the usual way, as though nothing had happened.

During the next two weeks of my stay, I understood that for the first time I was anxious to leave El Paso. The usual summertime diversions with Roger and Henry—taking the bus downtown to see movies or play pinball, hanging out with my cousins' friends in the neighborhood, lazing around the swimming pool —had become stale, and these ordinary pastimes mingled uneasily (in my mind, at least) with the tension I continued to feel within the household. Weekend family excursions into the desert, or to Juarez, or to White Sands, New Mexico, no longer seemed feasible; my cousins failed to bring up these familiar ideas, and I began to feel that everyone was privy to some secret dark knowledge from which I'd been excluded. In short, I felt like an outsider. My uncle, it seemed, became increasingly preoccupied with work, sometimes not returning home until nine or ten o'clock, and my aunt alternated long hours alone in her bedroom, the door closed, with her usual restless, animated activity, which no longer seemed charming to me, but rather frightful. She might take out the vacuum cleaner late at night, still dressed in her office clothes, and run it frantically over the living-room carpet, all the while shouting to Yolanda over the noise. "Like this, like *this!*" she would say, ducking the machine under a small table, or between two chairs. Or she would scold Yolanda for failing to rinse the dishes before putting them in the dishwasher, or for using too little bleach in the laundry, or for forgetting—once again!—to keep the glass sliding doors closed all during the day. As always, Yolanda stayed quiet and abashed during these tirades, a tiny crease deepening in her smooth brow as she tried to listen and understand. (At times Carolyn, her attention focused more on her fierce vacuuming or scrubbing than on trying to communicate with Yolanda, would revert to English, seeming to shout at herself rather than at Yolanda, who understood nothing.) Carolyn's behavior, in fact, seemed to bother Yolanda very little (had she been taught to expect such treatment, from Anglo employers?) and my cousins not at all. They talked idly of returning to school, of a ski trip to Ruidoso that Hugh had promised them for Thanksgiving vacation—talk that only increased my sense of exclusion. For the first time I thought of my own family's dull but peaceful routine back in east Texas not with a sense of boredom but with longing.

During these last days, too, I felt an increased curiosity about Yolanda—especially after the incident with the snake.

One afternoon Carolyn arrived home from the office about two o'clock, as had become her habit, and came out to where Roger, Henry, and I were lounging beside the pool. (Hearing her car in the driveway, we had quickly ground our lighted Marlboros into the huge potted cactus near the diving board.) Carolyn came quickly through the glass doors, greeting us absently— "Hey, boys"—and followed by Yolanda. Carolyn began talking to her about the line of scraggly shrubs along the fence, which Yolanda had apparently failed to water, when suddenly Carolyn shrieked and took several quick steps backward. She turned to us and stage-whispered, "Boys, there's a rattlesnake. Get inside the house."

The appearance of a rattler was an exciting event, however, and we did not obey. All three of us came to stand behind Carolyn, who had edged back toward the concrete surrounding the pool.

"Where?" said Henry. "I don't see anything."

"There, between those bushes." Squinting, I could just make out the snake's motionless coiled body, nearly invisible in the shade from the redwood fence. "Listen, boys, get inside that house," Carolyn whispered. "You too, Yolanda. ¡Rapido!"

Quickly, Yolanda obeyed. My cousins and I stayed where we were.

"What are *you* going to do?" Henry asked, in his caustic way. "Do battle with a rattlesnake?"

"I'm right behind you," Carolyn said. "Now get!" But she was staring at the snake, as if mesmerized. I felt that if we went inside, she would not follow.

"I could get Dad's gun," Roger said. "At this distance—"

"Don't you touch that gun, any of you," Carolyn hissed. "Now get inside!"

"Come on," I said, giving each of my cousins a poke. "Let's go."

"What for?" said Henry. "Are you chicken, Steven? Look, the snake's not even awake."

"But it won't sleep forever," Roger said. "We ought to kill it."

"No, *no guns*," Carolyn said. She seemed resigned, at last, that we boys would not go inside.

"Maybe we should call Dad," Roger said. "*He* could come home and shoot it. The last time we camped in the desert, he shot *two* snakes from a lot further away than this."

"No," Carolyn said quickly. "We're not calling your dad." I heard the bitterness in her voice.

"What are we going to do?" Henry said impatiently. "Stand here until it wakes up and attacks us?"

After a pause Carolyn said, "It should be killed, but . . . maybe we should call the police."

"The police!" Henry cried, and all three of us broke into laughter. But, laughing, we kept our eyes on the snake. It hadn't stirred.

Now the door opened again and out came Yolanda, carrying a hoe. The hoe seemed longer than Yolanda herself, who looked like a plump, overgrown child as she went past us and toward the bushes. "Yolanda!" my aunt cried. "No, no! ¡Es loco! ¡Es loco!" But Yolanda ignored her. She went directly toward the bush, aimed the hoe's blade at the snake, and gave it a couple of quick, no-nonsense jabs. The snake made a few jerky movements—we heard the dry, heart-chilling sound of its rattles—but then it lay still.

Yolanda turned to us. "Es muerta," she said. She gave a brief gap-toothed smile and went back inside the house.

"That foolish girl," Carolyn whispered, after a long moment.

Henry shrugged. "Where she comes from, they probably kill snakes every day. It's no big deal."

"Ho, listen to the big man," said Roger. "If you're so brave, why didn't you kill it."

Henry wrinkled his mouth, then laughed. "Yolanda," he said, shaking his head.

"That foolish, foolish girl," Carolyn repeated, and she stalked inside the house.

That evening, Uncle Hugh came home in time for dinner, and was regaled on all sides by stories of the rattlesnake. Even Carolyn, lately so quiet in her husband's presence, became animated as Roger, Henry, and I competed with our startling variations of what had happened. When I mentioned that we had almost called Hugh at the office, wanting him to come home and shoot the snake, Carolyn crossed her eyes at me, exasperated, and said, "Oh, we did not." She corrected Henry's fabrication that the snake had been poised to strike and that Henry himself had whizzed a few stones in the snake's direction, to scare it off. But she became genuinely angry at Roger when he said that Yolanda was braver than any of us, and ought to get a bonus for her heroism. "That's ridiculous," Carolyn cried. "What if she had missed? That snake could have turned on us— any of us," she said, looking hard at Roger.

"But she didn't miss," Roger said, glancing around the table for corroboration. "You're just mad because it was Yolanda," he added. "If Henry had killed that snake, or Ted—"

"Hush up!" Carolyn snapped. She wasn't accustomed to such back talk from Roger, who now put a hand across his mouth as though covering a laugh. The rest of us didn't laugh.

Uncle Hugh held up one palm, assuming his familiar role as peacemaker. "I'm sure it was all very exciting," he said, in a tone that sounded vaguely sarcastic. "As for Yolanda, and whether she acted bravely or foolishly—"

"Foolishly!" said Carolyn. She'd put down her fork, and though the meal had just begun she reached for her cigarettes. I saw that her hands were shaking. "You've heard what happened, Hugh. I *told* you what happened."

For a moment they stared at one another, Carolyn's face twitching and pale, my uncle's gaze holding an unmistakable coolness, a look of pure dislike.

I thought back to his absent evenings, Carolyn's long hours of crying in her room.

By now, Ted had come into the dining room, his girlfriend trailing shyly behind him. "Mom's been thinking of firing her," he said, cocking his head toward Yolanda. She had just entered from the kitchen, bringing a basket of hot rolls.

"Because of this?" Hugh said, irritated. "This thing with the snake?"

"No," Carolyn said, sitting back. She took a long drag on her cigarette. "But this might be the last straw."

"She's incompetent, Dad," Ted said.

"She does everything wrong," said Henry. "And she won't learn English."

Only Roger had continued eating. "She's not so bad," he said, around a mouthful of beans. "She's a good cook."

Now Hugh looked directly at me. "And what do you think, Steven? We might as well get everyone's opinion." But his tone implied that my opinion didn't matter, and I felt uneasy that Yolanda was in the room, whether she understood or not. I shrugged, affecting a Henry-like indifference. "I like her," I said. "Anyway, I don't live here."

Something in my voice—the pretended indifference, I suspect

—must have sounded funny, for everyone broke into laughter,
even Carolyn.

"An expert opinion," Ted said, rolling his eyes toward me.
He and Sheila left the room.

"Well, let's just keep an eye on her," Hugh said at last. "We
don't want to act too quickly. And after all, Steven likes her."

"Yeah, but he doesn't live here, anyway," Henry said, mimicking the tone I had used.

Everyone laughed again, including myself. Yolanda, not understanding, had kept her usual abashed, unsmiling demeanor.
When she left the room, I felt nearly overcome with relief.

Eager as I was to extricate myself from the household, I could
not have imagined that I would cause Yolanda's downfall.
During that last week, time passed briskly, and I thought of
nothing but getting away. I had packed and repacked my bags
several times, much to my cousins' amusement; but I sensed a
certain wistfulness in them, even in Henry, over my departure—
perhaps a shred of envy. Yet the tensions between Hugh and
Carolyn had relaxed considerably. They'd gone to a cocktail
party the previous weekend and had come home tipsy, giggling
together in their bedroom for hours afterward. I couldn't recon-
cile this with the dour, suspicious atmosphere of previous days,
with Carolyn's violent outbursts and Hugh's deliberate, cold
insouciance—how, I wondered, could two such people be married to one another? Having previously known only the example
of my own parents, whose union had remained placid throughout my childhood, I now thought of "marriage" as a passage
into the unknown, full of wild and fearful possibilities. During
my last days in El Paso, I scared myself with such unaccustomed
thoughts. I began questioning Roger and Henry about Ted, also,
asking about those long hours he spent alone with Sheila in his
bedroom. Why didn't Carolyn object? What if they had to get
married, Ted and Sheila, with Ted still a year away from high-
school graduation? What then? I insisted. Roger whispered to
me, in a confidential voice, that Ted used rubbers, and Henry
laughed that Carolyn bought them for him when she picked up
Roger's asthma medicine, and Roger indignantly said that wasn't

true. It was then I remembered the conversation earlier that week in the dining room, and I asked about Ted's obvious grudge against Yolanda.

Both Roger and Henry laughed, looking at each other.

"I thought you knew," Roger said, his plump face reddening. Henry raised an eyebrow at me. "You promise not to tell anybody?" he said slyly. "If you did, Mom would skin you alive."

"And us, too," Roger said, adopting the same sly tone.

I gave the promise, but had begun to regret bringing up the subject. The story that gradually unfolded, as Roger and Henry talked back and forth, interrupting and contradicting each other, amounted to this: late one night, five or six months ago, Ted had been caught in Yolanda's bedroom. Carolyn had remembered something she wanted to tell Yolanda, and though it was past midnight she knocked on the door and put her head inside. A narrow shaft of light just revealed the bed and her oldest son's startled, open-mouthed expression. According to my cousins, Carolyn had done nothing. She had whispered "Sorry," and had quietly shut the door, retreating to her bedroom at the opposite end of the house. Whether Ted had returned to his own bedroom immediately, or somewhat later, my cousins didn't know, but the next evening Carolyn had cornered her two younger sons and in her brisk, finger-shaking manner had informed them that the maid's room was strictly off-limits. Never mind why, she told them. (Though naturally, thanks to Ted's bragging, they already knew why.) Roger recalled his mother's obscure suggestion that Yolanda wasn't quite to be trusted, and in any case she wasn't to be bothered during her off hours. The main burden of all this, for Roger and Henry, was that they were being blamed for something their brother had done—a frequent complaint of theirs. They were always saying resentfully that Ted was the favorite of both his parents, that he was spoiled rotten, while Roger and Henry were treated like infants. "But what about Yolanda?" I asked them. "Did she like Ted, or did he—" and yet I couldn't finish. At fourteen, I couldn't quite frame the question in my own mind. Both my cousins regarded me suspiciously but then laughed it off.

My last evening in the house seemed very somber and quiet,

but I might have been imagining this. Uncle Hugh had become involved in another "major project" at the office, and hadn't arrived home for dinner; after helping Yolanda fix a quick meal of hamburgers and refried beans, Carolyn had gone to her bedroom to read. My younger cousins were watching television in the family room and Ted had gone off somewhere with Sheila. Bored, I had gone into the kitchen for a soft drink when I heard, from Yolanda's room, a soft and echoing wail that sounded for a moment like weeping. When I reached her open doorway, though, I understood that the sound came from the small plastic radio on the windowsill, which was playing a plaintive Mexican song. The female singer drew out every note in a low-pitched, agonized tremor that raised the flesh on my arms; it seemed evocative of a realm of irreparable loss and sorrow, a mystery beyond my ken but communicable through the staticky waves of the music. For a long moment I stood in the doorway, listening to the song and watching Yolanda, who stood at the ironing board in the corner, pressing a dress shirt of my uncle's. Her plump, rosy face—looking vapid but not thoughtless, immersed in the undulant keening of the song—seemed to me, for the first time, beautiful; and for the first time, too, I wondered at her certain loneliness and at the bleak forbearance of her dreams. Out of some abrupt, confused surge of pity I made a coughing noise and said "Yolanda?" and she looked up at me, seeming both embarrassed and shyly pleased.

When she said something I didn't comprehend, ending with "Señor Steven," I detected a trace of irony in her smile, which I found nonetheless friendly and reassuring. I came inside the room and, both nervous and elated, talked non-stop with Yolanda for perhaps twenty or thirty minutes. Aided by the broad, expressive gestures used by two people who speak different languages, we really managed quite well, our moments of successful communication celebrated by bursts of vigorous nodding and shouts of "*Si, si*" by both of us. I told her about the place I came from, with its humid air and rolling hills, its numberless massive trees, and Yolanda described the small town in central Mexico where she had been raised and whose dry, relentless heat and rocky terrain she conveyed with colorful, forbidding gestures, along with a dramatic raising of her heavy eyebrows that seemed to express both extreme pleasure and dismay. On the wall beside her narrow bed hung a yellowed map of Mexico, and side by side we peered at it, Yolanda tracing her route from home to El Paso with the tip of her squarish, bitten-down nail. This close, I detected an unfamiliar odor about her, as of strong soap mingled with the heavy scent of gardenias, or musk. When she dropped her hand from the map, giving me a friendly pinch on the arm, she made some loud remark that must have been a joke, for she laughed uproariously, her broad gap-toothed face tilted back, her glistening dark eyes fixed on mine, and in my giddy pleasure I laughed with her, not caring what the joke was. It felt that much better, perhaps, to be laughing about nothing at all.

It was then, however, that Aunt Carolyn's shrill voice reached our ears. We both turned in alarm to where she stood in the doorway, dressed in a pink quilted housecoat, her face denuded of makeup and her blond hair in curlers. I didn't know how long she'd been standing there, but I thought instantly of the pinch Yolanda had given my arm, and how snug and complicitous we must look inside this tiny room, laughing together.

Furious, Carolyn came toward me with her arm upraised. The quick, stinging slap came as such a surprise that I didn't move or react, except to lift one hand to my burning cheek.

"Steven, get to your room!" my aunt cried. "I'm really surprised at you."

"But Aunt Carolyn—"

"Don't say anything. Get!"

I began backing out of the room, one palm still laid across my stinging cheek.

"We were just talking," I said from the doorway, in what must have been a whining voice. "Yolanda didn't—"

Carolyn whirled on me. "You heard me, didn't you?" she cried. "Now go!"

I went down the hall toward the kitchen, still too shocked to think clearly. From Yolanda's room, I heard Carolyn shouting half in English, half in Spanish. The gist seemed to be that Yolanda was fired; that she would be leaving for Mexico in the morning; that her wonderful mother, Dolores, would be deeply ashamed of her. This went on for five or ten minutes, Carolyn's voice so shrill that it began to turn hoarse, Yolanda saying nothing in reply. I said to myself that my aunt was insane, and then I went to the family room and watched television with my cousins for the rest of the evening.

I was not surprised when Carolyn, the next day, behaved as if nothing had happened. I'd risen early to say good-bye to Uncle Hugh before he left for the office, and I slipped a note under Yolanda's door that contained a few words of apology and farewell in my awkward Spanish. At breakfast Carolyn was gay and chirpy, saying how awful it was that I had to leave for another year, but that next August would be here before we knew it. Ted was still sleeping in his room (with Sheila? I wondered) but Roger and Henry helped me load my few bags into Carolyn's station wagon, and then we all drove together to the station. As we had done the three previous summers, we said good-bye cheerfully, making awkward jokes and talking of summers to come. They all promised to write, even Henry, and I made the same promise in return. Soon enough it was over.

I don't remember much about that long train ride home, except that my sense of relief was far exceeded by a gray, glowering melancholy that I'd never experienced before. I no longer thought Carolyn insane, of course, but my sense of her injustice nagged and burned with an intensity felt only by the very young. Never again, I vowed, would I return to El Paso. Never again would I say Aunt Carolyn's name. When my parents asked about her, I decided, I would shrug my shoulders and refuse to speak. These childish fancies passed away soon enough, of course, and perhaps my generally glum and resentful thoughts had focused on my aunt as a way of avoiding the memory of Yolanda or the thought of her eventual fate, for which I would remain eternally, if innocently, responsible. I felt the unfairness of those casual and irreparable bonds that are often forged between two human beings, without their consent and without any particular design or beneficent result outside their own jagged, private dreams, their shards of memory.

But nowadays I often think of Yolanda. Where I once felt regret that we'd lacked a common language, that I hadn't been able to express sorrow or contrition or even properly to say good-bye, now I understand how banal such words must have been, and how much better left unsaid. I'm no less romantic now than as a child, though I haven't been back to Texas in years, and have no desire to revisit El Paso. It remains as a shining, snow-capped dream of my childhood, yet mired in a brownish haze of shame as if glimpsed through the tarnish of some ancient, sepia-toned photograph. As for Yolanda, I imagine her married and overweight, deep in the Mexican interior, with no recollection of me. She is surrounded by children, grown and half-grown. Perhaps I'm no longer so romantic, since I readily accept this. Though I am childless, and only casually married, in my daydreams I seldom ride through the desert and into the Mexican countryside, finding Yolanda disconsolate in her hovel, then carrying her off in my arms. And when I do, I don't take her to El Paso.

A Summer Romance

O N HER FIRST AFTERNOON at the beach, Hannah stood inside the screened-in back porch and with her usual pleased melancholy stared out at the waves.

This year she'd decided to drive out to the beach alone, bypassing her father's new place in Charleston. On the phone he hadn't bothered to act disappointed—his new wife and Hannah weren't mutual admirers—but he'd promised to meet her on Friday in time for dinner. So when she'd entered the back porch, hearing the crash of the waves and feeling her nose twitch agreeably at the salty breeze, she glanced at her watch: only 5:30, so she had several hours to herself. Breathing the heavy moist air, Hannah felt the luxury of absolute privacy, her sadness expanding and thinning to a form of contentment.

She'd been looking out for several minutes, her eyes misted over, when she saw the young man come walking along the beach. Hannah stepped back, narrowing her eyes as she watched him, her lips forming a cautious half-smile. What had Julie said on the phone, just the other night?—*Who knows, kid, maybe you'll meet somebody, some cute surfer or something, you know?* Then Julie had burst into bright raucous laughter, a new habit she'd developed about the time she acquired her first boyfriend, near the end of her and Hannah's senior year. Though she'd planned to come on this trip to the beach, she'd begged off at the last minute, giving that same laugh. Wouldn't she just get in the way? she'd asked slyly. Maybe Hannah *would* meet someone, find a summer boyfriend, a "summer romance"? Nothing was impossible, after all!

Hannah could imagine what would happen if Julie were here: she'd push Hannah onto the deck, stage-whispering, "Go on, don't be such a shy old thing." Or she'd call to the man, "Yoohoo! Over here, sweetie!" And when he looked she would point to Hannah, winking.

Watching the man, Hannah rolled up on the balls of her feet, then down again. She smiled her little half-smile.

He was tall, pale, and dark-haired, perhaps in his mid-twenties. He wore white swim trunks and walked quickly, almost urgently, like a man navigating a busy downtown street instead of a deserted beach. Hannah didn't think she'd seen him before. This late in the summer there was seldom anyone in residence along this exclusive, sequestered beachfront: she remembered her father saying on the phone that he'd driven down last weekend with Marthe, and it looked as if everyone had closed up their houses and left. "So we'll probably have the beach to ourselves," he'd said comfortably, adding with a chuckle: "I guess you'll like that, won't you?" It was a private joke between them that Hannah was "anti-social," mainly because she was so reserved and cautious around Marthe's college-age son, a tall light-haired surfer type named Fritz. Sometimes Hannah said "ha ha" when her father made his jokes, or she would cross her eyes in mock-exasperation. But on the phone she'd said softly, but clearly, "More than you will," listening to the curious adult evenness in her voice. Her father had quickly changed the subject.

When she saw the young man pause by the waves, looking down as the lacy foam rushed across his feet, Hannah took a deep breath, then crossed the porch and unlatched the screen door. She hurried along the cedar deck and had descended ten or twelve steps before he noticed her. He raised his hand at once and cried "Hi!" over the crash of the waves; he started toward her. Embarrassed, Hannah glanced down at the ripped cut-offs she'd worn for the car trip, and the pink sweat-stained

Emory T-shirt she'd lived in since taking her first college course this summer; for once she wished she'd listened to her mother, who often said angrily or flippantly, depending on her mood, that Hannah dressed like a bag lady. She waited awkwardly as the man hurried over, his hand outstretched.

"Hi, I'm Derek—from three houses down?" He gestured down the beach. "Glad to meet you."

He spoke in an eager, overloud voice, competing with the waves; his eyes looked anxious as he pumped her hand. He was older than he'd looked at first, maybe around thirty. Fine lines rayed out from the corners of his washed-blue eyes.

Hannah heard herself saying, "Hi, I'm Randi," blushing at once although Derek didn't notice. He stared downward, toeing aimless designs in the sand. "Randi" was a nickname some of her high-school friends had used, and Hannah had written the name for the first time, with her tight half-smile, when registering for her Emory math course in June. In ninth grade Hannah had idolized a fashion model being celebrated that year—an emaciated girl with huge eyes and a wild mane of blond hair— and the model's name was Randi, just *Randi* without a last name, and so Julie and the other kids had started calling Hannah that. They were being sarcastic, maybe, since Hannah had been a bit overweight even then, and had ordinary curly brown hair; but Hannah hadn't discouraged the nickname.

"Randi? That's a nice name," Derek said.

They started walking along the beach, Derek in the lead, gesturing her forward and talking amiably. Hannah felt a clutching excitement in her throat, her belly: her friends had often claimed that Hannah wasn't adventurous or spontaneous enough, that she was much too shy, too "stodgy." Julie had used that awful word, *stodgy*, not long ago, when Hannah had refused a double date with Julie and Rauf, and one of Rauf's visiting cousins. The truth was that Hannah wouldn't have minded the blind date; she just didn't care to be around the "new" Julie. With her sleeker looks, and her brash self-confidence, Julie had begun poking fun at Hannah, as though ridiculing some former version of herself.

Walking beside Derek, Hannah found it easy to forget what Julie might think or say. For Hannah sensed that Derek liked her, that he wouldn't put her through the ruthless period of assessment, and judgment, that Hannah suffered each time she met someone new. Derek spoke easily, unself-consciously, as if continuing with Hannah a lively conversation he'd been having with himself. He strode along rapidly, so that Hannah had trouble keeping up. She strained to hear his voice over the waves. Did she come to the beach often? he asked. Did she like it here? Was she sorry the summer was nearly over? He gave quick sideways grins as he questioned her; she felt her shyness ebbing, dissolving. No, she said, she wasn't really sorry—she was looking forward to her freshman year in college.

"Really?" he said. "Well, I guess I felt that way at first, but now I'm tired of it. It's my senior year, I go to this small college up near Myrtle Beach, you've probably never heard of it. . . ." He glanced at Hannah. "I guess you're thinking I'm too old, huh? To still be in college?"

He stopped and picked up a sand dollar, but it was broken so he pitched it out into the waves. He looked at Hannah.

"I don't know," she said.

"First I went into the Marines," Derek said, looking out to the horizon. "That was to please my father. And after that I was sick for a while, so I ended up getting a very late start. I haven't been all that motivated, to be honest. I skipped semesters here and there, I had to repeat a couple of courses. . . ."

Hannah felt the prickling of goose flesh along her arms. It had been so hot earlier, but now there were clouds to the west and the wind had gotten cooler, brisker. Derek was talking about his business courses—his father was in banking, he said, so he might try something in that line—and Hannah tried to listen. Yet she kept being distracted by Derek's affable manner and his manly, almost startling good looks—his hair dark and thick, his facial bones sharply cut, especially the prominent cheekbones and squarish chin. Derek's eyes were large, deep-set, the lashes long as a girl's. Although his body appeared solid, the shoulders fairly broad and muscular, his chest and arms looked vulnerable, Hannah thought, so smooth and white and unmarked. . . . Hannah knew that Julie would have considered him "sexy," or "cute," but Hannah responded to something gentle and even innocent about him—he might be the type who daydreamed a lot, she thought, or wrote poetry; or who'd been wounded badly in love and hadn't quite recovered.

"Which house is your father's?" Hannah said, looking back down the beach.

"I told you, three down from yours," Derek said. He paused for a moment, watching her. "You want to see it?"

"Now?" Hannah said, her shyness returning.

Derek smiled and grabbed her wrist, playfully. "Why not now? Of course *now*," he said. Keeping hold of her wrist, he led her back the way they had come. His sudden urgency charmed Hannah; he was like a boy, really, and he made her feel childlike, too. Soon they passed Hannah's father's house and at the same moment they glanced at it. The house looked alien, Hannah thought. She might never have been inside that house before.

When they reached Derek's place, he paused at the bottom of the wooden flight of steps. He released her and bent over in a mock-bow, gesturing broadly. "Madam," he said, "welcome to my humble home." Hannah laughed and preceded him up the stairs. She felt giddy but apprehensive. She was playing the role of a carefree, utterly confident girl—which wasn't herself, of course, and didn't even resemble the true Hannah. This was the same half-guilty feeling she'd had that day at college when she'd signed herself "Randi," then stared at the word as though trying to discover its meaning.

As they passed through Derek's back porch to the great room, Hannah saw that this house was even larger than her father's, though it was the same Georgian style as all the houses along this stretch of beach—gray stucco exterior, a sloping mansard roof with a large sundeck protruding from the upper story. The interior was dimly lit, so that the corners of the great room faded into shadow, coming to no definite end. Again Hannah shivered; she heard the faraway hum of the air-conditioning system.

"Are you cold?" Derek asked. She could feel his heated breath on her neck. "Look at that flimsy shirt you've got on, don't you know there's a storm coming?" He clapped his hands. "Hey, want to borrow a sweatshirt? Or you could use one of my mother's sweaters, or a shawl. . . . She wouldn't mind."

"No, that's okay," Hannah said quickly. "I really can't stay."
She stood with her arms crossed, feeling cold and suddenly
miserable. Noticing the antique mahogany furniture and the
doilies on several of the chair backs, Hannah supposed that
Derek's parents must be rather elderly, and had resisted the
"casual" nature of the house's original design . . . the effect was
discomforting, somehow. She turned to Derek and saw that he'd
fixed a dark dreamy scowl upon her.

"Why don't you hang around?" he said, nodding toward the
kitchen. Through the doorway Hannah had glimpsed an open
pantry, some copper pans hung along the wall. "I can cook,"
he said, winking. "That's one thing I *can* do. I could whip up a
little supper."

"Oh, no thanks," she said, backing away. "I have to meet my
father, didn't I tell you? I promised I'd have dinner with him."

Derek shrugged. "Okee-doke," he said. "But maybe you could
come back—you know, later on. I don't know many people at
the beach, do you?"

He'd begun walking her back to the porch; and now that she
was leaving, of course, Derek seemed even more handsome than
before. She felt a renewed scorn toward her own timidity, and
could see Julie's smirking face: *Stodgy! Shy old thing!*

"Thanks," she said quietly. "I'll try to come back. . . ."

"Please do, madam," he said, performing another little mock-
bow.

Hannah smiled and called out, "Nice to meet you!" and hurried down the steps. Walking up the beach, she looked over her
shoulder several times to see Derek still standing outside. He
waved each time, and Hannah waved back. When his house was
out of sight, she broke into a run; the wind had stiffened and
enormous raindrops began pelting her face. Out to the west, dark
clouds massed threateningly. The beach looked dusky and deserted though it wasn't yet six o'clock. Inside the house, Hannah
rushed around flipping on lights to dispel the gloom, but her
stomach fell when she entered the hall and saw a message light
on the answering machine. She quickly rewound and played
the tape:

"Hi, honey," her father's voice said. "It's the big bad wolf calling from Charleston. Look, it's raining like hell here, sweetheart, so I think I'll hold the show over for tonight, then pop down there in the morning. Sorry about dinner, but we'll have breakfast at the club, all right? The rain's supposed to clear out by then, but Marthe just don't want her old man driving in this weather. I hope *you* made it safely, sugar plum. Have a good sleep, okay? And batten down the hatches!"

Her fingers working idly, independent of her, she toyed with the machine, replaying bits of the tape briefly, listening with a small fixed smile as she heard *like hell here, sweetheart* and *then pop down there* and *don't want her old man* and then, tiring of the game, she rewound the tape and flipped off the machine. She said aloud, "I did make it safely, sugar plum," and without thinking much about it (later, she would try to pinpoint the exact moment she'd decided, but could not) she ran to her bedroom, grabbed her day-glo orange windbreaker, and in minutes was back down on the beach, half-stumbling through the stinging wind and rain.

The temperature had dropped by ten degrees, she thought; or twenty degrees. By now the swollen slate-gray clouds had filled the sky, bringing a steady, slanting rain from the west. Hannah rushed along, her jacket billowing. The beach seemed beaten into submission by the storm, the sand turned to a seamy, dun-colored mud that tugged like quicksand at her feet. She thought what a pitiful sight she must look in her rain-soaked clothes and stringy hair.

Derek waited inside the screened porch, wearing a pleased half-smile. He'd changed into a white sweat-shirt and jeans. "I knew you'd come back," he said, handing her a towel. "Our supper's almost ready, in fact. Fresh tuna, plus carrots and a broccoli salad. How's that sound?"

She couldn't speak: her wet skin against the refrigerated air had brought a violent fit of shivering. To hide her discomfort, she rubbed her hair briskly with the towel.

"Here, give me that jacket," Derek said. "I'll run upstairs to my mother's room, get you some dry clothes."

Hannah started to protest but he was already gone, returning a moment later with a white terry-cloth bathrobe and a pair of thick athletic socks. "I decided you should wear my stuff instead," he said. "It's not high fashion, but at least you'll get warm!"

While she changed, he stood at the window facing out to the beach. "This is an incredible storm," he said in a pleased voice. "The radio said the waves might reach twenty feet, which means this porch could be knee-deep by morning." He laughed, briefly. "But don't worry," he said, "it never comes up into the main house. At least, it never has."

"Okay, you can turn around," Hannah said quickly, wanting Derek to stop talking; something in his words—or in his dreamy tone of voice—made her uneasy. Taking her hand, he led her back to the kitchen and busied himself at once with their dinner. Despite her apprehension Hannah sat docile and quiet, in a straight-back wooden chair.

"Do you like to cook?" Derek asked. "I love it, especially for company." He diced carrots, he tossed the salad with his elbows raised in the air, lifting one hand in a flourish when he'd finished —"*Voilà!*" he said, "now we're just waiting on the rolls. You like sourdough, don't you? I hated it when I was a kid, but now I love it." He searched through the cabinets for plates and napkins, he opened and slammed drawers, moving very quickly as though agitated, over-excited. Hannah sat still and said nothing. She'd noticed Derek's habit of asking questions and then answering them himself, but that suited her fine. She felt an obscure but deep pleasure in just sitting here, while this handsome man scuttled crazily around the kitchen.

Outside the rain had settled in, darkly; occasionally they heard a distant crack of thunder. Herding her into the great room, Derek set their places on the elegant mahogany table, snapped off the overhead chandelier, and lit a pair of tall white candles. Sitting across from her, eating quickly and saying very little, he struck Hannah as a hero out of the Gothic romances she was always reading—his deep-set eyes thrown into shadow by the candlelight, his face gauntly handsome with its high cheekbones and strong chin. Hannah smiled at her thoughts, relaxed by the delectable glass of blush-colored wine, which she drank rather greedily; how shocked she'd have been, driving grim-faced along the coast just a few hours ago, to have pictured this scene lying ahead of her, this romantic adventure! It was no more than that, of course; she would excuse herself right after dinner, thank him profusely, then race back to her father's house and call Julie in Atlanta. "Listen," she might say, trying not to gloat, "you'll never guess what happened. . . ."

Derek finished within minutes, as though wanting to get the meal over with; he glanced impatiently at Hannah's plate. She had eaten only two bites of the tuna, which was delicious, and her vegetables were untouched. Embarrassed, she followed his glance to her empty wine glass.

"Finished?" Derek said, hurrying over.

When they'd cleared the dishes and tidied up the kitchen, Hannah thanked him and said she had to be going.

"What? Leave now?" he said. "But we haven't even talked, I haven't found out anything about you!"

"I know, but... Would you get my clothes, please?"

"All right," he said, sighing, and Hannah listened as he clomped downstairs; she heard the faraway humming of the dryer. But he came back empty-handed. Annoyed, Hannah began, "Derek, I—"

"Sorry, I'm really *sorry*," he said, watching her guiltily, "but I left your stuff on top of the dryer! I was thinking about the dinner, I guess, and so . . . look, it's just another forty-five minutes, that's all it takes. In the meantime, why don't I show you the house? I'm a practiced tour guide," he said eagerly. "Wouldn't you like that? A grand tour . . . ?"

He'd already started off, and so Hannah followed him up the dark-stained wooden stairs. He'd brought one of the candles from the table, which provided their only light; he led her to the bedroom nearest the stairs, and at the doorway Hannah quickly flipped the light switch. She went no further.

"This is—let's see, this is my mother's room," he said, glancing around. Hannah saw, on the oak bureau, the photograph of a smiling elderly couple—both gray-haired and well-dressed, wearing glasses. She thought to examine the faces for their resemblance to Derek, but she didn't want to follow him into the room or show much interest.

"It's nice," she said quickly, "but why don't we—"

"Jesus," Derek said, shaking his head. "What a cute kid!" He ran his hand across his face and laughed. "Come on, you haven't seen my room. You'll find it quite pleasant, I believe!"

She followed him numbly down the hall. She'd resigned herself to this "tour" and no longer felt embarrassed over her damp hair or the oversized bathrobe. When they got to Derek's room she fixed her attention on him, as though trying one last time to decide if his wayward energy were charming, or frightening; to decide if she were attracted, or repelled, by the look of sadness and defeat she kept glimpsing in his eyes. Entering, Hannah stayed near the closet with her robe clutched around her; Derek's room seemed gloomier and less inviting than the others. The walls were paneled in a dark dull-finished wood. There were no pictures or mirrors.

"Hey Randi," Derek said, from the window. "Come look at the view."

Keeping her distance from the bed, Hannah walked slowly toward him. Her legs moved heavily, stubbornly, as though wading through water. Derek rested his arm lightly along her shoulders, pointing with his free hand.

"See?—from up here you can see a lot further. There's your house—it's three houses away, right? Look, you left the lights on."

"I know—I meant to," she said, which wasn't exactly true. But it comforted her to see the few other houses stretching down the beach, one or two dark and abandoned-looking but the others well-lit, evidently occupied after all.... "It's a beautiful view, even in this weather," she added vaguely, her eye straying to the white-capped waves, just visible thanks to spotlights from the house next door.

"When there's a moon," Derek said wistfully, "I'll bet you can see a lot more. I'll bet it's beautiful, then."

Hannah stepped back, but now he turned in a fluid movement and grasped her shoulders. Slowly his face approached hers. "Do you mind . . . ?"

"Yes—I mean, no, you shouldn't," Hannah said. She looked down, confused by the sudden bright heat in her belly; she did want the kiss, of course. But now he'd dropped his arms and stepped back. He smiled ironically.

She began, "I'm sorry, I—"

"Look, maybe your clothes are done," he said, bending down for the candle. "I'll run down and get them, all right?"

"I could come down—"

But he was gone. She waited for a moment, eyes closed, more desolate than she'd ever felt in her life. Now that she'd rebuffed him, of course, he'd have nothing to do with her; already his beautiful image—somehow *beautiful* was the word, not merely *handsome*—lingered in her mind's eye with the pathos of someone lost forever. Of course it was her own fault, she thought, and she began wandering around the room, feeling a new curiosity about Derek. She'd heard nothing from the stairway, so she opened his closet door and peered inside. But it was empty: no clothes hanging along the wooden rods, no shoes along the floorboard. Still listening for him, she went quickly to the bureau and yanked open the top drawer: though she had known bleakly, before pulling the tarnished brass knobs, that the drawer was empty. The second drawer was empty, too. She had squatted down to open the bottom drawer, grunting, her stomach clenched with dread, when the overhead light went out and Hannah found herself in total darkness.

She stood, unsteadily. She started for the window, where the rain clattered fiercely against the glass, but then turned back toward the bed. She sat, then stood again. She could scarcely glimpse her own hand, though she waved it frantically before her eyes. . . . She'd already moved toward the door, supposing there must be a back stairway, some other way out, when she heard his clomping footsteps on the stairs. She had rasped out, "Derek, is that—" when he appeared at the door, his hand cupped gently around the candle.

"Hey there," he said. He was smiling. He seemed to be smiling. Yet the wavering candlelight sent weird, elongated shadows across his face, so that his expression looked friendly one moment, sinister the next.

"Derek?" she said, frightened. "What happened to—"

"A power outage," he said, putting the candle on the bedside table. "Courtesy of Mother Nature," he added in that wry, mock-solemn voice of his; but then he laughed. "Sorry about your clothes, Randi," he said, sitting down on the bed. "But I didn't want to risk the basement stairway, not with just a candle. Didn't want to break my lousy neck."

"But what about—how can I—"

Hannah could not put her thoughts together.

"Relax, will you?" he said. "Here, sit down"—and he patted the bed. "Here's the perfect chance to talk."

She sat; she had no choice, really. She must behave as rationally as possible, letting Derek say whatever he wanted. Though she could not turn to face him—her body had gone stiff, all but immobilized in her panic—she watched him out the sides of her eyes. He'd removed his sweatshirt and now wore only a sleeveless white T-shirt that had come untucked on one side. His arms looked pale and vulnerable in the candlelight; as he talked the arms moved in helpless flapping gestures, a constant whitish motion at the periphery of Hannah's vision. . . . She kept telling herself to breathe deeply, to remain calm. This was only a power outage, after all, and Derek hadn't really meant to alarm her. Wasn't he simply alone, and lonely, just as she was often lonely . . . ? He meant no harm, no harm. And the storm couldn't last long, not at this intensity; surely the power would be restored soon. Then she would go downstairs and retrieve her clothes and say good-bye to Derek.

". . . so it's tough, don't you think?" he was saying. "In contemporary times?"

"What—?"

She hadn't been listening to his words, only to the rambling and rather manic flow of his voice.

He laughed, shortly. "So you weren't paying attention, eh?"

"I'm sorry, I—"

"I was just saying how hard it is, these days—communicating with another person. Especially someone cute, you know?—someone you really like." His face seemed to float in the darkness, the features not quite visible; she kept trying to bring him into focus. "Everybody believes something different these days, everybody does their own thing and so you can't really fit in, can you? There's nothing to fit inside. I mean, nothing's *there*," he said, his voice edged with disgust. "Haven't you found that to be true?"

"I don't know—I guess so—"

"Ah, but you're young. Just *wait*," he said. Again that sharp, almost angry laugh. "You can lose your way, you know. It's so easy, really. That's the very thought I was having earlier today, when we met on the beach. I mean, you can't understand when or how you lost the way, you just wake up one morning and don't know who you are, like you've broken into fragments of people, somehow—like you're many different people, really, and you can't. . . ." He kept talking, more to himself than to her; she tried to listen but her head felt woozy, as if she hadn't slept for many days. And she wondered if it were really so awful, what might happen between them now, in the darkness? Perhaps this was only a version of what happened, sooner or later, to everyone? Dazed by such thoughts, she didn't bother to pull away when she felt Derek's hand begin stroking her hair.

"So pretty . . . such a cute girl," he was saying. "You understand, don't you? You appreciate my point of view, don't you?"

"Yes," she said at once. He brought his face to her cheek and pressed against her; she didn't feel a kiss, precisely, only the pressure of his warm damp face—mouth, nose, trembling eyelids—mashed against hers. For the second time today she felt that hot slashing pain in her belly, and then, as if to assuage that pain, Derek's groping strong hand moved slowly along her waist.

Now, dreamily, she let her gaze stray to the window beyond Derek's shoulder: she could still make out, through the rain-blurred glass, the other houses stretching down the beach. All these houses, including her father's, still had their lights on, which meant that of course there was no power outage, that of course Derek had disconnected the lights himself. Her heart jumped, but not really in fear. She gave an abrupt, nervous laugh. She'd laughed just at the moment that Derek, his opened mouth against her throat, had begun fumbling with the buttons of his jeans.

He drew back, sharply; she turned to him at once. "I'm sorry, I didn't mean to laugh, it's just that I—"

He was neither smiling nor scowling; he had stayed very still, as if lost in thought. She shouldn't tell him, maybe, that she knew he'd disconnected the lights. And she wished she hadn't laughed.

He said, very clearly, "It wasn't going to work, anyway. It doesn't matter, Randi."

"What? But I didn't mean—"

"It doesn't matter what you meant. None of it matters."

He spoke so slowly, so clearly—all at once she began shivering.

"What's wrong, Randi?" he said coldly. "Is there something wrong?"

She blurted, "I'm not Randi, I—"

"What? You're not Randi?"

"No, I—it's just a nickname, a stupid nickname—my real name is Hannah." She swallowed hard, against that terrible ache rising in her throat. "Hannah Greer," she said. "My father is James Greer and I—"

She was babbling, she wasn't making sense, and when she saw him reach to the bedside table—opening its drawer with what seemed a menacing slowness, a mockery of her panic—she could not move. She could not get up and rush down the stairway in darkness and out of this house. Even when he brought the candle toward her face with one hand, and the shiny knife-blade with the other, she remained perfectly still. She had even stopped shivering.

"Do you know who *I* am?" he said, drawing out each syllable as though speaking to a child. "*Do* you, Randi?"

She shook her head, briefly. She could not speak.

"No, and you don't want to know," he said, his contemptuous tone giving way to something hollow and melancholy, something very like sorrow.

"That's why I cut out the lights, Randi, to make it easier—so you would look and see anyone you wanted, *feel* anyone you wanted. Did you think I couldn't hear you, from downstairs? Rushing to the closet, going through the drawers?" He laughed, sadly. "No, Randi, I don't live here—I can feel you thinking that, and you're absolutely right. And yes, I've done things, I've done some terrible things—enough to frighten a whole roomful of girls like you! But does that mean I don't need to be—to be close to someone, Randi? And you didn't have to see, not really. You didn't have to *know*."

He held the knife-blade inches before her eyes, turning it over and over in the candlelight as though trying to hypnotize her; and in fact she could not take her eyes off the blade.

"I—I don't know what you want," she whispered.

"You don't?" he said mockingly. "You really don't? Then I'll tell you, Randi."

He stood, putting the candle on the table, then reached down and grasped her beneath one armpit; he drew her up to him, still holding the knife-blade close to her eyes. She had begun to cry, the steel blade blurring in her vision, but Derek seemed unfazed by her tears. He put his mouth close to her ear, whispering fiercely: "They're dead, Randi. A very nice old couple who lived in this house, I had to use this knife on them and now they're in the basement, dead as they can be. It's quite a sight, Randi. You're lucky that you didn't run down to the basement after your clothes, as I'm sure you were thinking of doing. You'd have gotten a pretty ugly surprise for all your trouble."

He had begun caressing her—somehow, "caressing" was the right word—with the blade of his knife, stroking its blunt edge softly against her throat. Again her panic and fear had stilled, hardened; had become one with her rigid body. Listening to Derek, she didn't tremble. She didn't even blink.

"And now, Randi," Derek said softly, seductively, "I'll tell you what I want. All I want is this: for you to stay here, in this room, for half an hour, which will give me time to make some, uh, adjustments down in the basement, and then get out of here. Do you understand? After that, you can come downstairs and get your clothes—I'll put them on the dining-room table— and you can leave. Okay, Randi? But you can't leave first—you can't leave *me*. Instead, I'll leave *you*. Got that, Randi?"

"But what—what about—"

"The old folks? Well, if I were you, Randi, I wouldn't get involved. The longer they stay down there, of course, the better chance I have to get away. Now I won't be able to control what you do. You'll probably call the police, but then I guess you'd have some explaining to do. Like, what were you doing here in this house, with a strange guy? And how will they know *you're* not involved, somehow? I think it could get quite messy, Randi my love."

He drew back, abruptly, and brought the candle to her face. She could feel its heat, and she stared tearfully at the flame rather than look into Derek's eyes. She didn't want to see those eyes. "Goodbye, Randi," he said, so softly the words seemed an echo, mere wisps of sound. "I had a lovely time."

Hannah did not watch as he left the room, taking the candle and the knife. She could hear him rummaging around downstairs, slamming the basement door, and after a few minutes the lights came on. Hannah blinked, looking around the room. Her knees felt weak, but otherwise she was all right. When the house had gone quiet, she crept into the hall, onto the stairway, then down into the great room.

Her clothes lay neatly folded on the table. She grabbed them, ran through the porch and down the steps into the rainy night. When she reached her own back porch, she discarded the clothes Derek had given her and struggled back into her own. But now they felt damp and foreign, like a stranger's clothes. She considered for several agonizing minutes whether to call the police, but she was too exhausted, too confused; she would tell her father everything in the morning, and let him decide. Safe inside the porch, she curled herself into the hammock, wanting to calm down, to rest her eyes for a moment, before going back to her bedroom for the night.

Sunlight woke her; she rose quickly, befuddled, and had time only to shower and change before she heard her father's BMW in the driveway. "Hannah-girl!" he boomed cheerfully, and after she came out, and endured her father's bear-hug and a round of silly questions—he was always energetic and boyish in the morning, and liked to flirt with his daughter—they went to the club for breakfast. She was relieved, at least, that he hadn't brought Marthe and Fritz along. That would make everything easier.

During breakfast, and afterward as they strolled along the beach, opportunities kept arising to tell her father what had happened; but one by one, they passed her by. As they neared the house of that poor old couple, Hannah looked stiffly out to sea, afraid that if she even glimpsed the house she might break down. Every time she thought about what had happened, her mind skittered off in another direction; she knew that her delay would only help Derek, but at the same time she couldn't imagine their apprehending him, hauling him off in chains. . . . It wasn't until the fourth and last morning of their visit together—her father, as it turned out, had business in Charleston and needed to leave earlier than planned—that her father slowed his walk, to Hannah's horror, and stopped only a few yards from the steps leading up to that house.

Outside the porch stood an elderly woman, sweeping the walkway. "Hello, Mrs. Tate, good to see you! How was your trip?" her father called jovially. He had cupped his hands, but the woman could not make herself heard over the waves. She nodded and mouthed the words: *Fine, fine.* "And how's your husband?" The woman kept nodding. *Fine, he's fine.* . . . Hannah felt her father hesitate, but then he yelled again, a bit louder: "And Derek? He's doing well, I hope?" The woman's face sagged; for a moment it seemed she would not answer. But then, at last, she nodded. *Fine, just fine.* She waved and turned back toward the porch.

"Poor old thing," her father muttered to Hannah. "Husband's got a heart condition, and her son's in the loony bin."

He didn't seem inclined to say more, so Hannah said, shyly, "Her son . . . ?"

"Yeah, name's Derek," her father said. "In and out of hospitals all his life. A sad case, really sad."

"But doesn't he—doesn't he come home to visit? Ever?" Hannah said.

"Oh, once in a while. He's in some type of halfway house, up near Myrtle Beach. He comes home occasionally—they let him drive back and forth, free as you please—and once in a while you'll see him out on the beach. A nice-looking kid, but totally out of touch. Waves at you, says hello—but that's about it."

"But what's wrong with—"

"Hey, let's don't talk about crazy people!" her father said playfully. Now he bent down and lifted something out of the sand. A sand dollar, Hannah saw, untouched and whole. She remembered Derek examining the broken sand dollar he'd found, then pitching it out into the waves. And hadn't he muttered something about his banker father's approval, or disapproval, something ironic about "dollars and cents," or "dollars and sense," his voice barely audible over the waves? Hannah hadn't quite heard. Now, as her father held up the sand dollar, it glittered whitely in the sun. Winking, he placed it gently in Hannah's palm.

"There, now your mother can't say I'm not a good provider!"

She looked up into her father's fleshy, sunburnt face; he winked at her, merrily, and Hannah winked back.

They walked along the beach, chatting lightheartedly. Hannah felt much better: the cool breeze was wonderfully fresh, the beach looked white and smooth as if the other night's storm had never been. She felt like herself again, and thought she could ignore, at last, those words of Derek's which had been replaying in her mind's ear... *you just wake up one morning and you don't know who you are, like you've broken into fragments of people, somehow —like you're many different people, really....* Yes, she could ignore them. When she returned home, Hannah thought, she would say nothing to her mother, or to Julie. She would never tell anyone what had happened. ... Hannah had put the sand dollar in the pocket of her windbreaker, and now she kept her hand in the pocket, feeling the sand dollar, turning it over and over. A souvenir, she thought. A last token of this summer, which now seemed so different from all the summers of her girlhood and one which might not recede so quickly into the past. ... As they walked and chatted Hannah's fingers, independent of her, began breaking the sand dollar apart, piece by piece. Hannah felt even better, doing this. There were so many pieces! she thought in wonder. It was very strange, she thought, but never before had she felt so happy.

The Burning

T HE SUMMER I WAS TEN, I spent two months in the hospital
with a head concussion, a broken collarbone, a broken left
wrist, and a face so swollen with bruises that it resembled an
overripe plum. Each morning they came to examine me, a doctor
and two nurses, and one of those nurses—a slight, red-haired
young woman of about twenty-five, who seldom spoke a word—
would give me a look of quiet sympathy that filled my heart
with shame. Though my bruises kept it from showing, the blood
rose into my face like a violent flame, causing my skin to burn
and throb, and bringing an ache to my eyes that somehow prevented tears. I was relieved when this nurse suddenly disappeared from the morning rounds, two weeks before my release
from the hospital. The other nurses, and the doctor, were polite
but businesslike, interested in my body rather than in me. I
endured them easily, and that terrible flame stayed down.

It turned out that I had sustained no "irreparable damage."
The doctor used this phrase in his report, which I examined
upon returning to the hospital some twenty years later. The
doctor himself, I was told, had died six years before in an auto
accident. None of the nurses who had treated me were still
employed at the hospital. I stood with the yellowed report in
my hands, staring down at those words. *No irreparable damage.*
The report was brief and perfunctory, with no hint of any mis-

givings on the doctor's part, any possible suspicion. When our neighbors or relatives marvelled, at the time, that all those injuries could have resulted from a simple fall from my bicycle, my mother always offered her joking, casual explanation: "Well, he's always been a clumsy kid," she told them laughingly.

My mother seldom laughed, and even in this laugh there was a note of bitterness that I alone could hear. Neither the relatives and neighbors nor the hospital staff had been around, after all, during that strangely humid spring when my father left us. They couldn't have understood how all those years of resentment and suppressed rage had been telescoped into a few short, dreamlike weeks, a time in which the air itself seemed to crackle with tension, any stray word or gesture having the power to spark a conflagration. Only I understood, and even in myself it was only a feeling, that kind of sharpened animal insight honed by fear and constant watchfulness. I couldn't have put the feeling into words, not then. I was only a frightened ten-year-old.

Although my father did abandon his family for another woman, and although my mother did become a rampaging, acrimonious creature who took no responsibility for her own actions, there is one thing I want to stress: they were both good people. I'm not making a grim joke—it's simply the truth. If you look back at their early photographs, as I have done—pictures taken during their courtship and in the earlier years of their marriage— I think you would see nothing to alarm you, no hidden glimmering of evil. They stare out of those old black-and-white photographs with a certain youthful forthrightness: my father small, wiry, usually wearing his khaki work clothes and smiling agreeably into the camera, my mother taller than he, her posture ungainly and awkward, wearing one of those oversized white blouses so common in the forties, and perhaps a pleated skirt of navy or deep brown, and always the tiny gold cross at her neck. In all these pictures they are obviously working class, ill-educated, rather naive; and to a trained eye, their specially intense Catholicism clings about them like an aura. It is the Catholicism of the provincial South, of the working people, a religion vaguely insecure in its consciousness of that loud, Bible-thumping fundamentalism encroaching on all sides, and thus the more stubbornly attached to all the symbolic paraphernalia:

statues of the Blessed Virgin and the saints, the stations of the cross, ash-smeared foreheads, novenas. In one of the pictures, my mother has a scapular entwined among her fingers, as any other girl might hold a flower. So they are a sympathetic sight, that shy oversized girl and her small, strong husband with his proprietary grin. Looking at their pictures, you can't help wishing them well.

Even at the age of ten, and earlier, I would glance back through those photographs with that certain hungry curiosity of one seeking clues to a puzzle. For I knew, perhaps two or three years before the actual event, that my father would eventually leave us. There was no particular, unmistakable sign, just a gradual change in the atmosphere—the way the air will seem to thicken, and even become eerily visible, as a prelude to bad weather. Later I would look back on this change and define it as a series of missing things, small ingredients of our lives that had always been there, taken for granted. Now they were sorely lacking. My father, coming home from his shift at the factory, no longer performed a certain ritual that had always punctuated my childhood days: calling my name the moment he arrived, grinning as I ran toward him; then grasping my middle with his grime-stained hands and quickly, gracefully hauling me into the air. I can still recall the delighted vertigo I felt as I ascended, my stomach contracting in the fear that he might drop me, or that my head might hit the ceiling, though I knew he would never let such things happen. I don't remember exactly when I began to miss this ritual—I must have been around eight—but I do remember sitting crosslegged on my bed, frowning, sorting through those old pictures. There were pictures of my father holding me, a dribbling three-year-old, at the neighborhood park, both of us squinting into the sunlight behind the camera. We struck a similar pose at the beach, and at an outing that must have been a picnic (in the background my mother stood, a grayish blur, holding a basket of food beneath the shade of a sumac tree). Even at the age of eight, I seem to have been capable of nostalgia—staring at those photographs, I seemed to understand that a change had come over my father, and that he would never really notice me again. That part of my life was over.

And there were other things I missed. I missed the way he and my mother would joke together in the kitchen, playful as adolescents, and at the supper table I missed their idle, rambling conversations about food prices, or about the neighbors, or about some upcoming event in the parish. Mealtimes became silent, interminable affairs, filled with the clanking of dishes and a submerged tension that I sensed but could not understand. And more than anything, of course, I missed their customary attention to me, their only child: questions about my day at school, about the nuns, about my preparations for first holy communion. They seemed to have forgotten I was there. My father was always remote, unsmiling, his mind far away from the small family circle we formed around the kitchen table. Whenever my mother did ask him a question, she always had to repeat it. Through the months she had come to focus on him totally, intensely— resenting his detachment, hurt by it, and morbidly preoccupied with this new, inexplicable turn in her married life. This was similar to the preoccupation that would, later on, send her gradually inward, to the core of whatever blindness or incomprehension or ignorance of power that had allowed the helpless deterioration of her life; and would keep her so perpetually bewildered that she would begin to lash out, senselessly, at the nearest innocent object.

He finally left one drizzly April morning, shortly after my tenth birthday. My mother stayed in her bedroom, and I sat with him at the kitchen table, not crying. He took my face in his calloused hands and made a little, awkward speech that he'd obviously been rehearsing in his mind. The words were forgettable enough, only a string of clichés. I don't remember being unhappy, but rather feeling relieved that some change was taking place; I had the thought, even then, that they'd be better off apart. But I also felt that my father was doing something healthy and forward-looking, even if cruel, and that he was abandoning my mother to a cloud of sickness, with no direction to go but backwards, or down. So I remember my saying, shyly, that I wanted to go with him. And I remember him saying, hoarsely, that it simply couldn't be.

Someday you'll understand, he told me.

So we were left there alone, my mother and I. A couple of pathetic orphans inside that tidy, fading house in an ordinary working-class neighborhood, and still only ten blocks from the church. Not surprisingly, it was the church that seemed to enable my mother, those first few weeks, to keep her sanity; and perhaps more important to her, to keep up appearances. I think that our neighbors, and certain friends of ours from the parish who chatted with us after church, had little reason to be suspicious. Our attendance at Sunday Mass had always been regular, but now my mother became unusually meticulous about our promptness and about the clothes we wore, so that the two of us often appeared half an hour early for Mass, and always in freshly pressed attire—a navy-blue jacket for me, a deep crimson dress for my mother; clothes that we ordinarily saved for special occasions. Getting me ready for church, my mother would position us both before her full-length mirror, kneeling down behind me and interminably combing, scrubbing, and straightening until my reflection satisfied her. She paid almost no attention to *me*, but rather considered my appearance—correctly, of course —as an extension of herself, and perhaps as a comment on her state of mind. If this was the case, and my mother was simply trying to prove that she had not been hurt and that her life went on even more efficiently than in the past, then the community no doubt saw her as a model of sanity and endurance. In public she was always gracious, almost queenly, assuming a behavior that in previous times I doubt she could have imagined, much less acted out. Leading me down the central aisle at church, and into one of the front pews—always keeping a firm, proprietary grip on my arm—she affected a certain stiffness in her walk, a kind of stoic formality. We attended every parish activity: the rosaries held on week-nights, the Saturday afternoon confessions, the bake sales and pancake breakfasts after Sunday Mass. No one ever asked her about my father, and she never brought up the subject. It was as if our family had always consisted of only these two formidable and well-groomed people, my mother and me.

This puzzling, intense, but outwardly peaceful routine lasted only a few weeks. At home, she always seemed preoccupied and virtually ignored me, except when we were about to appear in public. She spent long stretches of time alone in her bedroom, and since it was now the middle of May and school had let out for the summer, I had little to keep me occupied. My constant emotion during those weeks was a kind of wistful, bewildered loneliness, since the days no longer ended with my father's homecoming and therefore seemed shapeless, filled with monotony and a sense of drifting. I would watch television, or play by myself in the back yard, but part of my attention always remained focused on *her*—what was wrong with her, what would happen next? Would she leave me, also? And what then? The few times I managed to get her attention, it usually involved something I had done to displease her. What would a visitor think, she said irritably, who saw the dirt I tracked in from outside? Or who noticed my uncombed hair, or my unpolished shoes? One habit of mine she especially disliked: the way I would bring the box of old snapshots into the living room and spend hours repeatedly going through them. Those old pictures? she said distastefully. Who cares about *them*? But even that complaint wasn't directed at me, not exactly. Her gaze hovered nearby but never met mine, and her questions had an indifferent, listless quality, as if she were only muttering her private thoughts aloud.

One Sunday evening in early June, however, her attitude toward me—in fact, toward everything—changed dramatically. It began with a visit from my Aunt Julia.

Julia was our first visitor since my father's departure. Though my mother always seemed to anticipate surprise visitors, and kept the house immaculate just in case, no one had actually appeared: this may seem surprising, since small-town Catholics are the first to show up after a tragedy, but I suspect that my mother's manic self-sufficiency had discouraged anyone from attempting even the briefest consolatory visit. The telephone did ring, occasionally, but my mother never answered; eventually it stopped ringing. So my mother and I were both surprised to find Julia on our front step that evening, still dressed in the clothes she had worn to church.

I was sitting on the living-room sofa, going through the photographs yet another time. I had begun to feel that the photographs no longer belonged to the family, but solely to *me*: almost as if the events they depicted had not really taken place, but were only the product of some childish fantasy. Had my father existed, really? I stared hard at his pictures, especially the pictures showing him and me together, but I could not answer this question. I seemed fated to sort through the pictures again and again, seeking an answer yet knowing that no answer would ever come. My father had not visited or written since his departure, after all; nor, to do him justice, had he promised to do so. Later I would learn that he considered this "for the best." A child of ten could not understand these things, and was better left in the dark. In order to satisfy his concern about us, however, and perhaps to salve his conscience, he sent his youngest sister to visit us: a mission, I could see at once, that made her intensely uncomfortable.

My mother had merely opened the screen door, indicating with a jerk of her head that Julia could come inside. Julia had murmured some low, breathless greeting, but I couldn't make out the words; at any rate, my mother did not reply. As she entered the room, Julia's small, heart-shaped face had a look of pure fright, as if she were entering a house of horrors.

During the day, my mother kept all the curtains drawn, ostensibly to save on the air-conditioning bill—that summer, the temperature hovered in the 90s every afternoon—but also, I suspect, because she feared intruders taking random glances into our enclosed, rigidly controlled existence. She wanted no sympathy, and she certainly wanted no spying: which perhaps accounted for her coldness to Julia, whose visit contained elements of both. My mother made no effort to turn on a light, but merely stood aside with her arms folded while Julia peered into the room, squinting at the dimness and finally settling on me.

"Rory, is that you?" she said, trying to smile. "What is it you have there—are those pictures? Photographs?"

She came a little further into the room, her squint relaxing as she began to make everything out. I remember thinking how pretty she was in her light blue, frilly dress, and how vulnerable she seemed in this room with a silent, resentful woman and a silent, puzzled child. She did not belong here, and all three of us knew that; though she might have come here to pity us, it was I who felt sympathy for her.

I nodded, returning her smile. And I blurted out the words I was to regret for a long time: "It's my daddy," I told her. "Pictures of me and my daddy."

My mother shot me a look I would never forget. Later I would realize that everything had changed in that instant. It was as if my mother understood, suddenly, that she could no longer afford to ignore me, that I existed as something apart from her and as yet another person in her life capable of betrayal. For a moment I froze under that look, its hideous mingling of suspicion, shock, and rage.

"Julia's not interested in that," my mother spat out. They were the first words she had spoken since my aunt's arrival.

"Oh, of course I am," poor Julia said, coming toward me with a hopeful smile. She had no idea, evidently, of what had just transpired. She was too involved in her own fear and self-consciousness.

For a few polite, strained minutes we looked through the photographs together, Julia and I. My mother stayed where she was, near the door, her arms still crossed over her breasts. She was like a sentry, and I even seem to remember that she tapped her foot. It is important to stress the transformation that had taken place in my mother, within a few short weeks. She had been a shy, slightly incompetent housewife, deeply in love with her husband, and an adequate mother; in the manner of many docile Catholic wives, she had left the discipline to her husband and had never even raised a hand to me. Often, in the afternoons before my father arrived home, she would join in my play as if she were only another child, which in a sense she was. But now everything had changed, and I had to look upon her as an adult —someone capable of indifference, inexplicable behavior, conversation that I did not understand and that seemed, as I have mentioned, merely a kind of talking to herself. Her normally pale, rounded face now seemed creased, rather haggard, with tiny bitter lines at the sides of her mouth and eyes; though she had become so strangely punctilious about her makeup and general appearance, she could not hide these signs of strain. It was no wonder that Julia and I sat with our heads bowed over the box of photographs, talking together in low voices as if my mother were not in the room at all.

What happened next is difficult to remember clearly. It was as if a dam had broken inside my mother, propelling her across the room where she hovered over us, shouting at the top of her voice. Her skin had reddened, and her dark hair seemed shapeless about her face, as if lifted by wind or as if she had just risen from a long and bitter sleep. Suddenly she was a loud, unappeasable harridan, waving her arms in the air. Julia and I stared up at her, apprehensive, merely waiting. I had never seen my mother behave in this way before, but somehow I knew that the worst was yet to come. She was yelling at Julia about my father—each time she said his name, "Frank," her lip would curl upward in a sneer of distaste—and accusing her of taking my father's part, coming here merely to make trouble. One of my mother's hands, trembling in the air as she pointed, shaking her finger threateningly, seemed to hold me in abeyance while she shouted at Julia. That hand seemed to say that I was included in her fury, in the menacing gestures she used as she stood over us. At the moment she was shouting at Julia, but I was next.

Julia, her voice cracking in distress, kept trying to calm her. "No, Estelle, that's not true—that's—" but she could hardly be heard over my mother's voice. The more extravagant and ridiculous my mother's claims, the louder her voice became.

"You tell him," she shrieked, "you tell him I don't need any two-faced kid sister of his dragging herself around here, sticking her nose into my business! You tell him that! And as for that new woman he's got, that fancy whore, you can tell her that Estelle is doing just fine, she's happy to hand that no-good bum over to anyone stupid enough to take him! You getting all this, Julia? Are you listening?"

Poor Julia, nineteen and inexperienced and engaged to a young man in the parish who had recently left the seminary, convinced that his calling was to family life rather than the priesthood, sat on our sofa like a wilted, pale blue flower, her face drained of color and her hands lifted slightly in her lap, as if ready to ward off a blow. "No, Estelle," she said, in a voice that had gradually lowered to a whine of defeat, "that's not why I came at all. He did want to know how you were, that's true, but only because he's concerned—truly concerned. As for any other woman, you know that simply isn't so. There's nobody else, Estelle. I mean, I don't know what happened between the two of you, but Frank is certainly not the kind of man—no, my brother would never—" She faltered for a moment, suddenly taking up her purse and nervously rummaging inside. "Look, he even sent this check along, he wanted me to make sure you received it." She held it in the air before my mother, her fingers trembling. "He—he loves you," Julia stammered, "both you and Rory, and I'm sure he'd want me to say—"

But my mother had indulged this little speech as long as she could bear: she tore the check out of Julia's fingers and quickly ripped it into shreds. Some of the shreds fell back inside Julia's opened purse.

"Oh Estelle, you shouldn't—"

"Never mind your pack of lies," my mother said. Julia's speech (which *had* contained at least one lie: about my father not having another woman) had worked a perverse effect on my mother, hardening her features into a look of gloating triumph, lowering her voice to an ugly, victorious whisper. "There's nothing you can say, nothing at all. I know what Frank is like, and I know what you're like. You Jamesons, all of you, are rotten to the core —I was just too stupid to see it before. Even this one, this one here"—and at last the threatening hand pointed directly at me, causing a terrible leap in my heart—"even he's a Jameson, living right here under my own roof. Hell, I can't escape them!" She laughed bitterly. I was watching her hand, which kept pointing directly at me. "Even my own son, he'd rather look at pictures of his long-gone daddy than talk to his mother, who cooks and cleans and takes care of him, he doesn't pay any attention to *her*. Oh, I see how it all is," my mother said with a laugh. "I know the kind of people you are. You're all no good, every last one of you."

Julia and I merely stared up at her, dumfounded. My mother's words, taken together, produced a strange effect, mainly because these were things she had never before said in her life, to Julia or to anyone. She had gotten some of her phrases, evidently, from the soap operas she occasionally watched in the afternoons, and even the sly, hateful tone of her voice seemed taken from some other source, as if she hadn't known how to express her own anger and scorn. There had been something hollow and unconvincing about her accusations, her uncharacteristic shriek-ing. But somehow this did not diminish their effect, for if my mother did not know exactly how to express her anger and ended up sounding like a third-rate actress, still there was no doubt that the anger was real, lurking beneath the histrionic behavior. And it should be admitted that Julia and I did nothing to discourage her. With our pale, terrified looks—sitting side by side on the sofa, our trembling hands having instinctively joined —we only fanned higher the flame of my mother's rage. Had Julia been more self-possessed, or had I been a few years older, perhaps we could have reasoned with her somehow, brought her to the point of admitting her grief and pain. But instead we only stared up at her, unconsciously abetting her terrible need for power, and I remember thinking for the first time that every-thing had gone awry, that life would never return to normal, and that now there was genuine reason to be afraid.

Julia, pulling together the few remaining shreds of her dignity, slowly rose from the sofa. She had to force my clenched fingers from her own, and she glanced down at me the way survivors in a lifeboat might glance toward those remaining on the ship, standing in despair at the railings. But, to do her justice, she probably felt that she had already done enough. Almost certainly she had not wanted to come here, and of course she had not expected to face such blatant insults: this was the line she adopted, anyway, as a way of covering her fear. She said primly, "I'm sorry you feel that way, Estelle. I certainly won't stay if I'm not wanted."

But her voice cracked, and her hands were shaking. It was no good.

My mother smiled, as if Julia's pathetic attempt at masking her fear gave her a particular satisfaction. "That's right, Julia. You're certainly *not* wanted."

At that moment I saw that Julia would be allowed to leave, and that she wouldn't even glance back at the sinking ship. Her disgrace and humiliation were to be her punishment. I actually did think to call after her, to beg her not to leave me there, but

I understood the psychology of the two women too well for that:
Julia would not have the courage for any kind of bold or decisive
action, and afterwards my mother would hate me all the more
for having attempted to leave. So I merely sat there, holding the
box of pictures in my lap, while Julia made her escape.

No sooner was Julia out the door than my mother, her face
red and swollen, came heading toward me. I cringed back into
the sofa, flinching as she jerked the box of photographs off my
lap. Oddly, she wasn't screaming. She was only making some
desperate, inarticulate noise inside her throat, not really the
noise of anger but of some deep, frustrated effort. Perhaps the
effort of lifting the box full of pictures, since it was quite heavy.
For a moment, of course, I thought she'd been removing the
box in order to get at me, but I quickly saw that the box itself
was receiving the brunt of her attention. Once again I had that
peculiar feeling of being ignored by her, even though I was the
only other person in the house, and as she strode angrily out
of the living room, holding the large box against her chest, I had
the curious impulse to follow her.

I was barefoot, and I passed noiselessly through the dining
room and to the kitchen door, where I stood and merely watched
my mother. Having escaped her wrath, I felt so relieved that I
had the impulse to laugh—and, as I stood there, I believe some
kind of odd half-smile did come to my lips. Part of this impulse
toward laughter, however, came from the sense of excitement
my mother's movements and gestures inspired in me. I watched,
fascinated, as she took the box of photographs and dumped
them into the kitchen sink, then began furiously searching for
something, opening cabinet doors and then slamming them shut
again. Finally, in a cabinet over the sink, she found what she'd
been seeking: a small can of lighter fluid. With a liberal, abandoned gesture, she saturated the pile of photographs with the
fluid, and from one of her pockets she drew a box of matches
that might have been waiting there just for this purpose. Then
she stepped back, struck one of the matches, and tossed it onto
the wet pile of photographs. In an instant they blossomed into
flame. My mother took a step backward, and I stayed at the
kitchen doorway, watching her. All the anger had left her face,

and her skin had grown pale: she seemed mesmerized by the
flames (which had already begun dwindling rapidly, after the
fluid had burned off: the photographs themselves merely smol-
dered, sending a noxious odor into the air) and appeared, for
the moment, oddly contented. I drew back from the doorway,
not wanting to be seen. I no longer had the impulse to laugh,
nor did I feel afraid. That night, when I returned to the kitchen
for supper, there were no charred photographs in the sink, and
during our meal my mother chatted amiably, as if nothing had
happened. But the smell of burning lingered in the air.

Children, as I remarked to my wife the other day, are extremely sensitive to psychological fluctuations in their parents—
the subtle changes of mood, the buried tensions, the attempts
to mask unlovely, primal emotions—but their perceptions, no
matter how intense, fail to grasp the larger patterns in adult
behavior, the complex causes and effects that often work themselves out very slowly, over a period of months or years. They
have a dazzling moment of insight, but then the moment passes.
Then they are children again. Despite their amazing percipience,
we consider them as unsullied innocents or as victims. We blame
them for nothing.

We blame none of them, that is, except the one who was a
former version of ourselves. *That* child, perhaps, was guilty of
some heinous crime; *that* child deserved anything he got. These
thoughts don't voice themselves aloud, of course, but they pass
often through our currents of feeling in later years, when we
are adults and begin looking back wistfully, perhaps seeking
answers to questions we've only begun to formulate. What I
said to my wife, however, had only resulted from something
she had been saying, over a period of years, to me; but which,
either begrudging her superior insight or perhaps feeling that I
hadn't suffered enough, I hadn't wanted to hear. Gradually, I
did begin to hear. I'd awakened too many times from terrible
nightmares—dreams I couldn't remember except that inside
them I was once again a child, and that the dream was red-hued
and feverish and filled with urgent, rasping voices; far too many
times I'd awakened to my wife's touch, her anxious face bent

over mine in bed. *Rory? Rory? It's that dream again, isn't it? Can't you remember—?* For she had the idea that if I remembered the dreams, they would cease to plague me. I would no longer return to consciousness bathed in sweat and whimpering, but would wake blank-brained and peaceful as any normal man. Working down at the office, in the public relations firm where I hold an excellent position, or having dinner out with my wife and some of our friends, I would no longer have the curious sensation of not belonging, of not being worth the money I am paid or the company of people who often seek me out, who consider themselves my friends. I would not be a man harboring some terrible secret, fearing his own violent and unremembered dreams. But it has taken a long time to reach this point, to feel myself joining wholeheartedly in my wife's wishes for my own well-being. I am thirty-one years old, I've been married for seven years—and very happily married, considering the conflict between Marian and me over one particular issue: my insistence that we not have children—and yet I'm aware that the greatest effort of my life is only now beginning.

What my wife had been saying, all these years, was that I lacked compassion. Not toward my mother, who died three years ago and whom I'd always treated generously and kindly, and not toward my father, who has long been remarried and who often visits with his wife, a petite blond-haired woman (though the blond is now shading into silver) who protests repeatedly that she bears no ill-feeling either toward me or the memory of my mother. Nor did Marian claim, though she probably has the right, that I lacked compassion toward her—despite the vasectomy I underwent without her knowledge, because I suspected (incorrectly, as it turned out) that she had deliberately stopped using her pills, and despite my occasional indifference to her own suffering as a normal woman who must remain childless, as a normal wife who must endure her husband's moodiness, his irrational outbursts of anger, his unending nightmares. Rather she claimed that I lacked compassion for myself. I remember that when I visited that hospital, and stood examining the doctor's report, the recollection that had bothered me most was not the considerable pain I suffered during those two

months in the hospital, and not the terrible loneliness that had
overtaken me at night, when I was expected to sleep but could
not, but rather the memory of that young, sweet-faced nurse
who had come in with the doctor those first few weeks, and the
look of deep sympathy she gave me, and the hot shame that
rose flaming into my face each time her eyes met mine. Many
times during the years of our marriage, I would find myself
recalling that nurse whenever Marian expressed her own sympathy toward me, and usually I would tell her, irritably, that
the past was better left forgotten. That if she truly cared for me,
she wouldn't keep bringing up the subject. These hurtful words
usually silenced Marian, and within that silence I would always
feel a little smug, as if my rights had once again been vindicated—
my rights as someone who had suffered, and who must now
be allowed to forget. So we never got beyond that point, year
upon year. It took me a long time to learn that compassion did
not mean forgetting unpleasant events, but remembering them.

If it became my habit, in adulthood, to push aside discomfiting
memories as if to pretend they had no power, it may be that
the habit began on that day of Julia's doomed visit and of my
mother's burning of the family photographs. It pleased me, that
evening, that she had suddenly become talkative and cheerful,
and that the conversation included me as her only child, as
someone who must share in any decision she reached about our
future. The most pressing need we faced, of course, was finan-
cial: if we were not to accept any money from my father, then
it was essential that my mother find a job. Over our meat loaf
and mashed potatoes, she approached this subject with an almost girlish facetiousness. Should she become a sales person
down at Montgomery Ward? Or a waitress, perhaps, at the little
breakfast place a few blocks down the street? Would she be able
to endure one of those silly pink outfits, with her name stitched
in red on the breast pocket? I laughed or shrugged my shoulders
or even made little jokes of my own, happy and relieved that
my mother had returned to normal. Eventually she would find
a very good job with the phone company and would support
us both until I began working my way through college—she
never missed a day's work, not even during the painful divorce

proceedings that took place about six months after my release from the hospital—but for the moment the idea of her employment was a kind of joke, something we laughed over without quite knowing why. And it didn't matter why: what mattered was the way my mother winked at me, and piled a second helping of mashed potatoes onto my plate, and poked me in the ribs as though we were conspirators.

For several days our lives moved along normally—it was late June, the weather was clear and bright and hot, there was an ordinary childhood to be lived out of doors. On several occasions I stopped in my play to wave at my mother as she pulled out the driveway in our dented old Chevrolet: she went out every day for several hours, looking for a job. It was to the strain of job-hunting, in fact, that I ascribed her increasingly dour mood through the days that followed, for when she returned from these unsuccessful expeditions, her face would seem creased with exhaustion, her clothes wrinkled and awry. Occasionally she snapped at me—for tracking mud into the house, for failing to come for dinner the first time she called. After one of these occasions I sat quietly at the table, chastened, and watched her hurrying through the preparations for our dinner. She still wore the cheap, pale blue suit that she always wore when applying for jobs, and when she reached up to the cabinet for some dinner plates, I noticed the dark wet ovals of perspiration at her armpits. Then I noticed, once again, that sound I hadn't heard for several weeks: the sound of my mother talking to herself, murmuring desperately under her breath. She behaved as though I couldn't hear her, as though I weren't in the room at all. And so, although I knew better, I followed a sudden impulse and said in a loud, unnatural voice: "Mother, what are you saying? I can't hear you."

She whirled around, a slice of bread in one hand. At first she seemed so infuriated that she couldn't speak. Staring up at her, I noticed for the first time how much she had aged these past few weeks: the plump, rounded face had grown thinner, the lines deepening at the sides of her mouth and purplish shadows appearing beneath her eyes. The blue suit hung on her frame at an odd, unseemly angle, as though it were too large for her: as though her body were shrinking inside it. She kept staring at me, the slice of bread jiggling in her hand, and I merely stared back, white-faced and trembling. Finally she spoke, spitting the words out in a hissing, malevolent voice.

"I've had enough smart-talk out of you, kid," she said, gesturing with the slice of bread. "I've had enough, do you hear? Rory?"

I nodded, mutely.

"You're just like him," she said, in a voice of weary disgust, as she tossed the slice of bread aside and turned back to the counter. She was nodding to herself, and once again she began muttering words under her breath, as if commiserating with herself over my treacheries. Through that meal and the rest of the evening, I kept quiet and listened and watched her from the sides of my eyes. But she paid no attention to me. She seemed lost inside herself—muttering, arguing, dreaming. I wanted badly to share her thoughts. Yet I knew that I'd been pushed to the outer fringes of her awareness, and that a part of her mind—a desperate, feverish part, which had once again come to the fore—no longer knew that I existed.

And yet she was vaguely aware of me, as I came to find out during the following days. Oddly enough, she no longer left me at home whenever she had an errand to run, but began taking me along. She seldom said anything to me directly, but simply herded me out the front door and into the car, one hand vaguely touching my shoulder as if to keep me on course. It seemed that I was no longer a separate person but merely a part of her, a kind of satellite, and as long as I said or did nothing unexpected, she didn't seem to notice me. Her mind worked all the time, hectically, and as we drove along I could see her lips twitching, as if words that would match her constant, seething anger had struggled upward from a place deep inside her, but became garbled and senseless before reaching the surface. We went out every day, usually in the early morning hours, and I couldn't understand why: she no longer dressed for job interviews, seldom even running a brush through her hair before hurrying me out to the car, and often we made no stops at all; we merely drove around, occasionally through the shopping district but usually through the quiet residential areas, streets lined with ordinary, unpretentious houses like our own. One morning, having left the house at an extremely early hour—it was barely after six o'clock—and my mother seeming a bit less abstracted than usual, I decided to ask her why we were doing this.

"Is it for a job?" I said, with that false naiveté I had already begun to assume. "Are you looking for a job?"

She glanced over at me, irritated. "Never mind," she said. "We're just driving around."

We were passing slowly down a street lined with small, shabby houses. In the early morning dusk the very houses seemed asleep, with only an occasional window lighted from within. My mother, looking from side to side, seemed to scrutinize each house, peering over the steering wheel with her eyes narrowed. Once again she had forgotten me.

"But it's so early," I said, in a whining voice. "Why did we get up so early? And where are we going?"

"Just never mind."

"But why are we—"

"Shut up, do you hear me? Shut up!"

Near the end of that street, my mother brought the car to a stop. She was staring at a house about thirty yards down, on the other side of the street, and on her face was a hideous mingling of satisfaction and pain. Slowly I followed her gaze, and though I suppose I shouldn't have been surprised, what I saw made me take in my breath, sharply. There, parked in the driveway of a small, nondescript frame house with peeling white paint—a house like any other in this neighborhood, and very much like our own house half a mile away—was my father's old black pickup, a truck he'd owned since before I was born. He'd often said, proudly, that he would never part with that truck: the truck would run forever, he said, it would never give him a moment's trouble.

There it sat, parked in a stranger's driveway. Now I understood why we had been taking these early morning drives: my mother had wanted to find his truck before he drove it off to work. And I also understood, finally, that things had not returned to normal and perhaps they never would. So I merely sat there, edged up against my side of the car and waiting for whatever might happen next. I felt that my mother was crying, but I was afraid to look at her. After a few minutes she started the car and we drove away.

That afternoon she left the house again, not taking me along, and she returned half an hour later with a gun and a small package of bullets. The next morning we rose even before dawn, and when the sky began lightening we were driving along that street again, back and forth in front of the house. My father's truck was still there, as if it hadn't been moved since the previous morning.

My mother had the gun in a sack, resting on her lap. Her mental state on that morning is difficult to describe: her breathing was hoarse and labored, every few minutes she would begin to cry, and yet she kept making odd, casual comments to me—asking what I wanted for breakfast, and whether I'd like to go to the public swimming pool that afternoon—and once in a while she would give a short, reasonless laugh, as if responding to something happening in her mind. But I wasn't really trying to understand her: the emotion that had overtaken me, ever since yesterday morning, was a simple, blunt anger of my own. I had a pouting expression on my face, and when my mother asked her odd, conciliating questions, I refused even to answer. I no longer felt afraid of provoking her: I wasn't afraid of anything.

Finally she parked the car, this time only about ten yards from my father's truck. She waited nervously, alternately laughing or weeping; I waited sullenly, staring straight ahead, looking neither at my father's truck nor at her. But when my mother made a sudden, gasping noise, I looked over at once to the small, innocent-looking house. A light had been turned on inside, illuminating one of the windows; I decided it was probably the kitchen window.

Only a few moments later, the front door of the house opened and out came a small, blond-haired woman wearing a tattered pink housecoat. She walked with little, hurrying steps, as if afraid of being seen, and I understood at once that she was heading out to pick up the morning newspaper, which rested on the driveway and just a few feet from the left rear tire of my father's truck. As she bent over to pick up the newspaper, my mother took the gun out of the sack and slowly opened the car door.

What happened next is difficult to remember: it all happened so quickly. Evidently my mother had shouted something to the woman, for she had straightened and I saw that she had failed to pick up the newspaper. My mother had come around to the front of the car, so the two women were only a few yards apart. For one long, dreamlike moment they stared at one another: my mother talking and weeping, slowly raising the gun, and the other woman's face registering a quick series of emotions: simple shock, and then a sudden, bristling anger, and then—glancing toward me, then back toward my mother again—a look of dawning comprehension. And when the woman understood who we were, a hideous expression of pure fear took her features. She opened her mouth as if to scream, but no sound came out. I noticed that one side of her pale, rather ordinary face was still creased with sleep. She seemed paralyzed, as if she hadn't wakened at all but had found herself in the middle of a nightmare. My mother was speaking to her in a shrill, threatening voice, but the car windows were rolled up and I couldn't make out the words: I heard only garbled, crazy sounds, like words spoken underwater. Finally the woman had lifted her hands, palms outward in an imploring gesture, or as if to ward off my mother's attack. The woman took a few stumbling steps backward, a pleading expression on her face. It was then that my mother fired two ear-splitting shots.

Immediately afterward the gun fell from her hands, and a moment later she was back inside the car, grasping the steering wheel. Perhaps she was trying to make her hands stop trembling. Finally, taking a deep breath, she reached down to the ignition and turned the key.

The woman had fallen to the driveway, but there was no blood. I had watched the incident with that intense, hungry perception of frightened children, and I was almost disappointed that there wasn't any blood. When my mother fired the gun, I had seen a bright crimson flame exploding from the barrel, and my eyes had followed the shot to the hole it made in the woman's housecoat, a small hole that seemed suddenly to expand into flame, finally leaving ragged, charred edges around a much larger hole, perhaps six inches in diameter. I realized later, of course, that this must have been my overheated imagination,

for there was only an ordinary-sized bullet hole in the housecoat.
And I had probably imagined, too, the flame I saw coming from
the tip of the gun barrel. I understood all this the moment after
my mother started the car's engine, for the woman lying in the
driveway suddenly stirred, and after a moment got slowly to
her feet.

It was then I saw the small brown hole in her housecoat, and
realized that the bullet had missed her body entirely. Evidently
the second bullet had not even come close: later it would be
found to have struck the mailbox. Since the woman was not
hurt, in fact, there would be no criminal charges brought against
my mother; she would simply be ordered to undergo psychiatric
treatment for a minimum of one year—a treatment which, as it
turned out, greatly helped her. I have often thought how differ-
ently things would have worked out, had the first bullet struck
only an inch or two further to the right.

My mother, seeing the woman rise up from the driveway and
begin stumbling toward the house, let out a little cry of surprise.
For a moment I was afraid she would stop the car and attempt
to repeat the entire incident, but in fact she pressed hard on the
accelerator and within a few minutes we were home. In the
middle of that fast, desperate ride, I had finally dared to glance
over at my mother: her mouth was twitching again with her
unvoiced rage, and her face was queerly mottled red and white,
as if she'd broken into a rash. During that next hour and a half,
waiting tensely at home for the police to come, my mother said
nothing to me. She spent the time rushing from room to room,
compulsively straightening the house. Even though the police
questioned me in kind, gentle voices, and even though my father
later informed me that Mother was going to be all right, and
that everything would be back to normal soon, I hungered more
than anything for a glance or word from her, some private signal
that her troubles were over, that it had only been a bad dream.
No signal ever came.

It was my need to resolve these doubts, I suppose, or at least
to get some acknowledgment of my existence, that caused me
to bring up the subject only a few days later. It was after the
police had finally stopped visiting the house, and things had

returned to a semblance of normalcy. My mother's hearing was still several weeks away, and she was allowed to remain at home in order to take care of me and to continue seeking employment. She no longer seemed so tormented, but had remained obsessed with cleaning the house: she had cleaned out the attic, for instance, and had begun washing all the windows. But she still paid no attention to me. I sidled up to her in the kitchen, where she was mixing soap and water for the window-cleaning, and in a shy voice I asked about that woman now living with my father: Who was she? Why was he living with her? And why had my mother wanted to hurt her?

My mother turned around slowly from the bucket of water, and even after everything that had happened I could not have been prepared for the look of sinister, uncontrollable rage she gave me. Again her face had that mottled look, only her lips turning a pure deadly white as she opened them to shout at me.

"What do you care about her?" my mother cried. Instantly her breathing had become labored, and her eyes glistened with tears. "Why are you asking about her? You want to go visit her, eh? You want to be with her and your daddy?"

"No, that's not what I—"

"You're just like him, aren't you? Aren't you? You'll never be satisfied, no matter what I do! Never!"

I wanted to get away, but she had taken hold of my left wrist. With her other hand she slapped me across the face, hard. I cried out, begging her to stop, but she ignored me. She kept slapping me with the back of her hand, screaming about that woman and especially about my father, and how we were both alike. How all men were alike. She began punching me in the ribs, still holding onto my wrist, and with her other hand she reached back for something on the kitchen counter. It was the long, steel-handled brush she had been using to clean the windows. By now I was crying and my vision had blurred, and the blood had risen like a flame inside my face. There was nothing I could do but duck my head, dodging some of the blows, and keep trying to back away.

Passion Play

I

ON THE DAY Randall lost his job, he went home and opened the letter from his sister.

He'd received the letter more than a month earlier, but hadn't been able to respond: he'd been awaiting whatever moment of courage or desperate whimsy the act required. It was the fourth letter in as many months—long, rambling letters that terrified Randall, coming as they did after twenty years of virtual silence, broken only by cards at Christmas, Easter, and his birthday, and those containing only the *Love, Melissa* in her childish scrawl.

His life was ringed by women: he felt that when the phone rang, for of course it was Elaine. As they spoke he steeled himself against her disapproval, her easy scorn.

"Is something wrong?" she asked. "Your voice—it isn't quite right."

He told her that he'd been sacked.

"Well, you're not really surprised—are you? You've been expecting it."

He said: "When it finally happens, it hits you."

"They've got a lousy reputation, you know that. Anyone over fifty is always in danger."

Her voice was quick, impatient; anger enlivened her, he

thought. It was her staple, just as a certain staid melancholy had become his own.

"I'm forty-six," he reminded her.

"Yes, but—" He could sense her mind racing. She brought form to chaos, always; imposed logic upon the senseless. "There are other companies, Randall—much better ones. In the long run, this is a good thing. You'll see."

He let out a low whistle, inaudible. "Maybe, but I'm leaving town for a while. I've got to go down south, tend to Melissa."

He expected a loud squawk, for they had dinner plans that evening and had talked—that is, Elaine had talked—of their taking the train into Manhattan for the weekend. There was a play she wanted to see, and a new exhibit at the MOMA.... Normally Randall was content to let her plan their evenings, their weekends. Elaine was a trim, energetic woman a decade younger than he, a partner in a small law office only a few blocks from the insurance firm where Randall had worked for two decades; six years ago they'd met at a lunch counter, and he'd been impressed by her agile, clear-cut intelligence, and by her rather Nordic beauty that seemed both fragile and indestructible. She wore her pale-blond hair in elaborate coils over her ears; she was petite, talkative, restless. She'd been impressed, as she told him frankly, by his solid, well-muscled body, and by something solid, too, in his temperament: his unshakable poise, she supposed, along with the melancholy that had been noticeable even then. "I've got enough high spirits for two people," she'd said in those early, humorous days of their relationship—" and besides, I enjoy a challenge." Yet as his melancholy deepened in the past year or two—Elaine had found him a therapist, and assumed that Randall was still seeing him—she'd become edgy and dissatisfied, particularly as the specter of "failure" (Randall used the word often, rolling it off his tongue; it was one of the few ways he'd found to shock Elaine) began attending his life, as he felt, at every turn.

"Yes, I suppose you should get away," she said now, sighing. "You can get your head clear, and when you come back everything will look different. It'll be much easier for us to plan our next move."

Despite himself, he laughed. "My head is perfectly clear,

Elaine. I'm going south for Melissa's sake, not mine." He still
held his sister's letter in his free hand; he saw that the hand had
begun to tremble. "And besides," he said, laughing angrily, "my
life isn't some legal case for you to maneuver, to 'move' upon.
There are some things, my dear, that even you can't control."
The sarcasm wasn't like him, and for a moment there was
silence. Then she whispered, "That's an ugly thing to say. I
think I just learned something very important about you."
   "I'm not listening to this. I'm hanging up," Randall said.
   "Please do," Elaine said.

He'd only skimmed the letter, enough to know it was no
different from the others. There were complaints about his absence, *You always came home from college at Easter, why can't you
come this year,* about Marjorie, *She won't let me buy a pretty dress,
you send money every month where does it go,* about life in general,
*There's too much wrong with this town, they don't like me without
you, remember how we went to the lake in nice weather and you took
me in the rowboat, remember it then?* Evidently something had
happened, some problem had arisen, and he could imagine the
histrionic account Marjorie would send if he wrote to her. And
now there was nothing, really, to prevent his going. Five years
had passed since his last visit, and during that time his life in
Philadelphia had slowed, grinding nearly to a halt. Despite his
high threshold for guilt, he'd run out of excuses.
   During the long drive southward he steeled himself, rehearsed
set speeches to both Melissa and Marjorie, pictured himself as
a kind of automaton performing the necessary functions: visiting
doctors and bankers, solving this or that problem, smoothing
everyone's feathers as best he could. Yet he wasn't prepared for
the swell of his heart as he wound through the mountains of
north Georgia and found himself again among the tree-covered
hills to the south, already flooded with green here in early April.
He saw these familiar surroundings with an ashen face—that
imperturbability in the set of his bony jaw and calm gray eyes
that Elaine had once admired—but the stubborn muscle in his
chest rioted all the same, and in the last ten miles he pulled over
twice and tried to think of reasons for turning back. Nothing
came to him.

Entering the town, turning onto the bumpy oiled road leading to the house where he and Melissa had grown up, he felt like an intruder: that might have been why he sounded the horn as he jolted down the old driveway, and why he entered the house without knocking, instead calling out: "Halloo! It's me!" He strode through the dimmed living area, then back toward her bedroom just off the kitchen. He felt the jauntiness in his step: his brotherly persona (cheerful, a bit obtuse) instinctively took over. But when he reached the doorway he stared in shock, his jaw gaping.

"Melissa . . . ?"

She focused on him, slowly. "Ran-dall?" she asked, drawing out his name in the old way. Her eyes, Randall saw, were unreadable as ever, small grayish slits crowded by skin that looked vaguely swollen. The doctors had told Randall's parents that one day the puffiness would decrease, that Melissa's face would begin taking on "the semblance of adult features"—but of course they'd been wrong. They'd been wrong about nearly everything.

"Did you know I was coming?" he asked, not knowing what he said.

She turned her head to one side, then the other. "Nope. Margie didn't say."

He stared at her. Along her cheek lay a purplish bruise, shading to orange near the center. Her plump hands lifted awkwardly, as though worked by strings.

"I fell down, Ran-dall. Got up out of the chair," she said, her hands describing an arc, "but way too fast."

He nodded. "Where's Marjorie?" he asked.

She said, "Work"—then glanced away. She seemed disgruntled.

Already he missed something: the wide, wet, heartbreaking smile. Her cheeks flushing, she would expose her small teeth and pink gums fully, without shame. Even five years ago, it had been the signature to anything she said. Now she sat watching him, dully. Her expression did not seem particularly childlike.

She added, "My legs fell asleep, I was doing my pictures but I sat too long. So then"—her hands jerked upward again—"I fell right down, bam! Hit my cheek against the table."

She brushed one hand along her bedside table, fondling the

sharp corner. Randall took a step forward, his hand extended. She was lying.

"Ran-dall?" she said in her high-pitched, tremulous voice. "You okay?"

"Yes, of course," and finally his hand came to rest on her shoulder. He felt the need to silence her, to preserve the childish Melissa of his old and shameful memories. Though she had stayed a 12-year-old, as the doctors, right for once, had predicted so long ago, still he sensed a change in her, something he'd felt in the tone of her letters, too; in the very *fact* of her letters. For now, the touch was enough, a way of reclaiming her. As they talked his eyes had moved along her large, shapeless body, her breasts sagging beneath the seersucker dress of pale blue, her ankles a ghastly white where they showed above her habitual thick socks and plain slippers. Physically, she hadn't really changed; even her room was the same. Along the walls hung a variety of needlepoints, her "pictures," done in bold primary colors—puppy dogs, butterflies. Her curtains were the same red-and-white dotted Swiss that he'd bought impulsively during some long-ago visit, though the red dots had bled a little.

He looked again at her bruised cheek.

"How have you been?" he asked, lamely. "I've read your letters, Melissa. I was surprised to get them."

"I wanted you to come visit," she said. Again she looked evasive, her gaze returning to the windows. Her remoteness was almost womanly, he thought, though perhaps this was her idea of womanly anger, garnered from the television melodramas she watched in the afternoons.

He sat down on the bed, unnerved by this idea that after so much time she was a woman, no longer a child. For years he had visited annually, at Christmas, when he'd pull in the driveway to find her sitting on the porch steps, shivering in some absurd filmy-white party dress, a satin ribbon in her hair. She was twenty-five, she was thirty. Marjorie would start complaining the moment he arrived, as though Melissa were not limping along beside them: she was getting worse as time passed, Marjorie said, she'd gotten positively infantile, how could Marjorie hold a full-time job and still care for someone so sloppy, so uncooperative. . . . Sometimes Melissa would refuse to eat, their aunt told him; or would eat only the cookies and candy she hoarded in her room like a child. And she threw tantrums. She refused to bathe, she absolutely refused to let Marjorie shampoo her hair. . . . Melissa was thirty-five, she was nearing forty. Did Randall know what arthritis did to an old woman's joints, could he imagine the pain when she had to lift Melissa's dead weight after one of her spectacular falls, didn't he agree that sometimes she fell just out of spite, most of the time she had only a slight limp so why should she fall, the physical therapy *had* helped her. . . . Or maybe it was just her mind—here Marjorie leaned toward him, whispering—maybe she'd begun to deteriorate, you remember what the doctors said. . . . And Randall said flatly: No. The doctors said her mind works surprisingly well, considering. You know that. Oh? his aunt asked. Then why hadn't she gotten past the sixth grade? Why hadn't she— She has a good mind, Randall said stubbornly. And in her perilous, listing gait Melissa galloped at him from behind, clasped him with both arms and legs and he became the big brother again, jaunty, pretending surprise: Whoa!

Marjorie watched them play, her mouth a thin bitter line.

He'd recently met Elaine, and that had been his last visit home. He'd gotten a few shrill letters from Marjorie after missing Christmas that first time, but he'd doubled her monthly support and the letters had stopped. From Melissa there had been no complaints until recently. He'd preserved the limping, laughing girl of his imagination: that plump overgrown woman-child, clutching his strong body with all her limbs, her flow of talk spontaneous, unthinking, her laugh loud as a boy's. All things considered, he told himself, further visits would only upset them both. Elaine said pragmatically that past was past.

"Melissa," he said now, "I'm sorry to have stayed away so long. I should have visited or called, I should at least have written more often. . . ."

He'd always been bad with words. For years he'd let Elaine do the talking. The other day he'd sat quietly while his boss, old bald-pated Thatcher, spouted lies about his deep regret, his belief in Randall's future, his undeniable intelligence and skill. . . . Now

Melissa watched him solemnly, her cheek bruised, her broad forehead—once so smooth beneath her dark bangs—etched with tiny deep-cut lines.

"But I want you to know," he went on, his throat constricting with the need to cry, "that I'm not leaving until I get to the bottom of this. You'll be taken care of, I promise. So please don't worry anymore."

His heart had begun to pound; his passion nearly choked him. Already he knew better, but he half-expected a childish response, some airy *non sequitur*. Instead she sat back, looking thoughtful. She might have been recalling her invulnerable older brother, who had stridden so boldly out into the world.

II

Randall Trenner had been the only member of his family to attend college. His father, born in Atlanta, had moved north to this much smaller city in his mid-thirties to start a meat-packing business; he'd married Sara, a local girl, within less than a year. Raised as a devout Roman Catholic, he'd worshiped his young auburn-haired wife with something near to religious fervor. Just before their marriage, Sara joined her husband's church. Though the local parish was minuscule, Mr. Trenner's rather morose temperament and his wife's shy innocence of liturgy prevented their participation in church events: these obligations they transferred to their children, who took part in pageants for the Nativity, in coronations of the Blessed Virgin, in the annual passion play. At age seven each child took first Holy Communion, Melissa receiving the sacrament in her wheelchair; at twelve they were confirmed in the faith. Throughout these years Randall served as an altar boy, and Melissa helped preside over bake sales and charity bazaars. Much later, living a minimal but unchaste existence in the huge northeastern city that had become his home, Randall would feel that his family's home life had been claustrophobic, and would remember his childhood as restrictive, monotonous, and somehow passionless despite the blood-hued imagery of that religion and its Gothic, wildly improbable beliefs. In his quiet way, Randall had disliked the parish priest. One night after dinner Randall had made some abrupt, critical remark about Father McInerney, and this was the only time his father had ever struck him.

When Randall won his scholarship to Temple University, his parents had been pleased in an obscure, confused way; it pained Randall that their reaction unconsciously mimicked that of Father McInerney, who jovially congratulated both Randall and his parents after hearing the news. Guiltily, Randall felt intense pleasure at the thought of leaving home. By age nineteen he had developed into a loner, not unlike his father at that age; he had few friends, and had given over his adolescent years to his genuine interest in his school work and reading, and to that pastime common to adolescent males in the 1950s, body-building. Even this innocent hobby was attended by guilt, however, due to the physical contrast between him and his sister: though Melissa, struck by a sudden, raging fever soon after birth that impaired her both physically and mentally, had shown gradual improvement, she had been confined to a wheelchair until the age of twelve, and had used crutches for several years after that. She endured painful therapy treatments several times each week. Because of her illness, combined with a childish exuberance of spirit more common at age four than fourteen, she had even fewer friends than her brother. At the time he prepared to leave for college, Melissa had entered a difficult phase of life: her ability to walk under her own power coincided with the confusions of puberty, so that her careening, hobbled gait through the quiet household symbolized to Randall both her physical and emotional peril. Watching from the front windows as she clumsily chased one of the neighborhood dogs, or played whimsical games by herself, moving erratically from one tree to another, her mouth twitching as she sang or encouraged herself along, Randall would turn away in shame, his face burning. At fourteen Melissa was a plump ungainly child, nearly as tall as her brother, her face pink and smooth as an infant's. Her dark, thick hair was cut short, bowl-shaped, the bangs nearly meeting her heavy eyebrows; her gray eyes, inherited like Randall's from their father, were as pale and guileless as her brother's were opaque and guarded.

Watching himself in the mirror, a habit he indulged too often during those years, Randall would marvel that Melissa with her wobbly limbs and babyish personality could be his sibling, for in the mirror he saw a powerfully built and determined-looking young man ("stalwart," Father McInerney called him) who had already discovered his intimidating effect upon other people. His leaving for college seemed only to confirm Melissa's static, eventless life, but in the hard-eyed pragmatism he'd already cultivated Randall knew that his staying in this town would accomplish nothing. If he succeeded in a career, he thought, he might at least help her materially—an important consideration, since his father's business, never prosperous, had begun a slow decline. One scorching August afternoon Randall packed seven changes of clothes, a few books and supplies, and a passbook that represented several summers' work at his father's plant. He kissed his mother's cheek; he and his father shook hands, gravely. Before his father took him to the bus station, he exchanged an embarrassed, tearless good-bye with Melissa. In recent days she'd gone blank and silent, as though entering a kind of stupor. As Randall and his father pulled out the driveway Melissa appeared on the front porch, and without returning his wave sat watching as they disappeared around the end of the drive in a cloud of red dust.

Until October of his senior year, college had become a haven exceeding his adolescent dreams. He liked the regimented yet easygoing quality of dorm life; he liked eating in the cafeteria at appointed times. He even liked this cold, glowering city with its industrial plants and monolithic skyline: seldom leaving the campus, he felt himself in a snug pocket of calm, magically protected from the violence and chaos of the city. During the last two summers he had not returned home at all, but had worked odd jobs on campus and taken elective courses offered during summer school. Each semester his grades had improved; his professors could not praise him highly enough. Though sometimes put off by his solitary ways and the close-mouthed severity that might descend at any time—during a beer party, for instance— his dorm mates and fellow students seemed to like and respect him. They teased him about his thick Southern accent, watching his face to see how far they could go. It was true that he often felt tense and was unreasonably suspicious of others. To relax he lifted weights inside his room, or went to an occasional movie by himself or with another student. His acquaintances had learned not to ask about his family back home, but no one seemed surprised when he received an emergency call one October afternoon and left the campus abruptly, without explanation.

At age thirty-nine, his mother had become ill with a rare form of leukemia; by the time Randall came home, she was already hospitalized (for the fourth time since early summer, he learned) and could go at any time. She'd lied to Randall's father about the seriousness of her illness until she could no longer hide it, and then she'd begged him not to disturb Randall's studies when there was nothing that could be done. Mr. Trenner had agreed. He explained all this to Randall in a dulled but wondering tone as they sat together outside Intensive Care. The doctors had tried to convince Mr. Trenner to go home, that the ordeal could be quite lengthy, but he could not stay away from the hospital and Randall, not knowing what else to do, kept him company. Aunt Marjorie, his father's sister, had moved into Randall's old room in order to tend Melissa during this time, so Randall curled into a waiting-room chair of soiled vinyl (his father sat upright in the next chair) and tried to doze. He resisted thinking of school—the classes he was missing, the possibility that he would not graduate on schedule. He tried to comfort his father. But even though his father had become unusually talkative, Randall sensed there was no real communication; he was just talking. Randall might have been one of the nurses, or one of the walls. Yet he listened, he nodded; he said whatever came to mind, and could not help reflecting that he and his father were virtual strangers.

Late one night, Randall was summoned by a nurse: his mother was awake and would like to speak with him. As he rose, his father clutched Randall's arm.

"Be careful what you say—don't frighten her." His father's eyes had widened; they were ringed with exhaustion.

"She's not frightened," Randall said awkwardly. "Try to get some sleep, okay?"

"Say something pleasant," his father said. "Keep her spirits up."

"Keep your own spirits up," Randall said, more abruptly than he intended. He turned and followed the nurse down the hall.

He'd been inside the room before, but his mother had always

been sleeping. The nurse whispered that she'd just received her pain medication. "But she's gravely ill," the nurse warned him. At the bedside, his mother clutched his arm much as his father had done.

"It's all right, Mama."

"Don't worry about me," she said. Her face was drawn, her hair dull; but her skin was translucent and beautiful, faintly pink as though with health. He thought of Melissa's skin.

"I'm here now, don't worry," he said, surprising himself. His words did not sound hollow and even he believed them. "Melissa's fine," he said. "We're taking good care of her."

"It's not Melissa—" She broke off, her mouth twisted in grief.

"He's fine, too," Randall said. "I'm not going back to school, not for a long while. I'll see to both of them."

Her composure returned. She said that Randall's father had changed in ways that only she understood—she was frightened by the depth of his fear, his desperation. Randall tried to console her. She should think only about getting well, he said; she should concentrate on that. Gazing down, he was astonished that she looked so youthful, her skin reminding him of the Virgin's statue down at church—that same faint pink flush, a radiance whose source was not really physical. His mother was a simple, sweet-natured woman devoted to her family, but at that moment she seemed to him impersonal, somehow monitory—sent as a vision, perhaps, to guide him through the next phase of his life. An hour later she was dead.

He drove his father home. They told Marjorie. They told Melissa. Both women were subdued; they asked few questions. More than subdued, his father fell into silence. His skin was grayish, slack at the jaw and throat. He said he was going to bed, which surprised Randall.

"Let's have a drink first," he told his father. "A glass of wine."

Mr. Trenner shook his head. "Sleep," he said.

Uneasily Randall remembered what the doctor said: he needed sleep.

"I'm worried, do something," Marjorie fretted after his father had disappeared down the hall. She had taken hold of his forearm.

"He needs to sleep," Randall said.

Melissa sat in a wingback chair in the corner, watching them both.

Hours later the shot came. Evidently his father had prepared everything in advance. There was a will, there was a letter with careful instructions; there was an apology to them all. It was to Father McInerney's everlasting credit, Randall thought, that he allowed Mr. Trenner to be included in the funeral Mass. The Trenners had been married in this church and they left it together in two identical coffins. People spoke to Randall after the service, many of them people he did not recognize, and he tried to respond politely. It was a cool, beautiful autumn day at the cemetery, and people lingered around him, talking in subdued voices. All day Melissa had limped along beside him, saying little, and he tried to keep one arm around her shoulders as he nodded, listening to strangers.

III

"I can't be responsible for what happens," Marjorie said. "I *won't* be responsible."

She moved briskly around the kitchen, preparing tea and rolls, never quite meeting his eyes. Randall wanted to get up and grab her by the shoulders, give her a good shake, but instead he sat quietly, his thinking dulled; he did not know how to talk to her. Long ago Randall's father had remarked, casually, that Marjorie was a born martyr, and should have been an actress. She was a common version of Catholic spinsterhood—living for others, subsisting on her own rage. It had been a settled assumption in Randall's family that his aunt would never marry. After all these years she'd retained her abrupt energy, Randall saw, but there was a new sourness in the set of her mouth, and the quickness to anger that comes from long brooding over one's poor bargain with life. She returned to the table and stood clutching the back of her chair.

"As it is, we barely make ends meet," she told him. "Melissa has no conception of money, you know. She's always wanting this or that."

"Don't worry, I've got plenty of money saved," he lied. "And besides, there'll be other jobs."

"She's all grown up now, you know," his aunt said sarcastically. "Makes her own decisions, keeps her own counsel. That's fine with me, but I won't be responsible if something happens."

Her sarcasm weakened as she spoke; it appeared that her whole body had weakened. She'd become an emaciated, slump-shouldered old woman, though Randall remembered that in her youth she'd been buxom enough, with shining auburn hair and unblemished pale skin. He recalled the first time he'd seen the scoring of faint lines across Marjorie's forehead, as she stood over Melissa's wheelchair with her shell-backed hairbrush raised trembling in the air. (She hadn't used the brush, of course; it was only a way, she told Randall, of controlling Melissa who had become—Marjorie liked to roll the word out, precise as any schoolmarm—"incorrigible.") Now she sat, placing her thin hands on the table, palms open. This struck Randall as a meek, somehow ominous gesture.

"Marjorie, what is it?" he said. He felt the dull throbbing in his chest.

"You don't know what I've been through, Randall. I tell you, I won't be responsible," his aunt repeated. Her voice had fallen to a dry whisper.

"How did she get that bruise on her cheek?" Randall asked. "Tell me."

"I wrote to you, for months I wrote to you, asking for help. You sent money, but I need more than money. I used to have Father Mike, and you know how he loved Melissa, but it's gotten beyond me now. I'm an old woman, Randall, and I can't control her. I can't do everything."

Last year Marjorie had written him that Father Mike, an athletic, silver-haired man who had replaced Father McInerney, was leaving the parish, which had gotten far too small to justify its expenses. Each time Randall visited home he had talked to the priest, who often brushed aside his concerns by saying that Melissa was a delightful child. On his last visit Randall, irritated, had pointed out that his sister was nearly middle-aged, but

Father Mike had shrugged his broad shoulders, smiling amiably. "If we could all be so childlike!" he exclaimed.

Now Randall said, "The bruise, Marjorie. Tell me."

Her eyes lifted. "About six months ago, she met someone," his aunt said. "A man."

These simple words hung in the air. *A man.*

"What are you talking about?" Randall said.

In that dry whispering voice, she told him. She'd been having car trouble, and one day she'd called a mechanic's garage to have the car towed away. Melissa sat on the porch watching as the men arrived in the tow truck and began hooking Marjorie's car. The youngest of the two men seemed to be in charge, and as he stood in the driveway with Marjorie he kept glancing at the porch, where Melissa sat on the top step, chin on her hands. She wore her yellow sun dress. It was a September afternoon, very hot. The man, George Tillman, was small, wiry, deeply tanned, with wet-looking curly black hair. Marjorie noticed how he kept glancing back at the porch, only half-listening while Marjorie tried to explain about the car. When they finished preparing for the tow, the second man came up with something for Marjorie to sign, and George Tillman used that moment to step over to the porch and speak to Melissa.

When Marjorie got home the next night, Melissa wasn't there. Frantic, she'd called the young girl, Nancy, whom she'd hired that week as Melissa's new companion—one in a long series, Marjorie said bitterly, none of whom lasted more than a month. When the girl answered the phone, she was in tears. She said Melissa had fired her, had ordered her out of the house. Melissa had spent all afternoon in front of the mirror, the girl said, smearing makeup on her face, trying on her frilly, old-fashioned dresses. She'd said she was going out with George, she had her own life to live and could do just what she wanted. The girl had no choice but to leave, and Marjorie had felt terrible: the girl had been a nurse's aide at the hospital where Marjorie worked, and Marjorie had hired her away. She was only a typist herself, she complained to Randall, and now *she* might be fired if anyone found out. . . . Nancy had been such a sweet girl, though, and

this was a perfect example of Melissa's destructive, foolish behavior, her pure selfishness when people were trying their best,
as always, to help her.

His aunt stayed in her chair, in that slump-shouldered posture; she seemed to have forgotten about the tea and rolls.

Randall said, "This is hard to believe."

"He comes over when I'm at work," his aunt said. "There's
nothing I can do, you know, it's not against the law to visit a
40-year-old woman. Why, he even takes her down to Wool-
worth's and they buy new makeup, they go shopping for those
cheap flouncy dresses she loves so much. Everyone knows about
it, Randall. I can hardly lift my head in this town."

Randall sat quietly, stunned. "You should have called me,"
he said, his voice faint. "I would have stopped it."

"For as long as you were here, maybe," she said bitterly. "But
the moment you were gone?" She snapped her fingers.

He sat for a long time, staring. It was not the fact that Marjorie
lied, but the elaborate precision of her lying that amazed him.
For a few incredulous moments he'd believed her and, terrible
as the fiction was, it had admitted a solution. But now he sat
confronting the fact of his aunt's crazed isolation, which led him
to the image of Melissa alone in her bedroom, writing her pathetic
letters to him, to her brother who could offer her so little, even
less than in the past. . . . He could not comprehend the cruelty
of the world. He could not blame his sister's letters, he thought,
though they had sent his mind spinning backward, had set his
blood churning. Rather it was the heartless clarity of his present
life, a life that had slowly wound out into silence, emptying him
of all the distractions and trivial ambitions that had clouded his
adult years, rendering his mind a blank screen upon which
Melissa had scrawled, in all innocence, a poetry of doom. Yet
he felt no anger, not even toward Marjorie. He felt only the shy
beginnings of pain.

"What are you saying?" he asked.

"I'm saying that I've reached my limit, Randall. It's been bad
enough all these years, but I can't come home knowing that
only a few hours before—" She stopped, her breath catching.

"Yes?" Randall said.

"We've discussed it before, and I know you're opposed to the idea..."

"An institution?" Randall said.

"I know it sounds awful," she said, her voice wavering, "but you can well imagine what might happen otherwise. Even if you scare Tillman off, who'll come sneaking around next? No, we've got to move, both of us. I can move to Cartersville where there's a proper church, but Melissa needs someplace where they'll protect her, look out for her...."

Randall said, quietly, "All right."

"You know, it's a coincidence that you came home," she said, unable to hide her relief, "because I was getting ready to call you, I really was. Especially after—well, after that awful bruise sprang up. She won't admit it, but I know he beats her, and this isn't the first time. Last month there were these red marks on her shoulders, I saw them when I was shampooing her hair—"

"Never mind," Randall said. "That's enough."

"It's not that I haven't tried," Marjorie said, whining, "it's not that I'm mean or hateful—"

"It's all right," he said. "Please."

"And you'll tell her...?" she asked fearfully.

"I'll tell her," Randall said, thinking that yes, he had become an automaton, numbed and impersonal. "I'll handle everything," he said, "but please, let's not discuss it any more."

IV

Every life holds the seed of its own destruction, and for Randall the first blossom of darkness comes early, at the age of twelve. The memory will haunt him all his life.

The Friday before Easter, a glorious spring morning: Randall arrives with his younger sister at the church, driven by their father who has said very little today. Randall climbs out of the back seat, unfolds Melissa's chair out of the trunk, carefully lifts his sister from the car and into the chair. Their father stays in the front seat, not watching. "Okay, I'll see you inside," Randall calls, and he slams the door. The car drives off.

His mother is already there, inside the church. Waiting.

Unbothered, innocent, Randall grips the handles and begins wheeling his sister along the sidewalk. He's a big, muscular boy, well-liked in the town—especially by the parents of his friends. Father McInerney likes to remark, jovially, that Randall is the best altar boy in the parish. He knows every move, he never falters; he gives the Latin responses flawlessly. Even now, wheeling Melissa along, he is performing a ritual—memorized, unthinking. As they move toward the rear entrance of the church Melissa chatters brightly but of course Randall does not listen.

The back rooms of the church are dim, hushed. The Trenner children are the first to arrive. In the small anteroom just off the main altar, Randall waits with his sister, giving her words of encouragement though she does not seem concerned or nervous. She wears her usual church dress, a burgundy velvet with white lace trim, but clutches in her lap, like a prize, the small bag his mother had packed that morning. His mother had sewn the costume herself; for the past few weeks, her lap had been covered every evening in blue satin, white lace. Randall, who had acted the part of Pilate in last year's passion play, had been pleased when Melissa had been asked, this year, to play the Blessed Virgin. The play was something of an event in the parish: the brief opening ritual of the three-hour Good Friday service. A "dumb show" devised by Father McInerney, it lasted only twenty minutes; Melissa had only to sit there, in her blue satin, at the foot of a cross-shaped shadow cast upon the altar using floodlights and a pair of sticks tied together. Randall asks again, "Do you feel all right?" but Melissa doesn't hear: she clutches the bag, chattering about some trivial event at school this past week.

Randall is a good, dutiful brother. He often asks his sister how she feels.

Father McInerney arrives. The other "actors" begin arriving. After a few words with the priest, and a good-bye peck on his sister's forehead, Randall walks out of the anteroom, stops to genuflect in front of the altar, then walks down the center aisle and joins his parents in the third pew from the rear. "Is she okay?" his mother asks him, softly. He nods *yes*. Slowly the church is beginning to fill. Sitting stolid on the other side of his mother, Randall's father says nothing.

It is less a memory than a dream, perhaps, and here the dream turns upon Randall. He sits calm and unthinking beside his parents, waiting for the service to begin, looking forward to the passion play that will include for the first time his younger sister, Melissa. And the dream turns on him, at this point. Brutally. Though they have very little in common, he has felt protective of Melissa since earliest childhood. Disabled since her infancy, she has always been protected and coddled by the family; and perhaps, as their Aunt Marjorie complains, a little spoiled. Yet she is a happy, unselfish child. Not long ago Randall's father complained bitterly that her medical care had not been of the finest, her physical therapy should have been more aggressive, more carefully planned; clearly the disability, and the way she was treated by her doctors and teachers, only encouraged her to remain a bright babbling infant, coddled like a two-year-old even though she had now reached her ninth birthday. After first grade, she had been held back a year; near the end of the next year, one of her teachers had called Randall's father and suggested that Melissa be sent to a "special" school in Atlanta, very progressive, very expensive. That same week, Father McInerney stopped by for a visit. He was sorry to say that the school the teacher had recommended, while well-accredited, made no efforts to assure regular instruction in theology for its Catholic students, and he sincerely feared for Melissa's spiritual well-being at such a place. Randall's father had countered that they would of course visit her every Sunday, and take her to Mass, but Father McInerney had shaken his head, sadly. The school was simply not acceptable, he said. Melissa's disability was a terrible cross to bear, he said, but evidently it was the will of God, not to be circumvented by extraordinary means. Thus Melissa had gone back to her old school, and at the end of second grade was held back again. She was noticeably a bigger, older child than her classmates, though far less mature. She had little interest in her school work. Taking an indulgent approach, her teachers did not reprimand her for failing to turn in assignments or even for doing poorly on tests or other work. What could anyone expect, after all? Randall did not understand his father's anger and appreciated the kindness shown to Melissa by her teachers.

At other hands, however, Melissa was not treated so kindly. She had long been the victim of schoolyard pranks, but as time passed these grew more relentless and more cruel. Seldom did a week pass when Randall did not get into a fight with someone over Melissa, but he could not be everywhere, and he knew that most of the time she went unprotected. At recess, her teacher would wheel her into a shaded area next to the playground, then disappear into the teachers' lounge for lunch. During this 30 to 40 minutes, Melissa was the object of merciless ridicule, of whatever whimsical cruelty or stray ill-humors arose in her class-mates on that day. Once Randall had come up from the football field to find her tied inside the wheelchair, an "Indian" feather stuck in her hair, while a group of boys whooped and cavorted around her. Another day, near the end of the recess period, he glimpsed a teacher wheeling Melissa quickly back inside the building. Randall sprinted toward them, then saw that his sister's hair was full of leaves, her face smeared with dirt; blood had caked beneath one of her nostrils. "What happened?" Randall cried, catching up to them. "How did—" "It's nothing," said the teacher, a slim solemn-voiced woman in her thirties. "She was moving along too fast, I guess, and she fell—it's nothing, we'll go inside the washroom and clean her up." The teacher added, bending down, "Isn't that right, Melissa?" His sister nodded, blankly. She looked pale. Terrified. "Fell!" Randall cried. "She's never fallen out of that chair in her life. Tell me who did it, who pushed her—" "Never mind, it's all over," the teacher said, uneasily. Then she looked squarely at Randall: "These things happen," she said. She turned to wheel his sister inside the washroom; Randall hadn't been able to respond.

On that morning in church, that Good Friday, Randall sits wondering about next year, and how Melissa will fare without him—this fall, Randall will enroll in a junior high school located several miles from the elementary school—and with an ugly dreamlike inevitability the answer arrives at exactly that moment. For the passion play has begun, and a tall dark-haired "angel"—a girl Randall recognizes from Melissa's homeroom—appears at one side of the altar, wheeling Melissa before her. Next to him, Randall feels the change in his mother: she has leaned forward, a sudden tension in her body. Randall's own body has filled with a dull, leaden certainty that only in later years will he learn to call "guilt." Paralyzed, he stares at Melissa. She isn't the same Melissa he'd left in the anteroom an hour before. Now, looking both absurd and pathetic, she is wearing heavy makeup: thick white powder on her plump cheeks, blue paint smeared on her eyelids and even beneath her eyes, garish orange-red lipstick applied to her lips, rising to a pair of artificial peaks on the top lip. The makeup has been applied rapidly, clumsily. Because Melissa wears her white linen blouse and skirt, and because her head and shoulders and most of the wheelchair are covered by her blue satin veil, only his sister's face is showing—an hour ago so pink, shining, and innocent; now so ludicrous in this painted mask, so pathetic, that she hardly dares to raise her eyes. Yet Randall sees that she's been crying. He sees that beneath the makeup she is blushing fiercely. And he sees, his rage crashing like waves inside his heart, the small group of "angels" surrounding his sister, all of them girls from her class, all giggling behind their hands.

When Father McInerney comes out of the opposite anteroom and sees Melissa, his eyes widen for a moment but then, an old pro, he carries on. Father McInerney plays the role of Joseph of Arimathea. Near the end of the play, he looks on helplessly as the dark-haired angel reappears, her face strained to keep from laughing, and wheels the stricken Melissa out in front of the altar, where the cross now casts its long, familiar shadow. Randall sees that she cannot look up; no longer blushing, she is now chalk-white, trembling. He sees Father McInerney give a sharp, covert signal, and instantly the organ music rises. At the same instant all the actors rise, glancing shyly toward the congregation before filing out. A band of tittering angels descends on Melissa. Randall watches after them, craning his neck, as they wheel her away; they seem to be competing—giggling, swatting at each other—for control of the wheelchair.

Now that the resurrection is accomplished the altar is empty, still dominated by the slanting dark shadow of the cross. The passion play is over. The prank is over. During the last twenty minutes a collective tension has mounted inside the church but

Randall now sees, bitterly, that it collapses at once. People begin shuffling their feet; they chat back and forth, clearly relieved. Even his mother sits back in her seat, her eyes closing. Randall thinks, nodding to himself: It's over.

V

On Sunday morning he drove Melissa down to Carmine Lake, her favorite place since earliest childhood. She'd risen before dawn to prepare for the outing. Randall had lain awake, himself, and he could hear her thumping heavily from room to room, running the bath water, scraping clothes hangers along the ancient metal rod in her closet. Darkness pressed at Randall's bedroom window; he lay staring at the black rectangle, hearing beyond Melissa's innocent noises the first chirpings of the birds outside. Springtime, he thought. He'd entered another world. His stomach knotted as he watched the dark window, unable to imagine the pale streaks of dawn just moments away. His heart lay like a stone in his chest.

Marjorie, he knew, would stay inside her room until they were gone. Yesterday she'd been unnaturally polite, self-effacing, while Melissa had sat quietly in the back seat of Randall's car, seeming abstracted, only half present. Randall had driven them into town for lunch, and he noticed that the two women never exchanged glances or spoke to one another. He felt the silent pressure from Marjorie: why not tell her? Why not get it over with? Yet he'd been waiting, he didn't know what for. On the way home Melissa had suddenly perked up, had talked in a rushed, hectic voice, asking him whether they could take a picnic lunch to the lake, and if they could take a rowboat out into the water? He said quickly, *Yes.* Both he and Marjorie sat back at the same moment, relieved. Yes, of course, he said to Melissa. Tomorrow.

When they arrived home he'd said something about cigarettes and had returned to town, alone. Just off Center Street he found George Tillman's garage, an ancient structure of grimy dark-red brick. Randall sat in his car, waiting, and soon enough the man appeared, lounging for a moment against the doorway, smoking.

He looked much as Marjorie had described him, though perhaps a bit older than Randall had expected, his dark kinky hair thinned back on each side of his crown. He wore working clothes and a plain wedding band that glinted dully in the afternoon sun. He looked frank, healthy, oblivious. When he finished smoking he flicked the cigarette down, stepped on it, and went back to work.

Perhaps he had spoken to Melissa on that day, Randall thought; perhaps he'd even stopped by one afternoon and taken his sister for a ride, out of simple kindness. And Marjorie had fabricated the rest. Her jealousy kindled, perhaps. The whole incident mocking, after all these years, some desperate fantasy of her own. Randall did not know, nor did he want to know. For once the truth did not matter.

Thinking vindictively of Elaine and her pathetic addiction to the truth—to "utter frankness"—he drove back home.

Melissa came to his bedroom about six o'clock, calling out "Rise and shine!" in a cheerful parody of their aunt; this had long been a private joke between them. Coming into the kitchen, he was pleased to see her moving freely about as she made toast and set their places at the table side by side. Yesterday her limp had been awkward, heavy; today it was scarcely noticeable. "About time you got up!" she cried, motioning him to the table.

"Melissa, I'm not really hungry," he said. He smiled at her.

"Sit down, Ran-dall," she said, again mimicking their aunt. "You need your strength!" She smiled slyly, showing her small square teeth and pink gums.

Despite himself, he laughed. He sat down beside her.

"Remember, we've got to be back by eleven," he said. "I told Marjorie I'd take you both over to Cartersville for noon Mass."

Melissa frowned. "Don't want to," she said. "They're not used to me, Ran-dall. They point at me, like this." She wiggled her plump fingers in the air. "The grown-ups do it, too!"

For a moment this painful recollection dampened her good cheer. Everything showed on her face, Randall thought. She had escaped, at least, their father's staid melancholy that had hardened Randall's features since that Good Friday service so long ago, when his family had ridden home from church in their old bottle-green Dodge, not speaking; on that day, finally, Randall had understood his father's brooding silence, his mother's perplexity. Randall had sat in the living room, watching dry-eyed as his father went through the daily newspaper, turning each page methodically, giving no clues. Melissa had gone quietly to her room.

Now he recalled the bruised, silent Melissa he'd glimpsed two days before, when he'd showed up in her bedroom so suddenly, without warning; of course she hadn't stayed a child, as he'd have recognized long ago if he'd taken the time. *Past is past*, Elaine had said briskly, and the remark kept playing in his head, mocking him.

"We'll come home in time for Mass," Randall said, softly. "I promised."

Together they packed the car and were on the highway shortly after eight. There was little traffic this morning. It seemed they had the world all to themselves. Blinking at the sunlight, Randall thought in amazement that only a few days had passed since he'd left the city, his job, his old life; none of that seemed real. Next to him, wearing her yellow sun dress, his sister seemed unbearably real. The dress was plain cotton, with a full skirt, and it bared her shoulders except for the thin straps that formed a V across her freckled back. Her shoulders and the tops of her breasts still looked youthful, rosy. He could feel her intense, fleshy heat from his side of the car.

He said, "Thanks again for the letters, Melissa. I was proud to get them."

"I can write good letters, Ran-dall."

"You sure can. You can do a lot of things."

Her head bobbed up, then down. "Yep."

"But it gets lonely sometimes, doesn't it? With just Marjorie to talk to?"

This required a moment's thought. "Don't know."

"Wouldn't you like to meet some new friends?"

Another moment, then a slow headshake. "Nope."

They drove. He did not know how to talk to her. Straining, he tried to recall that muscular young boy pushing his sister's wheelchair, bending down every few minutes as they went along the sidewalk, under the April sun—what words had he spoken? what protection had he offered? They'd both been so innocent, so unthinking; and of course that boy wasn't a version of himself but someone else, lost forever.

"Can we go out in the rowboat?" Melissa asked.

"If they still rent them," Randall said. "It's been a long time—" "We'll rent one," Melissa said, confidently. She sat very straight, her eyes taking in the countryside, the passing cars. She watched eagerly, hungrily. Her transparent delight made Randall squeamish. He could easily imagine himself as Marjorie, reaching out to restrain her, to strike her with the back of his hand.... Cruel, he thought vaguely; so very cruel. Once or twice, as a child, she'd become so agitated that forcible restraint had been necessary, and after all she bruised so easily. She was so vulnerable, he thought. It was no one's fault.

"Calm down, Melissa," he said sternly. "You don't want to get overexcited."

It seemed she didn't hear.

When they arrived at the lake, she began struggling with the door even before Randall had braked the car. "Melissa, wait, not so fast—" but now they had stopped, and quickly Melissa pulled herself out the door. In the back seat were the picnic supplies, the blanket and sandwiches and soft drinks, but Melissa wasn't interested in food.

"We just ate, Ran-dall. Let's get a boat! Over there!"

They stood only a few yards from shore. The sky was overcast, the waves a dark gray-green, very choppy. The wind was brisk, chilly for April. "Don't you need a sweater?" Randall asked. "It's cooler than I thought—"

"A boat!" Melissa cried, beating her arms in the air. Randall saw whitish gooseflesh along her upper arms, her shoulders. Her round face had tensed in defiance.

Randall said, "It's too cold. Look, there's not another soul out in that water. It's too windy and cold, it's dangerous—"

She wasn't listening. She'd turned and begun hobbling down toward the water. Twenty yards away was a small unpainted pier, a few small rowboats tied to the railings. As she walked Melissa pointed, shouting excitedly. "Look! Boats!"

Grudgingly, he followed. "Melissa, we need to have a talk, do you hear? There's no time for a boat ride."

She stopped, turning to face him. "You promised!"

"I didn't promise."

She stood perfectly still, the yellow skirt whipping around her. She held her mouth tight.

Feeling boyish in his jeans and sneakers, he went over and glanced at the boats. They were very small, made of aluminum; they looked fairly new. Each had been tied by a single thick rope to one of the pier railings. Randall glanced all around. He saw no one.

He called, "All right, but only for a few minutes. And we can't go out very far."

She came galloping down to meet him. Her grin looked smeared, out of focus, like Randall's memory of her made-up face during that passion play, the lipsticked mouth painted larger than Melissa's own. There had been such pain, such confused fear inside the small slits of her eyes.

"Come on, now. Careful," he said.

Soon enough he'd untied the small oars, then freed the boat from the railing. Despite the wind, it was fairly easy to maneuver the boat away from the pier. This was a large, man-made lake, the opposite shore barely visible on this gray morning. Enclosing the lake, a silverish haze of fog lingered in the greening trees, and Randall saw that only a short distance out the water itself had the fog hovering over it, lightly caressing the turbulent surface. Randall kept his eye on the pier they'd just left and on his car parked beyond it; they would stay near the shore, he thought, they would paddle around for a few minutes until Melissa was satisfied. Sitting opposite him, letting her oar drag along the water, Melissa seemed at a great distance, her broad forehead tilted back, reflecting the faint light.

So much time had passed, he thought.

Such a heartless length of time.

"Look, I can row the boat," she said. She made crude, swiping motions at the water with her oar. She sat very straight in her end of the boat, a big ungainly child of a woman in her yellow sun dress, her bowl-shaped haircut. He watched her, both fascinated and repelled. The bruise along her cheek had already begun to fade. It looked like a faint smear of dirt.

Randall said, "Tell me about George."

Her gray eyes slitted against him; she kept her face bland, unreadable. "George?" she said.

She held the oar with both hands, lightly slapping at the water.

He felt no desire to press her. He felt nothing at all. "Quit playing with the oar," he said. "It's dangerous."

Her lower lip had protruded. "I want to," she said. She slapped at the water.

"I said to stop, Melissa."

His voice sounded toneless, otherworldly. Not Randall's voice.

She stopped for a moment, holding the oar suspended above the water. "Don't . . . want to," she mumbled. The oar fell, slapping the surface.

Small, choppy waves rocked the boat, so he stood very slowly, keeping his legs spread for leverage. He held out one hand. "Give me the oar, Melissa."

Her bottom lip descended further. "It's fun, why can't I . . ." But she lifted the oar toward him. As he reached down, the oar slipped from her hand and slid without a sound into the water.

"Now see what you've done?" he said, in a soft monotone. "See what a terrible thing you've done?"

She looked at him, fearful, her hands gripping the narrow seat. "I can't hear you, Ran-dall. What—"

Dazed, Randall felt his eyes close. Melissa tried to get up, she tried to reach out for her brother's hand, but she could not keep her balance and she fell, slipping over the side almost as quietly as the weightless oar had done. Her hand hit the side of the boat and held there for a moment, clinging.

Randall sat. He undid one sneaker, then the other. He placed his oar carefully along the bottom of the boat.

He whispered, "You see, don't you? What a terrible thing you've done?"

He looked down into the water. His sister's hand no longer clung to the boat. He must protect her, he must save her. . . . He saw the choppy iron-gray waves, dense, impenetrable. He lifted his arms in a graceful arc and dove.

He came up sputtering. The water was much colder than he expected; it had taken his breath away. He looked around and felt how suspended everything was, how silvery and quiet. Of course Melissa had not fallen, of course she sat silently watching him from the boat, her face set in a disapproving scowl; yet Randall felt no dismay. He felt nothing but his own heartbeat, continuing stubbornly in his chest. He saw that the boat was already some distance away—ten yards, twenty yards—but he didn't care. He didn't need the boat, did he? . . . He thought idly to himself, *It's over.* He took a deep breath. His passion spent, he straightened his agile body and swam on back to shore.

Grieving

O N ELIZABETH'S THIRD VISIT to the cemetery the girl was
there again, standing over the marker in a peculiar, tense
posture, as if she might crumple to the ground at any moment.
Elizabeth waited near the bottom of the green, grave-dotted hill,
only a few yards from where her car was parked on the winding
asphalt drive. She stood there quietly, watching. Her eyes narrowed. On the two preceding days she had noticed the girl,
who had seemed to be wandering among the gravestones aimlessly, only occasionally stopping near Elizabeth to glance once
again at the grave—she seemed to be checking on it, Elizabeth
thought, convincing herself that it was there. Elizabeth had tried
to ignore her. Both times she had kept the girl in her peripheral
vision, pretending she was alone (no one else was around, this
cemetery seemed always to be deserted) because she was in the
mood for solitude, wanting to experience her grief in a placid,
graceful way. That was Elizabeth's style. But now the girl stood
directly over the grave of Elizabeth's husband Albert, who had
died unexpectedly only a week before, and Elizabeth allowed
herself the sense of intrusion, even of insult, feeling a blush of
anger rise into her cheeks.

The girl wore a simple white dress, and its rather full skirt
was being whipped in the brisk autumn wind; the day was fair
and brilliantly sunny, but still very cold. The girl wore no coat

and the wind swept over her, yet she seemed to notice nothing, she was not even shivering. Something about the way she stood there—tense and strained, as if all her energy were concentrated in gazing down at Albert's grave—made Elizabeth blink her eyes, as if the girl were somehow not real, only a trick of Elizabeth's vision. But when she focused again the girl was still there, her reddish, shoulder-length hair blown in one direction by the wind, so that Elizabeth could see little of her face. The girl was very thin, wraith-like; her slender white arms hung at her sides lifelessly. She stood in a still, impossible attitude, simply gazing downward, her eyes partially closed against the wind. Even at this distance, Elizabeth saw that she had a wistful, delicate beauty that a certain kind of man might find appealing. She appeared to be about eighteen; she seemed frail, vulnerable, almost childish. Elizabeth wondered suddenly if this girl would have appealed to Albert, but since she had no way of knowing she pushed this outrageous thought from her mind at once.

Very quickly, she began climbing the hill; she kept her eyes fixed on the girl, who remained motionless even though she surely could hear Elizabeth, who was no longer trying to be quiet. Elizabeth felt her legs begin to ache, already she was almost breathless. She was perhaps twenty yards from the girl when she called out, "Excuse me—hello—do we know each other? Have we met?" By the time the girl turned to face her, Elizabeth had reached her husband's foot marker. She stood there, panting; she realized that she had practically run up the hill, and as if to atone for this absurdity she tried to smile. But instantly she hated herself: she had wanted to put the girl on the defensive.

"Have we met?" Elizabeth repeated. "Do I know you?"

The girl stared at her. Elizabeth saw that she was very pretty, her face angular and pale yet somehow girlish; her eyes were deeply set, an intense bright green and thickly lashed. The girl's vivid eyes, her paleness, the outdated, rather childish dress—all gave her a wild, unearthly look. And yet Elizabeth realized that she was not a girl at all: she was perhaps twenty-eight, even thirty years old. The two women stared at each other. After a moment Elizabeth felt an astonished, hurt look in her own eyes and glanced away.

"Do I know you?" she asked again. "Who are—?"

The girl said abruptly: "I'm awfully sorry, I didn't mean to stare at you that way. I'm always doing that—it's just that I was thinking, thinking of something . . . I'm sorry . . . no, I don't think we know each other. I'm just here to—to visit someone." She nodded toward the grave.

"But—Albert? Are you visiting this grave, Albert's grave . . . ?" Elizabeth felt confused and oddly frightened, for as the girl began to speak she had suddenly warmed toward her: she had an unguarded, childlike sincerity, something that resembled innocence. Elizabeth felt the urge to escape, to run away; she regretted having approached the girl at all.

"Yes," the girl said. "Albert Parkins. He was a very good friend of mine—we were very close. I didn't know that he'd died until Monday, so I missed the funeral—someone finally called me, afterwards—I found out—"

She began to cry. Instinctively Elizabeth reached out to her, taking one of the pale, bony hands and stroking it. Elizabeth's own hands were gloved—the gloves were suede, a soft pearly gray that matched Elizabeth's dress—and as she held the girl's hand she stared at her rough, chilled skin. The skin of her hands and arms was very pale, a whitish, doughy color, dotted with faint brown freckles. When she looked back to the girl's face, she saw that her cheeks were already streaked with tears; her entire body was trembling. Her head seemed to sag forward, as if she were wounded, her chin almost touching her breast. The girl stood there, weeping openly, quietly, allowing Elizabeth to hold one of her chilled, lifeless hands.

Elizabeth shuddered.

Then the girl drew away, taking a step backward. "Oh I'm so sorry, don't let me keep you any longer—I'll just stand here awhile, a few more minutes—then I have to go, I'm catching a bus at three o'clock. Are you here to visit Albert too? I shouldn't bother you. . . ." She was wiping her tears away like a child, with the palms of both hands. "I'll be all right in a minute—I just haven't known what to do—it's so strange, knowing he's down there."

"But I couldn't leave you," Elizabeth said. There was an earnestness in her own voice that surprised her. "And after all, we're both here to visit Albert—I was a friend of his too, so I understand. . . . Maybe we should walk back down for a while, my car is parked just at the bottom of the hill—"

"But I can't leave him, I only have a little while longer. I'm going home today, I have to take the bus back to Atlanta." She was shaking her head. "I can't leave him," she repeated.

"But you're not well," Elizabeth said, wondering at her own persistence. "And it's so cold out—don't you have a coat? Please come with me, perhaps we can talk. We could sit inside my car— see where it's parked, down there on the drive?—and talk for a while. Couldn't we do that?"

The girl glanced at Albert's grave, anxiously, as if mentally asking permission. Elizabeth was struck by her profile, which was severe but also delicate, the pale fine skin drawn tautly over the bones . . . her auburn hair looked freshly washed and glittered in the sunlight. She was a woman in her thirties, perhaps only a few years younger than Elizabeth herself, but in every way she reminded Elizabeth of a child—a rather nervous, imaginative child.

The girl turned to her and smiled brilliantly. "All right," she said. "This is so nice of you." Then she did a surprising thing: she put her arm inside Elizabeth's, familiarly, with the air of bestowing a gift.

They began walking down the hill, very slowly. The girl talked to Elizabeth in a high, musical voice, its sound dispersed by the wind so that her words were barely audible. . . . Elizabeth held onto the girl's arm, which rested in hers like a dead weight, something the girl had given up entirely, and tried to listen to this bright meandering voice which seemed to mingle naturally with the wind—but what was she saying? Elizabeth could not hear. She looked at the girl's face several times, smiling and nodding. She heard the words "dead," and "funeral," but it was almost as if the words were being deliberately blocked out— perhaps she didn't even want to hear them. By the time they reached Elizabeth's car, the girl had fallen silent. She turned to Elizabeth and smiled: a shy, sincere smile that somehow made Elizabeth go cold with dread, panic. Something about the girl disturbed her—especially these abrupt, unexplained smiles, which nonetheless trembled as though the girl were on the verge of tears. "Shall we just go for a ride?" Elizabeth asked doubtfully. She had raised her voice against the wind, but she had a sudden, surprising thought: she hoped the girl did not hear. She stared at the strange old-fashioned dress, at the smile which seemed too bright, unfocussed, and wondered if something were wrong with this girl, if perhaps she were unbalanced, even retarded. . . . But the girl only nodded. "That'd be nice," she said, and she got into the car.

Elizabeth drove slowly, taking extreme caution before pulling out onto the narrow, two-lane highway. Where would they go? The girl said that her bus didn't leave for almost an hour, could they simply go driving somewhere . . . ? Any place Elizabeth liked would be fine. Elizabeth nodded, but her eyes darted nervously along the highway, as if seeking something that might guide her, lead her to safety. She seldom drove anywhere; driving had always made her nervous, even in this small town where accidents were rare. She wanted to get off the highway, but after hesitating at every intersection she finally passed them all, reaching at last the outskirts of town and the open road. So she stayed on the highway, driving with exaggerated care. She wondered if her car would swerve into the opposite lane suddenly, plowing into the oncoming traffic. . . .

But this could not happen, of course: she was only going thirty miles an hour.

Elizabeth was relieved when the girl began to talk. She seemed obsessed with explaining things, wanting Elizabeth to understand why she had been standing there, on this windy cold day, over someone's grave. *My husband's grave*, Elizabeth thought.

"It happened about two years ago," the girl was saying. "I was only enrolled for that one year, I just couldn't afford to stay here. I'd just been divorced and had to do something, I had a little money saved up . . . anyway, everyone told me to finish college. Finish your education, they said. So I came here, just to get the degree and satisfy everybody—there was really no reason for it. I didn't want a career or anything. So I decided to become a history major, I was getting a degree in history. . . ."

Elizabeth nodded, keeping her eyes on the road. She watched

the grayish bare trees passing by them, their branches pulled
and tortured by the wind. Everything is so ugly here, she
thought. No matter where you look: ugliness. You couldn't escape it. Her husband had been a professor of History at the
University, and when they had first moved here—more than
nine years ago—they'd almost decided on a separation, Elizabeth
hated the town so much. It was a drab, self-centered college
town with barely twenty thousand inhabitants—and it was deep
in the South, in a land foreign to Elizabeth. She had grown up
in New York, and she had fought with Albert for months, years,
insisting that no career was worth this, she would make any
sacrifice if only they could go back, get away from here. But
Albert had quickly made friends at the University, and had come
to enjoy what he called this town's "serenity"—he had never
really liked New York—so that finally his stubborn indifference
to Elizabeth's complaints had worn her out, she had resigned
herself. Desperate and bored, she had taken a job at the University, as an assistant in an administrative office, and gradually
she had become adjusted, even content. She decided that it was
bearable, living here. She had a minor career of her own as a
poet, and she had begun to think that the seclusion might be
good for her work—especially the absence of certain friends,
the freedom from that hectic emotional atmosphere of large
cities. Over the years she had gradually mellowed, grown rather
quiet, even demure; she recognized with some bitterness that
she had grown into someone more likely to be Albert's wife, for
when they first married people felt she overpowered him. But
that had changed. Her own personality had softened, taken on
the same quality of meekness she had once despised in other
women, while Albert's energy and confidence had seemed only
to increase, to cast her further into shadow. Even now she felt
herself somehow diminished, slightly inferior to her smiling,
energetic, popular husband, who was dead.

The girl had fallen silent, but suddenly she said, as if answering Elizabeth's thoughts, "I can't believe he's dead." She shook
her head. "When I heard about it, when they called me—"

She seemed on the verge of tears again; Elizabeth reached
over and touched her arm. "But I don't quite understand," she
said politely. "Mr. Parkins, he was a professor of yours?"

"Yes, I was in his American History class. He was a wonderful teacher." Then she added, softly, "He was a wonderful man." Elizabeth hesitated. She said slowly, "So you admired him a great deal. You admired him. . . ."

The girl turned to Elizabeth; her eyes were a sharp hazel-green, glistening now with tears. "Oh, I loved him. I loved him very much. I always thought I'd come back here, you know—to see him. Maybe even to be with him. But I've got such a big family back home—my mother's getting old and I'm her only daughter, so I had to stay and take care of her. Albert wanted me to bring her up here, but I said no, Mama wouldn't want to leave her home. She's never been out of Georgia, not in her whole life."

Elizabeth let the girl's voice lull her into a kind of trance; she tried not to listen to the words themselves but only to the fragile music of the voice, a music softened by the girl's faint Southern accent. She knew she should be upset, but somehow she felt only a half-pleasant giddiness, the way she would feel looking out over a precipice.

Elizabeth glanced at her, smiling. "By the way, I've forgotten to ask your name."

The girl laughed, pleased. "My name is Betty. Betty Plunkett. What's yours?"

"Elizabeth."

"Really?—we've got the same name, then. Some people still call me Elizabeth, down home. My grandmother. Some call me Betsey, or Beth, but I like Betty. I guess it doesn't matter."

As Elizabeth drove she gradually let the words sink in: *Oh, I loved him.* A hushed, breathless exclamation. This girl had evidently loved her husband, Albert Parkins. Had loved him. Loved. *Love.* Elizabeth shook her head, as if to dispel these words, even Betty's voice. She was dumfounded, she could not think clearly. She wished she could feel rage, but there was nothing but this sense of blankness, a surprise so complete that no reaction seemed possible. She clung to the idea that something was perhaps wrong with this woman—she was so strangely girlish, after all, with that childlike insouciance to her voice, a voice that was somehow not quite real. . . . Elizabeth could not understand. The girl had said simply, *I loved him very much.*

"I like Betty too," Elizabeth said. "For some reason no one ever called me by nicknames, not even my husband."

Betty glanced at her. "That's because you're so pretty," she said shyly. She seemed embarrassed. "Betty wouldn't fit you, it would sound disrespectful."

She spoke these words very seriously.

Elizabeth said nothing. She had always known that she was a pretty woman—though in an undramatic way, with glossy, carefully styled blond hair framing an oval face, a face that was not striking but had no flaws. Few people who knew Elizabeth would guess that she spent almost an hour every morning in applying her make-up. Her beauty was deliberately understated, contained—she was certainly nothing like this girl who now sat beside her, whose face was gaunt, frail, yet so spectacular that it exhausted Elizabeth to look at her. And from the way the girl spoke, Elizabeth gathered that she was unaware of her beauty; she seemed to lack self-consciousness entirely. Elizabeth thought, *She doesn't even know that she exists.*

After a moment Betty said, "Did you know Albert very well?"

"Yes, very well. We were close friends."

Betty looked at her, her eyes filling with tears. "I wish I could be like you—I'm so emotional, such a crybaby. I hate myself sometimes. . . ."

Elizabeth reached over once again and patted her shoulder; she could think of nothing to say. After a while the girl grew calm, and Elizabeth had the idea she was enjoying the ride.

"Do you think we should turn back?" Elizabeth asked. "You don't want to miss your bus."

"No, we still have time. Let's drive a little further. I may never be up here again—I want to see all I can."

"Have you been here long?" Elizabeth asked. She noticed that the girl carried no luggage. "Where are you staying?"

"With a friend of mine," Betty said. "The one who called me about Albert. I was so upset, I dropped everything I was doing and went right down to the bus depot. I didn't even bring a toothbrush, just enough money to get me here and back and last a few days in between. I only have enough left for the fare."

"So you just came to the cemetery—every day—and visited Albert?" Elizabeth realized that her voice sounded incredulous.

"Yes," Betty said.

They both fell silent. Elizabeth knew they must be at least twenty miles out from town, but this no longer seemed to matter. In a careful, restrained way she began thinking of Albert, of his involvement with this girl. How was it possible? Betty had been a student of his, she said, but Elizabeth could not imagine their having met that way. She herself had once visited one of Albert's seminars, and her first impression had been of his impersonality in the classroom, his coldness. She remembered sitting at the far end of the seminar table, watching her husband as he led a tense, exhausting discussion of the Reconstruction, somehow building in that small room a mood of excitement, expectation, a tension which had all the students straining forward in their chairs, leaning slightly in toward Albert, as if he would end the class with some momentous revelation. Albert had been a very talented teacher, she had always known that, yet he had tended to abstract himself from his students; he never joked, never brought his personality into the classroom. His classes were formal, intense, exhausting. Elizabeth remembered watching her husband's eyes on that day, and she had imagined that the surfaces of his glasses were misting over gradually, concealing his eyes behind a sinister film, like a thin layer of frost. She remembered blinking her own eyes to rid herself of this absurd, displeasing image, and when she looked again there was only a lean, energetic, silver-haired professor bending toward them, waving his hands in the air in quick, short jabs, making a series of complicated arguments. He was a brilliant man, everyone said so. *There's nothing human to him,* Elizabeth had thought.

At home, of course, he had been another person entirely. Elizabeth had always considered him a good, loving husband, someone perfectly suited to her. They rarely went out, having few friends, and in the evenings they would usually part after dinner to work separately: Albert would retreat into his study, where he wrote his articles and book reviews and did his reading, while Elizabeth would take whatever poem she was working on and sit with it at the dining-room table, happy to be left alone. She worked on her poems very meticulously; sometimes an entire evening would pass and she might have written only a few lines. Somehow this pleased her, working so slowly. Albert worked at a frantic pace, she knew; she typed his manuscripts for him and she was always amazed at the swift bold strokes of his handwriting, as if he were literally assaulting the page . . . he wrote rapidly, carelessly, and when she did the typing she would silently correct his grammar, his spelling. But she always felt vaguely threatened by his handwriting—so large and bold and masculine —as if there were something in it she could not quite recognize. Her own writing was tiny and precise, perfectly readable.

It was Elizabeth's lucidity, in fact, which had made Albert decide to marry her—or so he often told her, jokingly. She was dependable, he had said; she would never surprise him. She had at times been offended by this but she knew it was true. She never had surprised him. She sat in the silence of their house night after night, while her husband worked nervously in another room, shuffling his papers, sometimes pacing the floor, and she would try out lines in her careful, elegant hand, usually marking through a phrase—with a single neat line—as decisively as she had written it. She worked very slowly, happily. She had managed to publish a few poems over the years, some of them in excellent quarterlies and one, several years ago, in *The New Yorker*, but she continued to think of herself as an amateur; most of her poems she never submitted at all. And when poems were published, she had not shown them to Albert —he never asked about her work. She wrote poems about beauty, the surfaces and textures of things she found beautiful, she wrote about the gradual changing of the seasons which always created some obscure pain in her, she wrote about the faces of people, usually strangers who had only passed by her in the street but had left her feeling some vague, undefined emptiness. She did not think these ideas were important, she did not even think the poems themselves were very important, and she was certain Albert would not have cared for them. He had a career, after all; he was a very busy man.

But she had loved him, though she seldom used the word "love," and she never wrote about love. And it surprised her that she felt nothing more than a vague startled confusion to hear this girl, this Betty Plunkett, speak so openly of having loved her husband, who surely had not encouraged her. Perhaps he had only pitied her; Elizabeth decided to console herself with this thought, and to pity her also. At the cemetery, she remembered, the girl had been crying in great, heart-rending sobs: all this for Albert, Elizabeth thought, all this because she no longer had Albert to love.

They still drove rather slowly along the highway—they had gone perhaps thirty, thirty-five miles, Elizabeth could not be sure—but somehow her desire to turn back, to take Betty to her bus, had left her. Betty continued to chat about her life back home, "back on the farm," and Elizabeth gradually formed a mental picture of the girl's past: she had been part of a large, rather poor family, she had attended school intermittently but the quality of education was so low, and her schooling was so often interrupted by family crises, illness, the necessity to help out on the farm, that she had not even finished high school until she was in her twenties. She had married soon after that, but the marriage ended in divorce: "John was a good man, but I didn't love him," Betty said simply. "I married him because my Papa was so sick and couldn't work, and Mama said if I didn't marry John what would happen to the family? We didn't have anything. John had a good job in town managing the new supermarket and he loved me and I knew he'd help Papa out—so I had to marry him. He wasn't mad when I wanted to get divorced —he cried though, he would go in the bedroom and close the door and cry quietly by himself, just like a little boy. I could hardly do it, I could hardly leave him . . . I guess I did love him, in a way. Almost like I was his Mama—that's really what he needed me for."

Her voice had fallen to a whisper.

Elizabeth took in everything Betty said, she listened intently; there was a kind of intelligence in Betty's words which fascinated her because she could not define it—it had nothing to do with education, or experience, but seemed simply a part of her feelings. She remembered how often Albert had spoken of the opposition between reason and the emotions, how it was necessary to control one's emotional impulses through reason, even when it seemed unnatural, an imposition . . . he had admired this ability in Elizabeth, he said. That was why he had married her, he said. Elizabeth remembered staring at him, not really comprehending.

"But you did leave him?" Elizabeth asked gently.

"Yes, I had to," Betty said. She spoke in a hushed voice; she had become solemn, almost reverent, in talking about her past. "I had to—I can't explain it. And I couldn't go back to the farm either, I had to get away . . . so I took the money John gave me— we'd been saving for the six years we were married, and he gave me half of it—I took the money and came up here. I started working for the telephone company and going to school at night —the girls at work all told me not to drop out of school, no matter how hard it was." Betty laughed, embarrassed. "They seemed to think I belonged there—in school," she said. "But I'm not really very smart, sometimes I have the hardest time understanding things . . . but anyway I went, I kept at it, I would send my paychecks home and live on the savings, I decided I would stay there and go to school until the savings ran out, or I could find a better job. . . ."

Elizabeth said nothing; the girl was from a world Elizabeth had never known, had seldom even encountered, and now she shied away from the ordinary facts of that world—where the lack of money governed everything, where an unmarried girl had to struggle not only for freedom, but for mere survival.

"But you didn't marry again."

"No," Betty said. "I met Albert then, and he was already married. And anyway I loved him, I wouldn't have married him for any reason but that. He said he wanted to marry me, he really did want to, but he didn't think it would work out. He didn't think he could make me happy."

Elizabeth steeled herself, taking a few deep breaths. She said evenly: "Did he—did he talk about his wife? Didn't he love her?"

Betty hesitated, as if this were really a difficult question. Finally she sighed. "He wouldn't talk about her," she said. "Of course I was curious, but he never really told me anything. He said we were very different, that's all. He said he had been married a long time and he was used to it. With me it wouldn't be the same—it wouldn't be a real marriage, not like he was used to."

"But why not?"

"Because it wouldn't be safe—that's what he always said. It wouldn't be safe, being married to me. I didn't understand what he meant but he wouldn't explain it to me—he would never explain things, not really—and once he even cried. That made me so sad, I felt like it was my fault. It makes me so sad, thinking about him now—I wasn't really very good for him."

"He cried . . . ?"

"He cried," Betty said. Her tone was apologetic.

Elizabeth sat perfectly still, stunned. She drove woodenly, not feeling the steering wheel beneath her fingers.

Betty kept talking, dolefully. "And now I've upset you," she said. "You were a friend of his too, you probably knew him better than I did, but here I've been carrying on like this, as if no one cared about him but me." Then she paused, as if some new idea had struck her. She said slowly, "But what about you—do you know her? His wife?" Her voice seemed shy, rather frightened.

Elizabeth did not even glance at her. "No," she said tightly. "I don't. I don't."

Anger seemed to choke her, gathering in her throat. She knew now that the girl was lying—of course she was lying, she had made up everything! Elizabeth blinked her eyes at the bright sunlight and seemed to be shaking off sleep, as if she had only been dreaming . . . she had a gradual sense of amazement at herself, at her belief in this girl's words. Now she glanced at her, from the sides of her eyes. Betty sat very primly—the way she sat there, her shoulders slightly hunched, was itself a kind of apology—but Elizabeth saw through her now. She was only a conniving young girl from the country, born by some fluke with a beautiful face, with a little luck and cunning. She had used Albert, had taken advantage of him!—a bright fierce anger jumped in Elizabeth's veins, she could hardly keep her hands on the steering wheel. She wanted to reach across and take hold of that coppery sunlit hair, to yank it out in handfuls, to drag her nails across that face, rip that soiled absurd filmy white dress into shreds, tatters. . . .

She pulled the car over onto the shoulder of the highway; they stopped with a jerk. The girl looked at Elizabeth blankly. She had enormous eyes: a sharp stinging green with flecks of hazel, of burnished gold, an uncanny brilliance to them. Elizabeth felt her body go cold. She stared into the girl's eyes and yearned to

see the light of cunning in them, a layer of something ghostly,
like frost, covering her evil. But the eyes only stared into her
own, puzzled and blank and entirely exposed.

"Why are we stopping?" Betty asked.

Elizabeth glanced away; she could no longer look at this
girl. . . . She knew this was a dream, that she had invented "Betty
Plunkett" from somewhere out of her own past, perhaps from
her own girlhood that had been shed when she married Albert,
lost forever. There was no girl really here, waiting patiently to
be taken to the bus station. She was alone, suffering a terrible
hallucination, the kind of thing people in great pain suffered
every day. . . . It was not unusual. But Elizabeth had not known
she was in pain: that was unusual, perhaps. Her hands were
gripping the steering wheel—she had to close her eyes against
the cold brilliant sun, its light glinting off the hood of her car,
reflected eerily back to her by the bare branches of the trees
surrounding them, held mistily by the tall, yellowish grasses
that stretched away into the hills, swept by the bitter wind into
distance. . . . She lowered her head until her forehead touched
the rim of the steering wheel, her fingers still clutching it, her
body shaking with long shuddering gasps, sobbing—she was
so happy to be alone, she thought, to be free of hallucinations,
of dreams. When she opened her eyes again—in twenty minutes, in three hours—she would see no illusions and there would
be nothing to protect her from pain. That was all right, she
thought. That was what she wanted. She did not want comfort
at all—she wanted to be very hard on herself, to open herself
brutally to pain.

Yet something brushed her shoulder, soft as a moth's wing—
what was that? She did not want tenderness, she wanted the
brute fact of her wasted life to fill her, assault her, so that she
might be pure. But some faint voice spoke into her ear, like the
voice of some younger, milder, more compassionate self: "That's
all right, you go ahead. You're just grieving, it's something you
have to go through. . . . " The voice was hesitant and girlish and
knowing; it knew everything. "You just go ahead and cry, cry
for as long as you want. This is good for you, so good, this is
the best thing in the world. . . . "

The Metamorphosis

T INY DISTANT LIGHTS, prickling this soft, uncertain, rumbling darkness—star lights, spot lights! She thinks: here it all begins. He thinks: *here I am, again.* That portentous hush, little flickers of light near the ceiling—wavering, dancing, mocking a night sky to still the waiting hundreds in suspense, to quiet their voices and widen their eyes for *her.* For Lacey. Who also waits, not knowing herself when the tiny ceiling stars will vanish and give way to the light-flood and her own radiant smile and thunderous welcome.

She waits, her heart pounding. The normal lighting disappeared to prepare for her, voices fell into expectant silence—broken only by scattered whispers, exclamations, giggles—and now she stands onstage, alone. Invisible except for the weak unpredictable lights hovering far above her and reflected by her sequins if she breathes; or the sudden flare of a match being struck, out there; or the faint glimmering of cigarettes in the distance, moving in slight dizzying patterns. When the lights go up she must smile, she must not scan the audience except in her vast, sweet, impersonal gaze that takes in all of them, loves them all. How she loves them! She thinks: Look at them but don't see them, their faces. Don't really see. He thinks: *I am afraid.*

But darkness persists and she sees nothing, no one. How she

once reveled in these brief breathless moments just before the lights, the cheers . . . her heart had pounded in excitement, not in fear. Her heart pounds, hammers. What had Teddy said?— "Sweetheart, don't be afraid—it's not the same place anymore, not to worry! This is your homecoming, they all love you, everyone loves you!" "But what if I look out there and see—and see—" "Lacey, don't worry! I'm taking care of you now, nothing should make you afraid anymore—you're well again and beautiful as ever and you're coming home a star—they'll love you, they'll worship you! You're a goddess, Lacey—nothing less." "But—" "No buts: a goddess."

Teddy's words are like bits of ice shooting through her veins. The air reeks with Fear and she can smell it. He gave her something: small orange capsules. She took them greedily—two, three, five, she can't remember—so that now she feels the Fear but can't remember why. Something out there, something dangerous, but there is a constant faint buzzing in her head and a slight film over her eyes and she will be all right. When the lights go up she does not want her eyes to flick outward to the crowd as if searching for someone, for one particular face. Nothing is there, nothing her eyes could catch onto. Past is past. Four years since she stood here last, since then she has played clubs in every major city in the States and in Europe, she is Lacey Clarke, *Lacey*, a star, the queen of all queens and adored by everyone. They worship me, she thinks.

He thinks: *She is a star and no one can hurt her, not anymore. . . .*

A tradition: walking onstage in silence, in darkness; but they *know*. It excites them, her presence they cannot quite see. Only a teasing flash of sequins, so many minutes of suspense! Most of them, tonight, have probably never seen her. But they love, adore, worship her. A goddess! They know she began here long ago—in this dingy, smallish club in the seedy section of a middle-sized, crass, unglamorous city—and went on to New Orleans, Atlanta, New York, London Amsterdam Paris and wowed them all. She didn't have to come back here and so they love her all the more. They remember the story in *Newsweek*, what an honor! *Lacey Clarke: Dragging Her Way to Stardom*. Her picture—those wide-set violet eyes, the blond flawless waves of hair, that angel mouth!—was placed alongside that of John Wesley Herrington, a nondescript young man in glasses who stared dully out of a black-and-white photo, probably from a high school yearbook. The caption read: "John Wesley Herrington/Lacey Clarke: The Metamorphosis." She remembers how popular it became, putting the pictures side by side. She remembers feature stories in the New York *Times*, the Cleveland *Plain-Dealer*, the Washington *Post*, the Atlanta *Journal*, the Dallas *Times-Herald*, even three staidly written columns in *The New Republic* with the two pictures placed neatly above them, side by side. She read all these stories cynically, her eyes narrowed; or Teddy would read them to her, while someone did her make-up. Together they laughed over all this publicity, since it helped make them rich and was so absurd . . . and she laughed to herself, privately, because the newspapers and therefore the world would never understand who she was or why she created such love, they could never understand these sweet moments of fear just before the music, lights and cheers, their crude perceptions could never sharpen down to moments such as this!

Yes, she thinks, this darkness is pulsing with love—and at once the Fear subsides. Whispered conversations continue, out there; she senses the excitement in their voices. She can be anyone, her act is carefully planned of course but she can be anyone at all: she can be a goddess of her own making, she can be Diana Barbra Liza, or she can be simply *Lacey* for they will accept even that, she is that big a star. She feels the tension rise, here in this large room and its enveloping darkness pierced by the tiny star-lights and her sequins and the match-flares, everything hinted at and nothing disclosed, she feels a tingling in the muscles of her thighs, her calves, something burns half-pleasurably in her throat and she feels a slight ecstatic stinging in her eyes. Tears. Such love and excitement and tension can hardly be withstood, the moment is too rare, too brief, too fleeting—and the past is past, forgotten, she is home again and she is loved and everything is reborn, she feels something like a small exquisite flood deep inside her—only a flood of love!

In an instant music blares and the crowd cheers and her body sparkles in light.

She thinks: I am loved.
He thinks: *I do not exist.*

"God, you were so fine. So beautiful..." For once he isn't
screaming: his voice is a reverent whisper.
"Don't call me God," she jokes. "I'm a girl."
Teddy lowers his eyes. "A goddess. A goddess."
"I'm tired, Ted."
"But of course, you worked hard—a solid hour. Can't you
hear them?—they're still cheering, Lace. They love you. They
want you."
She sits in a rickety chair before the huge mirror that accompanies all her travels; the mirror is surrounded by light bulbs that
make her face eerily bright. The dressing room itself is decrepit,
ugly, dirt in all the corners, paint needed everywhere, but she
pays no attention to that. She remembers the first night she'd
used this room, four years ago—she'd thought it grand enough.
Now she sees only herself and the mirror, they are in love, she
has forgotten why she is here. She has forgotten everything.
Teddy hands her something: two orange capsules.
"No more, Ted."
"But the second show isn't for two hours, Lace. You don't
want to lose it. Don't forget Amsterdam."
"But I *want* to forget Amsterdam—"
"God, how they loved you. They were so hyped for the second
show, I thought they'd tear the place apart when you cancelled.
I hung around, listening to them, while we were waiting for the
ambulance—I thought they'd burn the place down!"
She stares at Teddy: a big man, wearing glasses with heavy
black frames that are always sliding down his moist nose. She
watches Teddy sweat. He is very excitable and he sweats uncon-
trollably, he never stops sweating. He manages her tours and
promotes her career and soothes her fears and stands just backstage at each of her shows and shouts praise at her constantly
and always sweats. He *loves* her. She'd found him in New York,
when it looked as if her career might be flagging, he'd fallen in
love with her at once and since then they'd spent every moment

together. He must be forty-five at least, though she isn't certain. Neither of them asks questions. He's never met John Wesley and he doesn't want to.

"Relax, Ted."

But when she says these words her voice wavers and she wonders if he can tell. She does need the capsules. But no. No. She remembers Amsterdam. Toward the end of the first show, that night, her eyes had suddenly stuck on one of the faces out there, they stuck and could not move: she stared. Stricken, paralyzed. It was him. He wasn't smiling like everyone else. He wasn't swaying with the music or leaning forward eagerly into her magnetic presence onstage or shouting cheers and encouragement like everyone else. He sat back, scowling. He watched her. She froze. She finished the number in her chilled flesh, her eyes slightly widened with terror, her legs stiff as a doll's.

Backstage Teddy said, "Honey, what happened?"

"He's there. He's—out there."

"Baby, *who* is out there? Who is this guy—?"

"I—I—Ted, cancel the second show. I can't—I—"

"Is it somebody you know? Lacey?"

She pushed past him. She locked the door to her dressing room and stood there, panting. Already Teddy was pounding at the door. *Lacey, sweetheart, open up—Lacey, I love you, I—* She tore off her wig and threw it in the corner. That face: sometimes she becomes careless and her eyes flick out toward the crowd and one of them catches at her, one particular face. She remembered how he scowled. His mouth a thin dark supple line. That mouth was like a small crack, her eyes had frozen onto it, onto that little dark squiggling line like a dangerous crack of unreason, a dark delicate river that might lead her riveted eyes away from here, out of herself entirely . . . she could not look away. Mechanically, her own mouth had continued moving to the recorded voice blaring out from somewhere but the movements of her body had slowed, weakened, she stared at his dark unsmiling line of a mouth and then, with a quick jerk, glanced back up into his eyes, terrified. They stared. A recognition.

She remembers Teddy's hysterical voice, outside. With a cloth she had wiped off her make-up, pawed at it viciously like a child trying to wipe away dirt; she was careful not to glance into the mirror. Her skin hurt. She ripped off her earrings. *Lacey, Lacey, please unlock the door—please answer me. The crowd loved you, sweetheart—there's no one out there, no one bad—don't be afraid—* She had heard the muffled hammering of her heart.

She hears it now: it is telling her something.

She says to Ted, "I feel like hell. Did you have to bring up Amsterdam?"

"I'm sorry, sweetheart."

She tries to be ironic. "They want to eat me alive, don't they? Don't they want that, Teddy—to eat me up until there's nothing left?"

Teddy snickers.

She thinks about the crowd—usually she doesn't mind them. Most of them are lonely, unbeautiful pricks, she thinks sadly. Most of them would slit their throats if she asked them to. She makes a mental note for her next act: ask one of them to slit his throat, get him onstage, smile, raise a flirtatious eyebrow, hand him a razor blade and say in that sweet simpering voice: *Slit it, honey. Slit it for Lacey.* It would be justice, after all, for hasn't she wasted every night of her adult life in crowds like these, waiting for something, always waiting?—even before she became a star. Especially then. She remembers John Wesley at eighteen, searching among those faces every night for the perfect man, the ideal— he was there, of course! Somewhere! It was only a matter of time. Poor John Wesley, just out of high school, sneaking away from the house after his parents had gone to sleep, still wearing a crewcut—hopeless, living on hope. He had wised up, eventually. The faces had turned into fearsome masks, eventually, and he began wearing one himself. John Wesley found four lovers in the crowd and died four separate times and was reborn.

He became acquainted with the Fear.

As a child, he had not known fear—though he'd been a disappointment, certainly, that was always made clear. What was it his father called him? "The runt"—of course, he was *the runt of the litter.* Frail, sickly, with that unaccountably girlish face. His older sister, Marcia, had dressed him in her own clothes one rainy summer afternoon and he'd never forgotten it: only ten years old, yet he'd stared into the mirror in fascination at the long pale-yellow dress, the pinkened lips, the powdered flawless skin. His eyes had gone wide in disbelief. A transformation. "Johnny, you look just like Marilyn Monroe!" his sister screamed, delighted. He himself had not screamed—he only stared and stared. Years later, when the idea of performing first entered John Wesley's head, his mind had reeled back to that afternoon in his childhood and to Marcia's delighted, half-envious stare. . . .

Onstage at twenty-one, in that seedy ordinary club, her first appearance, she had seen him at last: her eyes had caught on him. . . . But he had changed: there was no love in those eyes. It happened again in New Orleans. And in Denver. In Amsterdam, finally, Teddy had pounded on her door: *Sweetheart, why don't you answer, please say you're all right. Who's out there, Lace?—I won't let them hurt you, don't worry—Lacey? Lacey? —Hey! You guys! Somebody do something, help me break down this door—go get somebody, a locksmith—oh my poor Lacey, oh God—please, sweetheart, talk to me—just one word—one syllable—*

She was dazed with fear and she'd made a mistake. Slouched at her dressing table, trying to ignore Teddy, she had glanced for an instant into the mirror. She saw: something horrible, grotesque, freakish, only a mass of smeared blues, pinks, reds like blood dried but still bright, tiny lurid black rivers runnelling down her cheeks. She stayed silent, staring. They looked like tiny cracks in a doll's face, but they moved. She bared her teeth. Her hand reached for something—a bottle of sleeping pills, bought in London at the "chemist's" but still half-full—but she did not move her eyes. She stared. The rivers widened into little faint ribbons as her face got wetter, she heard her own whimpering, a sound that did not seem to be hers at all—a man's unaccustomed, belabored whimpering—and she ignored Teddy's hysterical banging on her door. She swallowed pills without water. Four pills, then four more. Then six. Eight. They were small pills with a slick coating and went down easily, the bottle was soon empty, she let herself slide down into her chair until she could no longer see that face in the mirror and then, some-how, she was on the floor, holding onto the curving legs of her little vanity table, sobbing. . . .

Now she thinks: there is something out there, it wants me, it doesn't love me at all but it wants me—

"Relax, Lace, do you hear? Shouldn't you take something? Lace?"

She stares at Teddy. "No second show," she says coldly.

"But Lacey!"

"No—I can't do it."

"Baby no, you're just upset—I shouldn't have brought up Amsterdam, I'm sorry. Listen Lace, they love you. I love you. Not to worry, Lacey, not to—"

"Call me John," she says.

He stiffens. "Don't lower your voice like that, honey, it's not like you, you're too beautiful for that kind of voice, I can't stand—"

"I'm through with this, Ted," she says. "It scares me. The crowd scares me. There's something they want—I don't know, but sometimes I see one of their faces, accidentally, and I realize what could be out there, that anything at all could be out there, waiting. . . ."

"Honey, I don't understand you."

"Once I thought it was a man out there, a certain man. And I'd find him. I'd be beautiful and he'd see me and we'd find each other."

"But what about me?"

"Then I began to see other things, something in a pair of eyes, or the gesture of a hand, or someone's mouth—sometimes I get so afraid—"

"Lacey, this is nonsense!" Teddy is angry. He stands up and moves around the room, irritated, pacing. He says, "You re-member what Dr. Adcock said, that time—a neurosis, Lace. It's only a neurosis. You've got to fight it. Now look." He pauses rhetorically, standing over her until she raises her meek eyes. Her brain is blank, she is listening. His long white finger points and nags. "You just look: you don't need this. You don't need to be told anymore—you've beat this once and you'll beat it again. You *know*, intellectually, that no one is out there, that there's nothing to be afraid of, that no one wants to hurt you. So you don't have to let this happen. This is life, Lace: overcoming fear, struggling through this shit. You've got to live your life!"

"But this isn't my life, it isn't real—"

"Of course it's real—you're a star!"

"But I wish—I wish I could give them something—something real. Not Lacey. Not going through someone else's movements and mouthing someone else's words. But I know they wouldn't love me then—they only love Lacey."

"But Lacey, Lacey—that's who you are."

She thinks: No.

He thinks: *You've got to live your life!*

She shakes her head, staring at the floor. There is a silence.

Teddy bends down. "Sweetheart, just take these. They'll help you through. You know the doctor said it's all right—they're just to help you through. Lace—?"

She lets him lay the capsules in her palm.

He smiles. "On with the show?" And when she nods he smiles again, he backs away in deference: "I'll go away for a while, honey, let you get freshened up—take your time, Lace, you've got an hour—call me if you need me. . . ." He backs out the door.

She thinks: Bastard. She gets up and goes into the toilet, watches the pills swirl down. Bastard!

He thinks: *I need you. . . .*

Nothing to fear, she thinks. The show is almost over and she writhes in light—the final number! She floats around the stage in white chiffon, yards and yards of it, trailing a white feather boa she uses on the crowd to make them laugh. One moment she is simpering, coy, a tease, the next she opens up and has them on their feet, cheering. Lacey! *Lacey!* They cry out her name, they are frenzied and ecstatic and in love with Lacey. She smiles, feeling her lashes touch the tops of her cheeks, swaying with the music, knowing they are in love with her every movement. When she looks out she can glimpse, far in the distance, posters covering the walls of the club—announcing the homecoming appearance of Lacey Clarke, her name in high, pink, swirling letters! As she passes her sweet vapid stare among the crowd she notices many of them wearing large round buttons, pink letters on a white background: I LOVE LACEY. There is nothing to fear out there, she did not take the pills and is perfectly clear-headed and she even lets her eyes rest upon their faces, their eyes, their smiling mouths, but there is nothing to fear. The number is coming to an end and the lights are hot, bright, glaring, she can scarcely see but knows they have risen to their feet, cheering, stamping, calling her name—

Shouting, *Encore! Encore!*

Of course the show must not end, they want more, more. Always more. She bows and grins, she keeps them in suspense, and finally signals to the rafters: of course she will oblige. It is planned. She senses Teddy in the wings, smiling. The lights grow softer now and the music starts up again and she begins to "sing" in a strident, strong, sarcastic voice— "Free Again." Her favorite song because she never knows if they believe the words.

They are listening but still they seem tense, expectant, barely restrained. She moves, gestures. Grimaces. She is giving them everything but still it is not enough. Her heart hammers in glee. They love only the mask of her but that is all right—she is a symbol, an ideal, a star. She knows they too are wearing masks and she has often thought, up here, working her heart out, how necessary are these brash outlandish masks, how indispensable to protect the secret, feeling self. Smiling onstage. Backstage her make-up streaming away in tears, sweat, grimaces of fear. . . . She understands it now. She is all right. She sings:

> *Free again . . .*
> *Lucky lucky me, I'm free again. . .*

But something is happening—the song is winding down, ending, the last song, but they will not let her go. They are chanting something: *We want Lacey! We want Lacey!* Where is the music?— somehow the record is over. It is over too quickly. The crowd cheers, stamps, screams. *We want Lacey!* Yet here she is, in full view. What do they want? She stands there, trying to smile, to make a joke of it—she does a little dance. She rolls her eyes.

But this does not appease them. *We want—* Finally her smile vanishes. She stands there awkwardly in the hot lights; she feels a dribbling of sweat down her back. Cold insidious moisture breaks out on her temples. What is happening? Her body seems awkward suddenly, exposed, swaying slightly... the violent heat of lights bears down, she breaks into sweat. The crowd is screaming, calling—she can't make out the words. She turns to them, her arms spread wide in a helpless gesture, an appeal. She begins to speak: "Please—I want to say that I love—no, please—please listen—I want—" But from a distance, of course, she appears to be moving her mouth silently, they cannot hear her words; she knows this but keeps on. "Please wait—no, please wait—" They yell, applaud, jeer. She squints out, trying to see past the lights, trying to make contact with something out in that total, restless, wavering darkness.... Then there is a throbbing in her temples, making her throat ache with fear and her eyes widen in fear and her bones chill with fear: her eyes stick on something. A smile. His smile.

Behind her she hears a familiar voice, probably Teddy's, stage-whispering her name—somehow she hears it through the crowd. Their cries. Hissing, chanting. *We want—!* She thinks: Is this love? He thinks: *Is this love?* The music has disappeared, drained away into that little crack between his lips, that blackness, that tiny river... she stares, fascinated. The crowd has gotten to their feet but she has no eyes for them. She stares. Somehow they are closer: the darkness, the vast sea of faces, like living pale flares in the darkness, bobbing. The bright lights vanish. She discovers she is no longer onstage but is being sucked down gradually into them, she feels hands upon her, she knows that the minute crack of unreason has ballooned around her— how has this happened? Her eyes are suddenly freed and they dart everywhere, like a frightened bird's.

She imagines herself in the eye of a tornado, feeling nothing. Harsh, high voices all about her, raucous, greedy, a cacophony strangely distant, unreal. She ignores it. She is pushed and turned and mauled. Her eyes rest on nothing, she sets them free. She hears her name in the screaming calls of voices, a frenzy of callings, she feels deft hands paw at her from all sides, pummelling, she sees the white chiffon go drifting across the darkness in shreds, like white delicate birds fleeing a tempest. Hands tear at fragments of the dress that still cling to her body until there is nothing—she feels her wig sucked away, her earrings yanked off, her shoes wrenched from her feet, something twists and tears at her stockings, something yanks at her underwear, something dangles out. She drifts in this dark turbulent sea of noise. Fists appear, pummelling, angry, then retreat dripping red. Stained red. She glimpses a face: its bloodied nose, glasses aslant (broken?) across it, eyes white with terror. "Lace, grab my—" The face dissolves back, disappears. She is pounded, clawed, mauled, hands on all parts of her body, poking, prodding, getting in.... Someone's teeth raze her cheek: a bright spurt of blood. She wants to say, to scream: "But I love..." but she cannot say these words, they are a lie, all the love is being sucked out of her, drained out, like energy sucked out of stars until they become great black holes, ugly pockets in the universe. Now something flashes before her eyes: a blade, a knife blade rising out of the dark like a silver fin approaching on a black sea.

Teddy's face appears again—strained, contorted. Struggling. He takes her arm. "Lace, hold on to me—" He won't let go, she thinks, won't let me be free.... And then she feels it, the harsh bright stab of pain. It spreads downward through her legs and up through her chest, her arms, up her aching throat to her wide, blank, staring eyes. The pain cleanses her—it is pure, absolute, a miracle.

Her eyes roll back inside her head.

The crowd sends up a cheer. Something bloody is passed from hand to hand, in triumph.

Teddy holds on, pulls her slowly away. Naked, battered, unhuman, like some hideous plucked chicken, some great bleeding insect—he pulls it away slowly, back toward the stage. And it seems he will pull it free, drag it away and backstage and into hiding, for the crowd does not notice and continues with its festival.

Wintering

THE ALEXANDER BALDWINS never argue, but they are arguing now. Urgent whispers, rising up the stairway. Their three-story colonial is massive, beautifully restored (thick champagne-colored carpet installed throughout, even in the bathrooms; double-paned windows; an expensive new central heating system that works inaudibly), and so solid that it retains all sounds, all passions. The Baldwins stand in the dining room, where they've just eaten lunch, or perhaps in the wide foyer with its teal-blue Persian rug, where Laura confronts Alex before he can escape out the front door.

The foyer, just at the base of the stairs. Where Alex has begun to shout.

"For heaven's sake," Laura hisses, "keep your voice down."

"You know he can't hear us—it's affected his hearing, the doctor said so."

"I remember very well what the doctor said. That's why I can't believe you're doing this."

"My God, you act like I'm throwing him out! He *wants* to go, you heard him yourself. It's December, Joey's expecting him. The routine is established, Laura."

"Routine, that's a hell of a word to use. And as for Joey—"

"Let's not get into *that*."

Silence. Alex has that way about him: a gift for deflecting you,

for having the last word. I can remember him one evening thirty
years ago, slamming his small fist on the dinner table, very
precisely, then announcing that he *must* be excused, he *had* to
continue work on his science project or how would he win first
prize? His mother and I stayed silent, watching his erect little
frame march defiantly from the table. Joey giggled in his hand.

Laura, cowed but still resourceful, now says in a wounded
voice, "How would *you* feel, being expected to leave at a time
like this. We have so much room, Alex, and he's gotten to like
the new doctor so well—"

"He has a doctor in Atlanta, remember? It's the weather, you
know that. He always winters down there."

"But this winter is . . . different."

Alex pauses, considering. "Maybe so, but you know how he
hates Chicago when the weather turns. And anyway the plans
are made—he has his reservation, I called Joey and gave him
very clear instructions—"

"Your plans, your instructions—is that all you think of?"
Laura interrupts. Her whisper is thin, disgusted. "What about
feelings? Your father's more than—than part of your damn
schedule."

Alex, severely: "Speaking of which, you're making me late."

"And Joey is so inept, so irresponsible. What if something
happens?"

"I'll be back by six," Alex says obstinately. "We'll drive him
to the airport then."

"What if *you* had a child?" Laura says, her voice cracking.
"What if someone did this to *you*?"

The front door, opening. "But I don't have a child," he says
sarcastically. "I only have you."

When the door slams, there is the sound of Laura's soft weeping. With a kind of malice, it seems, the house contains us all:
our every sigh or whisper. I back away from the polished oak
banister, thinking this.

Old men are permitted such thoughts.

Consciousness, anger, dread: do they diminish with advanced
age, or do they retrench, slyly, for some final and invidious
attack?

The first quarrel with Marguerite concerned, ostensibly, my contemptible dread of airplanes. Her father, one of the richest men in Georgia (farming and real estate interests, mostly, and a profitable dabbling late in life in the international oil business) and the first in his club to purchase, and then learn to fly, his own airplane, had offered us a free ride to New York, the boys (then four and six) included, where he would wrap up a land-purchase deal and where I could meet a few of his stock market cronies. My fledgling career as a "broker" would be helped by such contacts, and there would be plenty of time for Marguerite and the boys to see the sights. My wife, who had led a typically sheltered Southern-debutante existence followed by two difficult pregnancies and two intense, protracted postpartum depressions, was elated about the trip. Not that she was concerned about my brokerage career, since the tacit assumption had always been that she, already possessed of an immense inheritance from her maternal grandfather and eventually to become even richer when her own father died, would be my only client. Nor, oddly, did her enthusiasm come from her own need to get away, prodigious as that must have been. Rather it was the six-year-old Alex, his alertness and curiosity already showing themselves as serious, focused, and forward-looking, who needed the stimulation of new sights and experiences, and she even insisted that Joey, though lethargic and fussy as his brother was lively and precociously well-behaved, was old enough to profit from the trip. When I had tried, the night before our departure, to dissuade her by admitting the real reason I wanted to stay home—my heartstopping fear of that flying machine, the nightmare of my conscious wide-eyed self caught helpless within its tumbling, fiery descent—Marguerite exploded. She was brushing her long hair, angrily. She hissed that I was a coward, and a poor example for my sons. Behind her, I was a shadowy reflection in her gilt-edged mirror. We argued for a while, but quickly the argument became a monologue, a tirade—my wife's anger was disproportionate, wild, and I sensed that during most of our seven-year marriage I had lived on time borrowed against the Southern code of wifely submission and my own disinclination to hamper Marguerite's quietly forceful style. Now, she'd had enough; from that night forward, she abandoned her oblique manipulations and daily proved that her power had always involved more than money. We went on that trip, of course. While her father and his copilot happily prevailed in the cockpit, she and Alex perched at the window and exclaimed over rivers, mountain ranges, swiftly moving rags of cloud. In the seats behind them a whimpering Joey huddled against his father, whose bowels had turned to lead.

Since my wife's death of cancer, six years ago, flying has become easier for me, and the biannual exercise in dread can even, at times, seem instructive. For this evening it came to me that I didn't dread the flight itself but rather my destination; and I knew that although my son remained deliberately obtuse, his wife had seemed, somehow, to understand.

Laura has always felt an instinctive sympathy for me, perhaps a displacement of some unacknowledged pity for herself, and in deference to this I kept quiet during the ride to the airport. To trade upon the "poignance" of the moment would have been distasteful, and anyway I've never been a vindictive man. (Alex was correct, after all, when he claimed that I wanted this trip; for I had told him so.) I sat between them in the spacious front seat of their Continental, wearing the benign, even slightly addled expression I've developed as a way of reassuring Alex that I mean no trouble to him, that preternatural docility has become a way of life. Not surprisingly, he chatted and laughed during the long drive (the Alexander Baldwins live in Lake Forest, more than an hour from O'Hare), talked about their plans to visit Atlanta frequently this winter (plans that are talked about every year, and which never materialize), lavishly praised my new doctor in Atlanta, a young neurologist at Emory University Hospital (whom Alex has never met). As he talked, his cheeks seemed to glow. His suede-gloved fingers flexed on the steering wheel. My son's smell was as fresh, new, and leathery as the interior of his expensive car, and I felt embarrassed for my sour odor of old age, of illness, that must have been apparent to both Alex and Laura. To avoid such thoughts, and to insure that my silence wouldn't be misunderstood, I made feeble comments about the weather as we drove along: how surprisingly warm for December, how the low-slung, soupy clouds appeared to hold summer rain rather than malevolent bits of ice.

"Yeah, but it won't be long," Alex said comfortably. "They say it'll be a severe winter, much worse than last year's. You're lucky to be getting out."

I nodded. "Yes, and last year's was hardly mild. Even in Atlanta, it snowed three times."

"Really, did it? Three times?" Since boyhood, unusual facts had always pleased him. But again I feared being misinterpreted.

"It melted quickly, though. Usually the next day."

"That's good," said Alex.

Laura, who had stayed morose and self-absorbed thus far, said abruptly, "Where did you hear that?"

Alex looked over, irritated. "Hear what?"

"About this winter. Its being so severe."

He shrugged. "I don't know. The newspapers."

"Those predictions never amount to anything."

I wasn't watching him, but I could imagine his lips flattening against his teeth—a gesture that meant he'd had enough.

"Chicago winters," he said evenly, "are always severe."

This brought a few moments' silence. I had begun to feel unusually awkward, sitting there between them. The Alexander Baldwins, after all, are a very good-looking young couple. Alex has his mother's high, prominent forehead, her clear, imperious green eyes, her fine olive-dark complexion. Laura, dark-haired and demure, has the faultless poise of upper-class Southern wives, cheeks and hands of an unearthly paleness, and unexpectedly full, sensuous lips. Next to them I'm a sack of bones, wispy yellowish hair and patchy skin where unexplained purplish marks, like bruises, come and go without warning; my eyes are faintly bluish, watery. I didn't blame Alex for wanting to get rid of me, and I wished Laura would not protest. But the awkwardness came out of a sharp, familiar longing that, during that silence, rose ungovernably in me: a longing to stay here, to spend the winter with these two healthy, well-dressed adults, safe inside their well-managed and well-insulated house.

Perhaps that was why I said, out of nowhere, "One thing your mother disliked about the South was the weather—she always loved the snow. She never felt happier, she once said, than when she could stand at the window and watch the snow falling."

Alex glanced aside, irritated yet curious. "Mother said that?"
"Oh, were you thinking of her too?" Laura broke out. She
had, suddenly, the exuberance of nostalgia. Looking her way,
I saw that her eyes were moist. "I do remember," she said,
nodding, "how she used to talk about the snow. Whenever the
two of you came for the holidays, she always hoped for a big
snowfall on Christmas eve."

Alex picked up speed, though rain had begun to spatter the
windshield. "I don't remember that," he muttered.

We stayed silent for the rest of the drive. I sat thinking how
despicable it was, trying to use the specter of Marguerite on
Alex. To the guilt I'd felt when overhearing their conversation
was added the guilt I've always suffered, helplessly, at the spec-
tacle of my own self-pity. Advanced age makes self-pity even
harder to bear, because no one minds it. People pat your hand,
they smile reassuringly. So I was grateful for the silence. Com-
pared to this weight of guilt, my consciousness of dread or anger
shrank to nothing. I could even imagine Joey's quick, furtive
smile of greeting without a shiver of revulsion.

The point of no return. That is what we've reached, the flight
attendant says with a wink, when I had only asked her for the
time.

"Will the flight be late?" I ask now.

"What?" she exclaims in mock surprise. "Our flights are *never*
late."

Sourly, I look away. Here in my first-class seat, mainly a salve
to Alex's conscience but nonetheless welcome, I impersonate
the old curmudgeon I should have long ago become. I order hot
tea, then complain that it's too strong; I demand to change seats,
wanting to escape a chain-smoking executive seated just behind
me. The flight attendant, who pretends amusement at my high,
whinnying voice and general irascibility, keeps glancing into my
eyes as if to find a telltale twinkling there, but she finds nothing
and eventually stops asking if there's anything I want. In the
half hour before landing there is just enough time to remember
how Marguerite, during our last flight to Chicago, pointed out
that beneath my irritated behavior on airplanes lurked profound

fear (which she no longer found contemptible, but "interesting") and to recall my own weak protestations that I'd conquered that phobia years ago. She had turned to look out the window, smiling. Even during her final illness she'd had that serenity and assurance about her, as though death were only another challenge for Marguerite Holloway Baldwin to confront with a nearly surreal grace and dignity. It strikes me, now, as unfair that Alex's memories of her should so often seem abstracted, as though she'd become a character in an old novel; he speaks of her with a polite, soldierly reverence but seldom with warmth or any sense of personal bereavement. Perhaps she is still with him, somehow, in a way she was never with me, so that there's no need for him to grieve.... This thought now causes my fingers to shake, in some blending of feebleness and terror, as I attempt to drink the cooled, black-looking tea that the flight attendant (stupidly? defiantly?) has placed again on the plastic fold-out tray before me. She appears just at the moment the airplane dips sharply, in its first gesture of descent, and the tea sloshes first onto my papery fingers, then onto the white, well-starched cuffs of my shirt.

"Oh, have we had a little accident?" she asks in the cooing, nanny's voice I've begun to inspire in the very youngest people.

"No, *I've* had an accident," I tell her.

She vanishes, then reappears with a cloth and some colorless cleaning solution. She wipes frantically at the cuffs, making little grunting noises with her head bowed as I sit stolid above her, scowling.

In a moment she straightens, eyes crinkled with regret. "Tea stains are tough—I've managed to get most of it, but still..."

I retract my arms like a pair of claws, hiding the soiled cuffs beneath the tray. "It's all right," I say gruffly, but then, noting that she seems genuinely depressed—she is responsible for my welfare, this perky twenty-year-old, and senses her failure—I add, irrelevantly, "If it weren't for my wife, I wouldn't be on this trip. She made me promise I'd always winter in the South, but somehow it never works out. This is only the first, I'm sure, of a string of mishaps."

She looks at me strangely. Her face, in that cruel transparency

suffered by the young, passes through befuddlement to pensive-
ness to a slow, blushing delight whose source I cannot imagine.
But of course she hasn't listened: she is only responding to the
new, milder tone of my voice. In a moment, her impishness has
returned in full force. She grins. She winks.

"Well, give her a message from me," she says. "Tell her not
to let a handsome guy like you go flying off alone—he's liable
to get into all sorts of trouble."

I don't respond. As the plane continues its descent, I recall
the innumerable times Marguerite would remark upon my handsome, even formidable appearance.

Standing alone amid the crush of travellers, his shoulders
hunched, Joey is hardly "formidable"; he looks defensive, as if
fearing contamination. When he glimpses me, however, he
springs forward like a wind-up toy, long-limbed, grinning, all
gangling solicitude. He snatches the flight bag from my shoulder.
He queries me about the flight, his breath reeking of gin.

Unlike Alex, my second son drinks to excess.

"It was fine," I tell him. "Excellent weather."

"Oh, that's a relief. I'd heard about this rainstorm, out in the
midwest. So I wasn't sure . . ."

"You fly above the clouds."

Already walking along, father and son. He keeps lurching
ahead with his long legs, then stopping while I catch up. He
makes bantering conversation, he grins sheepishly. Tonight he
has a rabbity, woebegone look, longish hair a bit tousled, nostrils
pink and sore-looking. Anyone encountering him, I think un-
charitably, might be the one to fear contamination, for his boyish,
half-sickly grubbiness has never left him. When we reach baggage claim, he actually does turn aside in the middle of a sentence
—he was narrating the story of this airport, the largest in the
world, his excitement obviously genuine—for a long, raucous
sneeze. When he turns back, his cocoa-brown eyes are glistening.

"Sorry, I have a cold. Whenever the seasons change, I get
one. And then it stays for a week."

"You should take vitamins."

Guiltily, "I know."

We wait for the baggage, a prim and well-dressed elderly man with his son, a thirtyish slump-shouldered man/boy wearing Levi's, a khaki shirt, a fawn-colored suede jacket that has seen better days. Yet not an unhandsome man, my Joey. He has the Baldwin sturdy build and strong jaw, his mother's clear skin, high forehead, good bones. These advantages, however, are apparent only to the most sympathetic observer; what people notice are the pink nostrils, the slack posture, the ridges of dirt beneath his nails. Comparison with his brother is, and always was, inevitable. Even their mother remarked, when they were boys, that she felt she'd given birth to Jekyll and Hyde.

The carting of luggage, the maneuvering of Joey's rattling, malodorous car—only two years old but already despoiled—take up the next few minutes, but then we're on the interstate and an eerie tension arises between us. Joey shifts in his seat, fiddles with the rear-view. I sit looking at the shimmering skyline, limned by a crisp starry night.

"It was raining in Chicago," I tell him, conversationally. "And much warmer than here."

"Are you cold? I'm afraid this heater doesn't work." He fiddles desperately with some knobs on the dashboard, then curses.

"No, I'm all right. Keeps the blood moving."

"I meant to have that fixed, I'll do it tomorrow. You want this jacket? Here—" and he's already halfway out of it, letting the car swerve abruptly. A car in the other lane blares its horn.

"Keep the jacket, Joey. And watch the road," I tell him.

The jacket falls on the seat between us; Joey grabs the wheel and glances aside at the passing car. "Bastard," he mutters.

Patience. With this son I need patience, and fortitude, and a certain measure of abandon. If you ride with him, you know that your life could end momentarily. His mother often remarked, in a rueful tone, that the first funeral in the family would be Joey's—he was so vulnerable, so clumsy and helpless. The first day of spring training for his junior-high football team, he broke his collarbone. On his sixteenth birthday he received his driver's license and, from his mother, a new Thunderbird, and three weeks later was hospitalized with a head injury and countless minor lacerations, the car having become scrap metal. As a young man he was given an honorable discharge from the navy only three months after his impulsive enlistment; he never told us why, but there were predictable jokes that he had wrecked a battleship, or had been unsuccessfully offered to the Russians. Poor Joey. And yet he survived. Though his mother left him very well off, he has worked for the past several years as a magazine illustrator, a tame nine-to-five job that has occasioned no mishaps we're aware of. He does drink too much, and his marriage to a willful, discontented woman—a failed ballerina— has been quite tempestuous, not to mention a considerable embarrassment to the family, but as Alex remarked only last week, he does well simply to remain among the living. I try, as best I can, to share my eldest son's condescension—as though I too, the whole year round, could boast a thousand miles dividing me and Joey.

"So," I ask now, "how is Barbara doing?"

"She's all right," Joey says gloomily. "She's gotten this part-time dancing job. It makes her feel—validated."

"Well, good for her. We all need that."

"It's her word, not mine."

So they've had some argument, and this accounts for Joey's dour mood. I've begun to breathe easier when he half turns to me and says, imploringly: "I hate to ask this, but what did the doctor say?"

"The doctor? Which one?"

"The one in Chicago, Dad. They did some more tests last week—?"

"Right. It's not benign," I say quickly. "I wish you'd keep your eye on the road."

Unconsciously he has slowed to about forty, and on either side the traffic whizzes by. Obedient, as always, to the letter but not the spirit, he sits with his eyes trained vacantly ahead, all his earnest attention still on me. I seem to feel his body heat, radiating from his side of the car.

"We knew that already, Dad"—I feel a pang at his tone of weary patience, like an adult dealing with a precocious, intricate obduracy—"but I thought these new tests were meant to—to determine—"

Why should his faltering give me a surge of joy?

"They estimated anywhere from three months to a year," I say prosaically, "depending on what decision is made down here."

"But why would anyone choose a shorter—" but then, comprehending, he stops himself. Audibly, he takes a gulp of air. "This young guy at Emory, you know, he's had amazing success with these so-called hopeless cases. They even did a story on him on the six o'clock news."

"We didn't know that," I say idly.

A brief pause, as if stymied by the "we," but then: "And Alex seems impressed with him, just from talking with him on the phone. And the two doctors have been in touch, of course. Alex thinks—"

"All of Alex's opinions are well known to me."

I spoke more harshly than I intended, but decide to let it stand. Poor Joey, who's only trying to assume his part in all of this, glances quickly aside, hurt, then accelerates the car and, after a moment, sneezes. I sit erect and watchful. The skyline, once we've left the freeway, becomes an unassimilable surrounding of lighted towers, neon signs, slowed traffic. With a maximum of jolts and cursings Joey maneuvers us along Peachtree Street where, in the midtown section, Joey and Barbara live in their high-rise condominium. I find myself hoping that Barbara won't be home. The car's chill has, after all, begun to affect me, bringing a dull ache to the joints of my knees and hands. I imagine lowering myself, slowly, into a tub of lukewarm water, my glasses left beside the sink so that only in a blurred, wavering fashion can I contemplate my hollowed-out chest and abdomen, desiccated genitals, long thin bluish spindly legs. If I should feel a familiar throbbing near the base of my skull, then a slowly radiating darkness whose source is that spoiled part of me, that smallish clump of festering, rotted fruit, perhaps I'll sit in my twelve inches of colorless water and wait for the final dark wave and not even cry out for help.

We are stopped for the ticket at Joey's parking deck, and though my thoughts have exhausted me I say, irrelevantly, "I wonder if your mother could have intended this."

For reasons of his own, Joey doesn't answer.

*   *   *

Irrelevance. I am prone, lately, to sudden stray remarks, mur-
murings; though enunciated crisply enough, and ranging from
the jocose to the vituperatively bitter, these are, I must assume,
brushed quickly aside by my auditors as the mumblings of an
old man's dream. My saying to Alex that Marguerite had loved
snow and frigid weather. My offhand comment to the flight
attendant about "my wife" and how she had planned out my
winters to the end. The cryptic remark to Joey, which contained
the implication that his mother had possessed a certain morally
ambiguous omniscience, a prevision of the long, sterile aftermath
stretching beyond her death, and even some notion that my
summers and winters, arranged in this way, might keep her
image perpetually clear and glittering before me. An implication
that elicited, appropriately, a reproachful silence even from the
tolerant Joey, whom I suspect of a sentimental, unflagging devotion to the memory of his mother.

His mother. My wife. Marguerite.

Several days pass, and then one afternoon I find myself at
the door of my smallish middle bedroom, straining to hear an
argument between Joey and Barbara that is taking place in the
living room. The door is opened an inch, half an inch. Here the
doors squeak; sounds carry cruelly through the small rooms; the
children don't think to lower their voices. When Marguerite and
I first walked through here, eight years ago, she remarked that
the place didn't seem well-built—the floor creaked in places,
she felt a draft coming from somewhere—but that nothing was
well-built any more and at least it was new. It would suit Barbara
and Joey for a few years, until they decided to make a normal
life for themselves out in the suburbs. I can still see Marguerite's
precise, sharp gestures, noting a wallpaper she liked or a doorframe that seemed slightly crooked. Here, there. Pro and con.
Finally she had pronounced herself satisfied, and naturally the
children were very pleased with their wedding present—though
unaware that years later Barbara would still be a failed ballerina
and Joey stuck in a time frame where, as if a mediocre, mildly
comical film were being endlessly replayed, he broke things and

walked into walls and fell victim to small, vexing illnesses normally reserved for children. Since arriving, I've noticed with an old maid's disapproval how they've let their home fall into an alarming desuetude—the furniture ratty and stained, the carpet soiled, every shelf or knickknack blurred by dust, ashtrays heaped with Barbara's peach-colored cigarette butts. The kitchen sink is full of unwashed dishes. A stale, sickly-sweet odor, tinged with the faint smell of rot, hangs in the air like heavy, invisible gauze. No, Marguerite could not have intended this for me. I stand with my ear to the door's crack, straining.

"Let him do whatever he wants," Barbara says for the third or fourth time. "It's as simple as that, really."

"There's a difference, Barbara, between what he says he wants and what he *wants*."

My son, the psychologist. When I informed him, this morning over "breakfast"—two pieces of burnt toast, a cup of cloudy tea —that I really felt I must return to Chicago, he gave me what, for him, is a penetrating stare, his exhaustion-ringed eyes narrowing and his own cup quickly set down, sloshing tea into the saucer. "Have you been talking to Alex?" he asked and then, more darkly: "Or to Barbara?" "I called Alex last night," I replied, "and told him what the doctor said. He was reluctant, he made me repeat the doctor's words a dozen times, but finally he agreed. As for Barbara, how would I talk to her? She's never home." Joey had stared into his teacup, frowning mystically. He was already half an hour late for work, and had yet to shave or change out of an old pair of iridescent-orange overalls that he wears around the house like a second skin. "I don't know what you told Alex," he said finally, "but the doctor told *me* that you should stay here. The weather's warmer, and the facilities are better." My lips formed a smile as I flung a skeletal hand toward the breakfast-room windows: "This is your glorious weather?" I asked. It was drizzling steadily, the temperature in the low forties. "As for the doctor, I don't like him much. He's a know-it-all, and far too young. And anyway," suddenly intense, self-righteous, "an old man should be able to choose where he wants to die." That took the wind out of Joey's sails. Getting up from the table he said, whining, "I really don't want you to leave," but in my imagination I was already back inside that large, solid, well-lighted bedroom, the smiling moist-eyed Laura bringing me something on a tray.

For the first time since my arrival I've spent all of today indoors. No doctor's appointment, and thanks to the cold rain I missed the prescribed morning walk. Joey telephoned from work every couple of hours, but aside from this I've had relative peace. Barbara was gone the whole day, as usual, to dance lessons or to the stylish coffee shops where she meets her rowdy friends, other "artists" whose lives are as pointless and unproductive as her own. Yet I don't dislike her—she has a certain feistiness, a blindness to her own mediocrity—and have not resented her neglect. For much of the afternoon I sat in the overstuffed wingback in the living room, staring out at the bleak drizzling cityscape and dreaming myself northward, back into the home of "the Alexander Baldwins"—as they're known in the society pages—where I am often, between the regimented Alex and the sympathetic Laura, a bone of contention but am myself left in some white shadowless sphere of contentment, a soul's eternal, placid winter that forces troubling memories and internal frettings and even physical pain to recede, to diminish, to become attenuated and drained of color. Here, that peace is threatened every moment. Accidents happen. Unexpected things are said. I sometimes find myself hobbling around my bedroom, in circles, or mentally drafting long, plaintive letters to Marguerite, crammed with devotion and senseless pleading. Is it any wonder I should want to escape, despite Marguerite's own wishes? Even the pain has increased since I arrived, my spine and the back of my head throbbing in the dead of night.

So this afternoon's taste of peace was blissful, a prevision of days to come, and later, still straining to hear, I'm pleased even by the children's argument, the antiphonal and almost predictable back-and-forth of it, as if some monolithic pendulum were to swing between weakness and strength, anxiety and comfort.

Joey is saying, weakly and anxiously enough, "You don't even give a damn, you're just like Alex. Purely selfish, absorbed in your own routine."

Barbara snorts with laughter. "And what are *you* absorbed in?"

I can picture the shake of her thin, rather equine head, its small ponytail swishing in punctuation. "The point is, he's not a child but an old man. He has the right to make his own decisions."

She speaks in her pragmatic, offhand way, as if she could simultaneously be doing other things—paying bills, knitting a sweater—and still comfortably win any argument with Joey. I can see him slouched in the wingback, pink-nostriled, staring morosely at the floor.

"You neglect him," he says pointlessly. "He might like it here if you'd be more attentive. I'll bet Laura doesn't leave him to make his own lunch."

"No, because Laura's a nonentity who doesn't have anything better to do. I've got a career, Joey, or anyway as much of one as you have. Why don't *you* stay home and take care of him."

Good for her. Joey is sighing, as he always does when he throws—literally—his hands up into the air. With weak sarcasm he says, "And I suppose Mother's wishes don't count for anything? Her saying that he should winter down here with us?"

Barbara exhales noisily; she must be smoking. "You're not conscious of it, I know," she says tolerantly, "but you speak of her as if she were a dictator, laying down the law for everyone else. The fact is that she's dead, he's alive. So I vote with him."

"Don't speak disrespectfully of Mother," Joey warns. But his voice is about to crack.

Barbara's manner can soften, very suddenly, once Joey is thoroughly vanquished; she is a graceful winner. I see her crossing to him, putting fingers in his tousled hair. She says, "Just try not to worry, you sweet dope, things will work themselves out. You're really a lot like him, in certain ways—I've noticed that through the years. And that's why you don't get along."

There is just enough time for Joey to say, in a strangled voice, "But this is the last winter, Barb, and if he goes back now—" before I manage, struggling, to get the door closed.

Marguerite, on her deathbed, had said in a clear bell-like voice, "You'll sell the house, of course. It would be pointless, your living here alone. . . ." She gestured weakly, indicating not only the two dozen empty, high-ceilinged rooms but also the forty-odd years of our life together (the house had been, of course, a wedding present from Marguerite's father) and a future that, once she was gone, would be hopelessly diminished. Her hand was pale, ringless; it fluttered briefly in the air. "Yes, it would be impossible," I murmured, though she hadn't looked at me and didn't now.

What a difference the final illness makes!—her honey-colored hair had turned a limp iron-gray, her flesh had thinned cruelly along the bones of her face and hands, her lips were dry and sore-looking. Standing beside the bed in a dark suit, white-haired by then but still physically robust, I felt awkward in my good health, and suddenly very afraid of Marguerite. I could only repeat, "Impossible," and then Alex stepped forward to take command. I took a step back, relieved. I maintained the gravely attentive, deferential air of a family retainer, and while Alex talked with his mother in low, businesslike tones, Laura quietly took my hand. In the shadows beyond the foot of the bed stood Joey and Barbara, also holding hands; they both looked terrified.

"Don't worry, he can come live with us," Alex told his mother. "He doesn't have the—the ties to Atlanta that you have, so I'm sure that Chicago will suit him fine. . . ."

Watching Marguerite, who was staring intently into Alex's eyes, I remembered how upset she had been when Alex, a graduate from the Emory business school, had accepted a position with a Northern firm; she had consoled herself by proclaiming his behavior rebellious, independent-minded, and characteristic of her family, which it was, and as a temporary aberration we would all laugh about someday, which it was not. She could never like the idea, of course, that Alex's life could take root so far from home, but because he prospered she accepted it, and he made partial amends by marrying a girl of impeccable Southern background. After his marriage, regular trips to Chicago became part of our yearly routine. We even invested in a shopping center and several residential developments there—"business interests" which I kept an eye on, whenever we came to town, while Alex and Marguerite visited. I'd never thought of Chicago as a future home, of course; but, my own family having long since died off, home for me had become wherever Marguerite was, and now that she was dying it seemed appropriate that she make any decisions about my future. While she and Alex talked I listened disinterestedly, as if they were discussing the fate of a stranger.

"But what about Joey," Marguerite protested, vaguely, "I don't want the family split apart. . . ."

Alex patted her hand, all stoical patience. "It's been split apart for years, Mother, but we'll have Joey up regularly for visits. He can come whenever he wants."

My wife shook her head, frowning slightly and trying to lick her lips. Her tongue looked purplish and swollen.

"No, he'd never come, and anyway you'd forget to invite him. . . ." She thought for a moment and then, her voice clear and bell-like again: "Your father could winter down here, where it's warmer, and then spend the rest of the year with you and Laura. That would work, wouldn't it?"

Alex said, "Of course it would," and unexpectedly, from across the room Barbara piped up, "We'd love to have him." Even Laura said, "It sounds like a lovely arrangement." Joey said nothing, but perhaps he hadn't heard: by then he had begun to weep, softly. I was standing there recalling how much he had cried as a baby.

Old men spend a great deal of time recalling things, after all, and our memories are selective: I'm hardly confident that Marguerite's deathbed scene was centered on my own fate, as I seem to be suggesting, or even that the problem generated much emotion from anyone concerned. The entire memory has been spurred by Joey's weeping—he is weeping now, as we sit pointed toward the airport but stalled in bumper-to-bumper five o'clock traffic—and the tears I remember were surely over the loss of his mother rather than the thought of my own future homelessness. Even now I sense the source of his grief as somehow apart from me, something my presence has crystallized for a brief painful moment. Perhaps it's the memory of his mother, once again; or the thought of his own wasted life. . . . But in an hour I'll be on that airplane, flying north: I try to think of that.

My Joey is drinking. As we inch forward, here on this crammed expressway, he takes regular swigs from the small metal flask he keeps in the glove compartment, and talks a great deal—whining, pleading, arguing with himself or with me—and now is weeping openly, unashamed. I sit staring forward, trying to ignore his jagged sobs, the sweetish stench of the liquor. Outside the sky is gray, the clouds low-hung and threatening, and the air is unusually warm. I try to pay attention to this weather, to the other cars, to watch for signs announcing the number of miles left between us and the airport. . . .

Joey is saying, "It's always been the same, that's what gets me. It *never* changes. Even before Mother died, it was always what *Alex* wanted, what *Alex* thought. . . . Shit," he says, taking a long swig, "he had the wool pulled over *her* eyes, didn't he?" But he isn't asking me, of course; he's just asking. ". . . And he never was fair to you, even Barb noticed that. Always talking about the Holloway investments, the Holloway money, as if you hadn't earned some of that money yourself. You were a broker, you knew how to invest it. That's what counted."

At this I glance over, irritated. "You don't know what you're talking about."

But Joey is nodding to himself, not hearing. He began this drive with a plea for reason, insisting that I *must* stay in Atlanta, that my illness *could* be reversed with the very best treatment, and by now has become reasonless himself. He says wildly, "You see what has happened, don't you? You see what he did to us? He cut us off, made us into nothing, big clever Alex with his white strong teeth and his fancy brains and his charm, his charm. Even Mother fell for it."

"Quit blaming Alex for everything," I tell him. "He's just the type who likes to take charge, to keep everything moving along efficiently. Your mother was like that, too."

"Hah, he takes charge all right. He's like one of those computers he loves so much, spitting out the answers for everybody. Take it or leave it, that's what he says. I'm the Fascist and you people are the slaves, I'm the great white hope and you people out there, you little peons, you'd better just listen to me. That's what he says to himself."

"You're drunk," I tell him calmly. "Now look, that inside lane is starting to move."

"And the fucking hell of it is, everybody listens. Everybody bows and says Yes, Allah, anything you fucking say. Not just the family, I'll bet—everybody."

"Joey, don't make me late for the airport."

At this he straightens, begins trying to change to the faster lane. But still he mutters under his breath. He takes a drink from the flask. "God," he says, husky-voiced again, sentimental, "do I feel sorry for Mother. What she must have gone through, in those last years. Seeing how Alex had turned out."

"What, are you crazy? She adored Alex."

"No, she knew better." He jabs his finger into the air. "At some level, she knew better than that. I promise you."

He has changed lanes, but now the traffic is clogged again. "Joey, maybe we should exit and take a side street. We're in danger, really, of missing that airplane—"

"Everything would have been so different, without him. We would have had a normal family. Why should we be separated, anyway?—why are we always driving to airports, always wrangling long-distance over when you'll visit or when you won't visit? It's not natural, it's not *good* for people to live like this. . . . This stupid plan, having you fly back and forth all the time—"

"Joey, that was your mother's plan."

"—it's not right somehow, it's in*hu*man. You can say what you want, but I know Alex is behind your flying back like this— I know how he manipulates people, making them feel guilty. Even Mother, he even manipulated *her*."

"Listen, will you stop this talk? Will you pay attention to the driving? It should be obvious that I *want* to leave, I'm not feeling well and I need to go home. Even the doctor said so, he said I should be wherever I feel safest. Because they can't do anything, the doctors. They *can't*."

He looks over, blinking. "But—but this is your home—"

"No, this is not my home, this is crazy-land." It has begun at the base of my skull, that insidious throbbing. When this happens I weaken quickly, the blood rushing to the place of rot. And here is my son, thwarting me. Spouting these ridiculous lies. "It's true," I tell him, "that I often do things just to please Alex, just to keep the peace. But today, this is not one of them. In fact, he doesn't want me back, he wants me out of his hair, and I don't blame him. But today I'm being a selfish and stubborn old man, I'm going back where I belong. I don't belong here, and I never did. Your life is crazy, your house is a mess, I can't stand it there. After this past week, it's a wonder I'm not already dead."

"What—why are you—"

"Yes, *dead*. I'll get there soon enough, but at least I want some peace. I deserve that, don't I? Don't I deserve, at long last, to get what I want? Yes, it's true that Alex is somewhat manipulative, but you want to know where he learned it? Do you? From your bitch of a mother, that's who."

Joey, dead-pale, seems utterly stymied; he doesn't try to speak. Only a moment passes before we are jolted forward, my head slamming against the doorframe before I can raise an arm for protection. In his shock, Joey has relinquished control of the car and let it ram into the car ahead of us, which then hit the guard rail. Now both cars are stopped. Before it even began, it is over. We were driving only five miles an hour, no one is hurt seriously, we both sit for a moment in shocked silence. My head is throbbing. Spinning. I'm thinking that I must get out of here, there is somewhere I must go. . . .

Finally Joey opens his mouth. "You take that back," he says childishly. "You didn't mean that." But he is weeping again; he doesn't count. "We have to stick together, you and I. They're so damn cold, so heartless, but we can't let them—can't let them kill us—"

I struggle to open the door, keeping my other hand cupped at the back of my skull. Must get out of here; must get away. . . .

"My God," Joey cries, "what are you doing! The lane next to us is moving, you can't—" but I don't listen, I get the door open and stumble away from the car.

Outside, it has begun to rain. Enormous, tepid raindrops gently pelting me. I hear the blaring of horns, the sound of someone shouting from behind. But I must get away from here. Hobbling, clutching my head with one hand as I navigate toward the side of the expressway, I struggle blindly forward, as if coaxed by some imagined wintry sphere in the far distance, out there, where Marguerite is waiting. Around me there are screechings, raised voices. So much noise and strife!—so much confusion! I move aimlessly through it all, a stumbling and contemptible old man. How fitting his destiny, this old man pathetically sick, dying, seeking to brush his knuckles against a stranger's car window in heavy traffic, begging for mercy, for shelter. . . . My head throbs wildly, even my eyesight seems to fail, yet before that moment of crashing, inevitable darkness I'm able to think, quite clearly, *Yes, she must have intended this for me—*

Wildfires

THE PHONE CALLS from Dr. Bucknell and from Gerald's brother, Stan, come during that same afternoon. It is late August, and Janet has spent much of her day staring at the ragged, sloping lawn and dispirited trees outside her office—the green landscape is baking away, she thinks, everything left an indeterminate yellow-white. A death-color. The green has been drawn upward into the superheated air, dissolved in the fierce brilliance of sunlight. She is startled by the telephone calls, and made to feel rather guilty, for both calls focus on her husband—I'm phoning you about your husband, Mrs. Stillman, hello, Janet, I'm calling from the bus station, how is Gerald? Both startled and guilty, yes, for she understands that she had successfully avoided thinking of her husband during most of that day.

Stan is a tall, strapping kid of nineteen, the kind who can drain a tumbler of iced tea in two or three swallows. Janet pours him a second glass, feeling disconcerted by his presence although she has known of his visit for five or six weeks. It will be good for Gerald, his mother half-yelled into Janet's ear, through the crackling of long distance; they don't get to visit enough, they need to get reacquainted. Stan's such a sweet boy, old Mrs. Stillman had said, but Janet had not felt stung by the implication that Gerald was not—only mildly disappointed. After all, mothers always favored the baby of the family, didn't they? Janet would never know, yet such a small residue of affection for Gerald, after all that had happened, did disappoint her. Easy to say she'd have been a more loyal mother, but wasn't it true?

It is touching, nonetheless, that Stan has talked of little besides his mother since his arrival. He tilts back in the kitchen chair, a piece of ice held in his back teeth. "I swear, she cried a bucket," he laughs, sentimentally. "'Cause I'm the youngest one, I reckon." He crunches the ice.

Janet sits down with her own tumbler of ice, and a diet soft drink. "Well, you'll have to make her proud."

"Yes'm," he says, and Janet could swear a mist covers those artless blue eyes. "I suppose I will."

Wanting to break the tension Janet says, with a little laugh: "Stan, please don't call me ma'am!"

Stan has the country boy's radiant grin; it spreads from ear to ear. He flushes crimson. "It's okay," he says, winking. "I didn't mean you were old or nothin."

Stan is moving up to Atlanta from his boyhood life, the only life he knows, in order to attend Georgia Tech. Like Gerald he's big-boned, his yellow-gold hair cut short; unlike Gerald he's trusting, open, ready for a good life. He doesn't know anything, and Janet thinks maybe his mother's ambitions are a good idea, after all; even if he flunks out of college, he'll meet a few people different from himself, understand himself as a south Georgia farm boy and decide to go back. Janet wishes this for him. Gerald, she fears, has forgotten his extreme youth. She can't remember his last reference to the farm, his childhood.

"It's real nice of ya'll to invite me up," Stan says. "But don't worry, the dorms open on Monday and I'll be out of your hair."

"Oh, you're no bother," Janet says, laughing. Why is she taking this jaunty tone with him? she wonders. She is almost flirtatious.

"But I mean it," he says. "Everybody needs their privacy, married especially. Once I get to the dorm you won't know I'm in town."

Janet puts down her glass, feeling alarmed. Old Mrs. Stillman isn't behind this, she knows; she'd wanted Stan to move in with Gerald and Janet, claiming the arrangement would be "good for everyone." Janet understands with a pang that Stan does know a few things, after all. She'd seen his gaze cut downward on the word "married," and she wonders what Gerald's mother and the rest have said about them, what whispered conferences have taken place. And now the commonplace thought arrives with a jolt: Yes, she is married to Gerald. When they eloped at eighteen, Stan was only a toddler.

"We—we hope to see a lot of you," Janet says blankly.

"I'm looking forward to visiting with Gerald," Stan says. "When will he be home?"

She wakes, startled. The telephone, the doorbell . . . ? Today at work, Friday, she'd fallen into a daze, nearly mindless, as often happens on these summer afternoons. She is head of the drafting department for a medium-sized construction firm, and she does enjoy her work, especially since they moved to a new building adjacent to a shopping mall and only a few blocks from where Janet and Gerald live. Now that she has her own office— the cubicles of her subordinates are down the hall—she often falls into daydreams, stares blankly out the window, unaware of time and genuinely unconscious of herself; even when she is working hard, she has begun to notice, she is similarly abstracted. One day she had joked with Gerald, trying to comfort him, by saying her work was moronic: it required skill, but not really much thought. Gerald has complained for years that his own work is meaningless, but he hadn't liked the joke. "If that's the case, why don't you quit?" he said, irritated. She didn't dare respond that they needed the money—though she wanted to— since she makes twice what Gerald does, and that's another sensitive issue. "Maybe I will, one of these days," she'd said vaguely, and then she laughed. Gerald gave a little smirk and left the room.

But today she hadn't been working, just staring out at the colorless landscape. The jangling phone had startled her, and when a deep voice said, "Mrs. Stillman, this is Dr. Bucknell," for a moment her pulse raced. Then she understood. She quieted.

"As usual, it's nothing," Dr. Bucknell said, rather shortly, and Janet could only say, "Yes. Thanks for your patience." The line went dead.

Now, deep into the night, she understands that the phone hadn't rung, nor the doorbell. Across from her Gerald sleeps heavily in his own twin bed, face down, one arm thrown across the top of the pillow. In the distance she hears something: a car's squealing tires, a horn honking, then a bottle shattering against pavement. Neighborhood teenagers, she thinks. Friday night. Janet's face is unlined but she is thirty-nine years old, and alarmed by such things.

She lapses back into the pillow, remembering Gerald's paranoia those first few years, his jumping like a wild man at the slightest abrupt noise. (Just part of the "shell shock," people had said—even the doctors. It would go away soon.) Then followed the years of depression, his hypersensitivity leaking into a great dark hole, into oblivion. And now the petty grievances, the fatigue, the hypochondria of an old man. Perhaps the phone rang inside a dream, Janet thinks, making her nerves sing, her heart pound. Perhaps she has caught her husband's earliest symptoms, after a lapse of years.

She remembers the uneasy, somehow knowing way Stan had pronounced the word: Married.

Sunday is never an easy day, and now there is the pressure of company in the house. Stan sleeps long and deeply, like an infant, but Janet is up by eight o'clock, making coffee and setting out the breakfast things while Gerald sits at the dining-room table, rattling the big newspaper page by page.

He has been reading items aloud from the Arts & Entertainment section, trying to find something to do with Stan this afternoon. He brings up a movie, then a play, but Janet points out that Stan is new to Atlanta, shouldn't they show him something of the city? Gerald makes a grunting noise of assent. He rattles another page.

Janet makes the coffee, each movement deliberate and slow. She is stalling, she muses, but against what she isn't sure. Yesterday was somewhat awkward, made tense by the need to

entertain Stan and also assure him that all was well, but she'd
been surprised to see Gerald relax in his presence, even fall for
a few brief moments into his old, kidding ways. She'd had, here
and there, heartrending glimpses of Gerald at nineteen, and the
buried memory revealed that he hadn't been so different from
Stan; a little thinner, a little smarter, but really the same eager,
innocent kid. Yesterday they went to a baseball game, and she'd
watched as Gerald and Stan jumped up at the same moment to
cheer a ball sailing out of the park; she'd seen their identical
Adam's apples bobbing as they downed beer after beer. Later
in the day Gerald had seemed to tire, the burden of talking with
Stan gradually shifting to Janet, but naturally Stan hadn't
noticed: he'd sat in the living room eagerly talking about his
future, about the University and the girl back home he hoped
to marry, about his excitement at finding himself in this enormous city.

"Pretty soon I'll be a real slicker," he'd said to Janet, winking
and cocking his head toward Gerald. "Just like my brother here."

Gerald had been staring, dazed, at the television set: another
baseball game. Though they'd turned off the sound right before
dinner.

"Brother, be happy the way you are," Gerald had said flatly.
He hadn't taken his eyes from the set.

Now, pouring her and Gerald's first cup, she looks at him
through the kitchen doorway. "I've got an idea," she says. "How
about the museum?"

Gerald pauses a long moment, as he generally does after Janet
speaks. "But that's indoors," he says, turning back to his paper.
"I thought you wanted him to see the city."

"But Gerry, the museum *is* the city," and for a moment her
hand, lifting the cup to her lips, trembles in anger. She takes a
deep breath, understanding that really this is an old argument.
When the highly publicized new museum had opened, Gerald
had refused to go because of the long lines. Later, as national
articles began to appear detailing the innovative architecture of
the museum building, and the dramatic additions to its perma-
nent collection, he'd scoffed at the publicity. So Atlanta was
becoming an international city, was it? We were leading the way

toward the 21st century, were we? He'd made some crude refer-
ences to the city's racial problems, its street people, its violence
after dark. It pained her to see his anger so unfocused, so desperate, but she hadn't known what to say. They still hadn't visited
the museum.

"And besides," she adds now, "it's time you and I went, too.
It'll be fun for all of us."

She has approached him from behind, talking in her smooth
caressing voice all the while: an old habit, taking pains not to
surprise her husband. Yet he looks up with a child's pained,
wondering face, as though "fun" were an obscenity shouted in
viciousness or anger. Fortunately for Janet, Stan comes in from
the hall at that moment, and they both look up. Wearing only
blue jeans, he rubs his puffy eyes with one hand, scratches his
flat belly with the other. His arms and chest are huge, Janet sees,
the skin a smooth pinkish-brown around the sculpted muscle.
Stan says, yawning, "Hi everybody, what's for breakfast?"

Once a young woman of considerable fire and passion—so
she had enjoyed thinking of herself, in the days when she might
toil for eight or ten hours straight over one of her canvases—Janet
often consoles herself by remembering that "art" was more
noticeable as a feature of her youthful persona than it was evident
in her finished paintings. Having diverted that single-minded
energy into a job that demanded skill but not art, a marriage
that required more tact than love, she now looks indulgently
upon her extreme youth—the oversized paint-spattered flannel
shirts, the ostentatious disregard for makeup or her hair, the
late hours of work that shocked her early-rising parents and
then her young husband, from whose side she would steal away,
at one or two in the morning, for a few additional, fervid hours.
The resulting canvases were really quite tame (once or twice a
year, Janet visits the basement and opens again the big water-
proof locker, then returns upstairs half an hour later, chastened)
and what gives her the sharpest throe of nostalgia is not the
thought of what might have been, but rather of who she was.
Perplexed or not, Gerald often woke again when she returned
to him, as if roused by the fever that glowed in her veins while

she worked, their mutual passion incendiary in those few months as it had never been since. She often thinks, in these late and diminished times, of her early fervor as an artist, of her passion with Gerald, and finally of the war itself as a series of quick fires, outbursts of feeling that defied containment, exploding the flimsy boundaries of flesh and time. Although Gerald had suffered no physical injuries, and though nothing prevents Janet from buying an easel and canvas tomorrow if she chooses, there are silent moments between them when she caresses his body slowly, reverently, as if the limbs had been blasted, the skin irreparably scarred; or he will hold and fondle her artist's hands as if they were a pair of dying birds.

Though Gerald loves his brother, it's clear to Janet that Stan makes him uncomfortable; the sooner this visit is over, the better. Perhaps the Sunday morning routine, in Gerald's mind, has made the unlimited expanse of Stan's future too painfully clear. Paging through the newspaper, he glances at neither Stan nor Janet; his deeply set eyes seem half-closed, wincing. The same expression, Janet thinks, as when he opens the drapes in the morning to a flood of sunlight. Not long ago he remarked that he prefers cloudy days.

Janet has been telling Stan about the museum, and he reacts with polite interest. Now he sees Gerald bending over the paper, however, making a series of dark slashes with the ballpoint gripped in his hand.

"What's that, the want ads?" Stan asks, in all innocence. "You're not job-hunting, are you?"

"So will you, soon enough," Gerald says.

Stan looks at Janet, puzzled.

"He likes to keep his eyes open," she explains, non-committally. "You never know what will turn up."

"But what about those government benefits, bro?" Stan asks, though the joshing tone doesn't suit him. Gerald says nothing.

"I think he's bored with it," Janet says, rising. "How do you like your eggs, Stan? I'd better get started."

Stan follows her into the kitchen, and though their voices are audible from the dining room she can take a different tone in here.

"His co-workers are much younger, most of them," she tells Stan, "and I think he feels outnumbered. There's no communication, it's a big office and very hectic, and after all, the work isn't very fulfilling. ...." She goes on to explain, in her quick rushing voice, that although he still works in the government welfare office, he seldom gets to meet with clients. Most of his time is spent operating a word processor, and filing an endless stream of papers. Stan clucks his tongue in sympathy. "Gee, that's a shame," he says.

Janet doesn't tell him that Gerald has been on probation three times for "excessive sick leave," or that his supervisor told him bluntly that he would never be trusted with work requiring interpersonal skills. She doesn't tell him about the morning last spring when Gerald found an unsigned note in his mailbox at work: BABY KILLER it had read, in big block letters. For all this, she can't really explain why she hasn't encouraged his job-hunting, or that she knows he isn't serious, anyway. He has returned from all his interviews over the years with the same grudging attitude, assuming he hadn't done well, pointing out flaws in the interviewer or the position or the company in the same way he discovers imaginary flaws in his body, then makes new appointments with Dr. Bucknell week after week. As with his job problems, Janet is neither sympathetic nor unsympathetic about her husband's hypochondria. She makes the doctor appointments when he asks her to; she reports the test results when Dr. Bucknell finally calls back. There is nothing more she can do, Janet thinks. Before long they will need to change doctors.

Now Gerald's brother does something which, at the moment, astonishes her, though later she'll look back and wonder at her own surprise. He comes from behind her, while she is cracking eggs inside the bowl, and draws his bare arm up along her side. He says, bending to her throat, "It must be tough for you sometimes, huh?" and so weirdly mingles dastardly bravado and countrified awkwardness that she might laugh if she hadn't experienced any deeper reaction. As he presses his solid chest against her back, crushing her on both sides with his biceps, her girlishly warm, swooning response causes her to drop an egg unbroken into the bowl. It makes a small, insulting splash. Her eyes closed, she manages, "Get back, Stan, please get back."

And instantly mourns the loss of warmth, of solid male heat, as it retreats into the empty space behind her.

Janet drives them to the museum, all three of them packed into the Stillmans' Cutlass, the air conditioner blowing at high speed. It has been years since Gerald drove a car; he takes the bus to work, and Janet does all the other driving. Today Stan had offered to drive, but Janet quickly shook her head. Now he sits behind her and Gerald on the back seat, like their overgrown child.

"Guess I might as well tell you," Stan says sheepishly. "I've never even been to an art museum."

"This one is fairly new," she says, turning onto Peachtree Street. "It's quite spectacular."

"We haven't been, either," Gerald tells Stan.

"Not to this one," Janet says. "We went to the old museum, of course. Quite a few times."

"I don't remember one of those times," Gerald says.

There is an awkward silence. Janet doesn't know if he is needling her, deliberately, which isn't like him; or whether this is an obscure reference to the memory loss, both short-term and long-term, that he frequently claims as one of the results of his war experience. Janet finds both possibilities unsettling and decides to change the subject.

"Maybe you'll decide to take an Art History course, when you're a junior or senior," she says to Stan. "You know, as an elective."

"Well, maybe I could," Stan says slowly.

"He's going to study biology, remember?" Gerald says. "Why would he—"

"I meant as an elective," Janet repeats. "For his own enjoyment."

Gerald looks straight ahead, saying nothing. He is wearing sunglasses.

After a moment Stan says, "Well heck, why not? I could do that."

They park on a side street only a block from the museum. As they join the other Sunday afternoon strollers on the broad sidewalk, Gerald lagging a few steps behind Janet and Stan, Janet begins to feel a buoyant, light energy filling her, especially her legs. They feel elastic, springy, but she tries not to walk too quickly. At the museum entrance, Gerald keeps his sunglasses on while Stan gallantly pays their admission. They wander inside, a little dazed by the cool glaring whiteness of the walls, the pale flood of light from the numberless windows and skylights. The interior gives an illusion of weightlessness, a pleasant nullity, despite the hundreds of milling visitors, the spiraling walkways, the incessant vague rush of whispered voices, exclamations. . . . They stand on the ground floor, staring upward at the walkways that lead in a slowly ascending circle around the dome, rising to three additional floors. Watching as visitors ascend the ramp, Janet feels a familiar stab in her abdomen: the half-pleasant vertigo that has plagued her since childhood. Despite herself, she is eager to begin ascending the ramp.

Then she turns, abruptly, to see Gerald and Stan waiting next to her, looking helpless and bewildered.

"Isn't there a tour or something?" Gerald asks, embarrassed. "I hate just wandering around a place like this."

Janet gathers her patience, takes one of the brochures at a desk marked "Information," and pores over it quickly.

"The next floor is furniture and decorative arts," she explains, "and the main art collection is above that. Why don't we start up the ramp—"

"No, let's go this way," Gerald says. He points to a sign at one end of a long corridor: ELEVATOR. "It'll be quicker."

Janet looks longingly at the ramp, fascinated by its weightless suspension around the inner shell of the building. People on the ramp appear to spiral upward along the walls, released from gravity. "But—"

"You take the elevator, Gerald," Stan says. "We'll meet you upstairs."

And they separate before Janet can react. Gerald trudges toward the elevator.

"Janet, I wanted to talk for a minute, anyway," he says. "Listen, I really don't know what got into me, you know? Maybe it's because—"

He continues to apologize, awkwardly and at length. Janet scarcely listens. She is fascinated by this building, its cunning yet somehow beneficent design, seeming to cleanse one's vision of all biases of weight or color; having entered this place, she is ready to *see*. Though smiling at her own thought, she knows it is true. Every few steps up the ramp she gets a new perspective, enabled to see the enormous atrium on the ground floor, a grouping of porcelains on the second floor; and now she glimpses the majestic stillness of the European paintings just coming into view, lined along the pristine walls in their own weightless glory, enthroned like a row of grandly gazing, independent monarchs. In a single glance she picks out Renoir, Van Gogh, Delacroix, Toulouse-Lautrec.... "Here," she says, touching Stan's hand. "This is the floor we want."

As they leave the ramp Stan asks, whining, "But you understand, don't you? Please say—"

"Oh yes," she says carelessly. "Of course."

In 1972, shortly after finding his present job, Gerald had seemed to take hold of himself: it was time, he said, to put the past behind him. He was sensitive to his wife's condition, he told her. He understood her distress. Recently Janet had quit art school, abandoning her dream of teaching part-time to gifted children while simultaneously developing her own talent. She'd never worked with any real sense of discipline, or direction; she'd never had her own teacher except in the enormous public high school she attended in an Atlanta suburb, and that wasn't an atmosphere conducive to serious work. It was the summer after high school that she began her "bohemian" period, staying up till all hours and wearing her sloppy clothes, and that same summer she met Gerald when he was in town for a big weekend with some of his pals. They were engaged within two weeks, married within another month. It was during the two years of Gerald's tour duty, which followed almost immediately, that Janet had the time to think of her life and her commitments, and to understand that her love for her husband somehow transcended everything. She was left dissatisfied, a little bitter, but certain in her self-knowledge. When Gerald returned to her, hardly the same person as before, they struggled along for a while on his benefits and her part-time salary as a cocktail waitress—the last vestige of her bohemian indulgence—but she wasn't making progress anyway, she felt; her canvases seemed to her lifeless, arid, each new one a tedious variation of the last. When her husband, whom she loved, continued to flounder in the confusion of his memories, his dreams, his terror, she abruptly quit both art school and the cocktail lounge; within weeks she had an entry-level drafting position, and to her gratified surprise Gerald began immediately to improve.

He began to share some of his experiences with her, something he had never done those first few years. He used those overfamiliar words from the evening news—napalm, Tet, Khe Sanh—but in her husband's flat, disaffected voice they had the force of some exotic and furious language, making her heart beat with morbid excitement, with its own fury. He was cool, non-judgmental, failing to use the word "atrocity" though she listened and hoped for it, but he told her of the bombing of a small village, deep in the Hue province; of thatched-roof huts bursting into flame as their occupants scurried out into the surrounding brush; of the way the fires spread, so easily, to the brush itself, so that Gerald could pause and hear the screams, hear the desperate trampling rush, then look upward to see the dull, hanging smoke like a soiled thumbprint on the sky. On any day, walking through the jungle, they found charred patches of ground, as though a cancer had erupted out of nowhere, eating everything in its path, then dying mysteriously as it began. They found bodies, of course; all ages, sizes; some blackened to cinders, scarcely identifiable at all, others clean and whole, unmarked, the cause of death another mystery, not that anyone was curious. We never buried anyone, usually we didn't even stop, Gerald had said, in a dry rasping voice. I don't know, somehow it didn't seem so bad—not at the moment. They were just part of the landscape.

Janet listened patiently. Out of long habit, she stored the imagery away, although knowing she would never use it; she felt herself and Gerald involved in a process, perhaps, by which she could share his pain, story by story, image by image. But as months passed he became worse instead of better. If she spoke unexpectedly, he jumped half out of his chair; if she suggested their going to a party, he looked at her with half-incredulous horror, or he laughed bitterly. He began visiting a psychiatrist, who prescribed antidepressants. He meditated alone in his room, playing a cassette tape with his doctor's murmur guiding him along, step by step. Late at night he wandered the house, his bare feet thudding heavily, while Janet lay staring at the ceiling, helplessly monitoring his progress through the rooms. Now the kitchen, now the living room. The small half-bathroom off the hall. Again the living room. Janet's eyes were opened wide, unblinking. She would lay thinking about those wildfires, sprouting randomly through the tree-covered hills. Imagery rose in waves like the undulating hills themselves inside her brain, riddled with smoke and flame, some primordial landscape stubbornly refusing to metamorphose into anything shapely or coherent. At her sides lay her white hands, unclenched and still.

They drifted gradually, Janet and her husband, from a perspective to which the future seemed a barely possible deliverance toward a place whose past, present, and future did not seem distinct; one could use, really, a single word to designate them all. Only the week before Stan's arrival to begin his college studies, Gerald had woken her from a sound sleep, his face a half-moon floating above her bed, and that night it had been her turn to jump. "My God, you scared me half to—" "Janet, shh," he said, and she had the strange thought that he'd been drinking, or were simply talking in his sleep. Yet she saw the opened slits of his eyes, a concentration of the surrounding dark; she saw the tension in his posture, in his white shoulders and downturned head as they hovered in her terrified vision. "There's still time, isn't there?" he said. "You remember, we talked about the baby, we said maybe in a year or two. . . . Janet? Are you listening?" Then he'd made a choking sound, and had turned his head to cough; she had risen gently from the bed and taken hold of him. He said nothing more, allowing her to lead him back across the room, toward his own rumpled bed. She got him settled in, aware that he was already sleeping, certain that he had not really woken; but sleep did not return so easily to her. She lay for a long time, her eyes open. She had performed that ritual countless times—returning him like a frightened child to his bed, soothing him however she could—but it had been years since either of them had mentioned any baby.

For a while Stan follows her, like a docile child. He shifts his weight from side to side; he makes vague, appreciative comments. "Now *this* is nice," he says. In the packed, complicated silence of this room, his enthusiasm is jarring. "I like this a lot." "Yes, it's beautiful..." Janet says. They are standing before a large statue—Randolph Rogers, "Nydia, the Blind Flower Girl of Pompeii." Slowly Janet circles the statue, amazed by the compressed urgency of the girl's posture. She is hunched forward, eternally poised in flight, her limbs and drapery conveying an elegant containment in her fear, a tragic integrity. Janet stops before the girl's face, the smoothed-over sightless eyes. She imagines such a girl, a blind girl hearing cries all about her, sensing the supernatural onslaught of heat, destruction, death; the girl's emotion is somehow preserved here, in the white glittering stone.

Her fingers itching, Janet reaches to touch the girl's eyes, but Stan grabs hold of her wrist. "See the sign?" he whispers. "You're not supposed to touch anything."

She drifts away from the statue, toward a long row of Impressionist paintings. Monet, Renoir, Degas.... "Look, oh look at this," she breathes. It's a painting by Renoir, "Mademoiselle Legrand." A shy, hauntingly beautiful young girl of about twelve, her hair a glorious light-filled auburn, a tiny jewel glittering at her finger. The face conveys timidity, innocence, an eerie poise. This child will become a child-woman, Janet thinks, fascinated by the balancing of elements—the child's elegance and beauty, the artist's sense of doom.

At her side, Stan is growing restless. "Shouldn't we find Gerald?" he says. "Is he—"

She refuses to hear him; her awareness is filled by these glorious paintings. She moves from one to the next, feeling herself alone at last, cut loose, floating—how was it possible that she'd stayed away so long? That the pictures hung here, day in and day out, without her coming to pay homage, to match their exhilaration with her own? Now she stands before a small, unfamiliar painting by Van Gogh—"Woman in a Wood." At first glance an unappealing work, heavy with dark greens and browns, muddy-looking. Like the numberless trees, the woman is little more than a stilled column, a slab of paint applied rapidly, angrily. But entering the picture, Janet feels its power. The woman is trapped, of course; even the sky offers no hope in this landscape so rampant with life, claustral, entangling its human victim. Janet can readily imagine a pinprick of flame arising somewhere in those woods, spreading rapidly, cleansing the landscape of all good, all evil. She takes a deep breath, then another. Trembling, her hand floats toward the painting, one finger outstretched as if touching the woman, or the slab of paint that represents the woman, might somehow comfort her—the way her mother had comforted her when she was a child, waking in tears. It's only a dream, Janet—only a dream. But as her finger nears the canvas, she feels a man's hands enclosing her waist; his breath is warm against her throat. She turns around, startled and angry.

"What are you—"

"What's wrong?" Gerald says, confused. Clearly, he is more startled than she.

"Oh, it's you—but you shouldn't—"

She breaks off. Can she blame her husband, really? But neither can she make him understand, of course, or even communicate her exhilaration, her sense of power. She gives him her old smile —conciliating, mildly hopeful.

"Where's Stan?" she asks, but she is watching Gerald. There is something strange about him; he seems shy, boyish. He has removed the sunglasses, revealing eyes of a pale, aching blue. Have they always been that color? she wonders. He takes one of her hands and kisses it.

"Could we leave?" he asks, gently. "I can't look at this stuff. . . ." His voice is flat, apologetic.

"You mean—the Impressionists?" she says. "Or—"

"All of it," Gerald says.

They find Stan and walk soberly back to the car. For several minutes they sit awkwardly silent, but then Janet says: "I'm coming back, you know. I'm coming back next Sunday."

They are stopped at a red light. Her hands rise to her face, fluttering—but why should she be nervous? She has not spoken in anger, but as if she were alone in the car.

Following a stray impulse, she puts down the visor and stares for a moment into the small mirror. She sees a blond-haired, reasonably pretty woman, wearing an unreadable expression. Tense, expectant, insolent? She is pale, perhaps too pale, excepting the small, feverish blossoms at the tops of her cheeks.

How long since she has stared into a mirror? she wonders. But yes, there she is. She remembers.

Gerald has turned toward the rear of the car. "So, how do you feel about tomorrow, eh?" he says to Stan, who leans forward, his big arms along the top of the front seat. "It's a big day, isn't it?"

Janet hears the falsity, the desperation in Gerald's words to his brother; they spark a flame in her heart so sudden, so merciless, that she literally clutches the wheel.

"Yeah, I'm looking forward to it," Stan says, grinning. "I'm looking forward to everything."

Distant Friends

A GYPSY CHILD of the Sixties, Lex travelled most of the year. He had money, but this was hardly apparent; he still carried a knapsack, wore blue jeans faded at the knees and seat. Though nearing forty, from a few feet away he looked youthful, if rather indistinct. A girlfriend once wrote to Lex that after a few months' separation she couldn't summon him in her mind's eye: he tended to fade, lose his outlines. The letter was catty, Lex knew, but it had absurdly cheered him.

When in late October he got a call from Marty Krieger, his friend who lived on the other end of the continent, Lex had been about to take off but hadn't yet decided where. Boulder, Colorado was still his "home base" because he'd gone to college there, and because the place where he'd grown up—a small city in southern Georgia—had in Lex's imagination entered the realm of myth. (His parents were dead, his memories of other relatives still in Georgia resembled cartoon figures from some grotesque Southern novel he might have read, but would never read again.) Nowadays he seldom went further south than Birmingham/ Atlanta/Richmond, and made those stops only briefly as he looped from the Southwest up toward New England, his favorite part of the country. Here in Boulder, he had a small efficiency in a building he owned and spent much of his time managing; it was overrun with college kids who had an intuitive grasp, it seemed, of who he was, why he was there. Headed themselves for hard-driving careers in business or high-tech, they perhaps saw in Lex a line of development, vestigial but sympathetic, they might gladly have followed except for some accident of politics or culture, whatever had pulled them into the shunting, hard-surfaced world that had replaced the world of Lex's extreme youth, that storm of bullets and flowers.

"Marty? You sound upset," Lex said into the phone. He listened to the faint roar of long distance, that obscure crackling. His friend sobbed again.

"Lex, I hate to bother you, but it's Priscilla. This time, she might not make it. So the doctors say."

The last time—just before Lex's previous visit to New York, a year earlier—she almost hadn't made it, either. Priscilla was the Kriegers' daughter, five or six by now, whose supposedly "mild" cerebral palsy had brought vicious complications more than once. "They said that before, Marty, don't forget—that's *exactly* what they said."

"No point in blaming the doctors, Lex."

"But they're always negative—you know, just in case. Got to cover their asses." He was almost shouting.

There was a long pause from Marty. "I feel guilty for calling you, I know you've had more than your share of hospitals, doctors . . . but this time, Lex, Diane is really wiped out. She won't even talk to me. Sits outside the room in this pitiful folding chair, just staring. The doctors say let her sit."

Imagery of his mother's slow death in 1969, uterine cancer, the place he'd started out gone bad, rotted; of his brother's quicker fading in 1971, flown back from Vietnam with "internal injuries," cancer in another form. *Don't die on me, Pete, we're the family now, we're the pitiful remains!* He'd done some sitting, some staring of his own.

"Well, they're right about that," he admitted to Marty.

"When you came that other time," Marty said, softly, "it was such a help—"

"Marty, I'll be glad to come."

He had nothing better to do than try to help Marty and Diane Krieger. He was a vagabond, after all; he was an "heir." Yet that evening he packed without much sense of motivation, and though he'd promised Marty he would arrive by noon, the next morning he cancelled his plane reservation and decided instead to drive the little bone-colored Valiant he used to crisscross the country once or twice each year. He'd make good time, and from the details he'd gleaned from Marty he gathered that Priscilla, for the moment, was stable—even if her parents weren't. Driving, Lex wondered about his own ability to help Marty and Diane. Back in college, when Lex and Marty were roommates during their junior and senior years, it had been Marty with his sure-fire accounting brain and tight-assed ways—as Lex liked to kid him—who had to look after his slovenly friend, whose laziness extended to his politics (he had to be dragged to protest marches) and even to his drugs (he bummed off everyone in the dorm). Lex could still summon a pleased nostalgia for himself in college —that same pair of jeans worn two years straight, the straggly blond hair halfway to the shoulder and tied with a red bandanna he'd frame now if it hadn't been lost in his wanderings, the indifference toward his classes that was often mingled, especially if the topic were philosophy or literature, with a thrusting, combative style of inquiry that the other students distrusted and his professors feared. He hadn't been likable, though Marty and a few others had called him on his "act"; they saw to the docile and plaintively bewildered soul underneath. When he graduated, and then suffered the loss of his mother in the same year, they hadn't been surprised when he cut his hair and took a job writing newspaper copy right there in Boulder and married an orthodox Jewish girl who had her own money. But they also hadn't been surprised when he divorced her two years later and when, after Pete died, he quit the job and spent long stretches of time away from Boulder, unreachable by telephone or mail. At least one had assumed, he later told Lex, that Lex had gone to "find himself," but Lex had been even less embarrassed by the cliché than his friend had been.

One thing he had found was another cliché—the open road— and in the decadence that accompanies bereavement he'd recovered, then indulged a boyhood romance with the lives of truck drivers, traveling salesmen. The great wanderers. (His father, who had died when Lex was ten without having touched a penny of his wife's money, had been a farm equipment salesman; the stories he told Lex on his return from sales trips, true or not, were now the staple of Lex's memories of his father. The romance was what was left of his father, just as what remained of his mother was an image of eternal grim patience and of his 19-year-old brother a wild, improbable hope for the future.) Because Lex's college friends had scattered in all directions, as if thoughtfully providing the dots for Lex to join as he moved in the grim and patient Valiant across state lines and time zones, there was never the fright in Lex's life of reaching a destination: he made stops, some brief and others protracted, but eventually he went away. For his friends, Lex supposed that something called "normal life" resumed after he left, though their lives were never normal while he was there. Hospitals, funeral homes, divorce courts had been some of his past destinations, and now he understood the romance of the endlessly meandering voyage; as his friends pretended to, as well, feeling their confinements vicariously released through him. It fascinated Lex that his friends were always the ones to call—*Come visit us! Come witness our triumph! Come share our pain!* they cried from Dallas, Lake Forest, New York City. Never once had Lex showed up anywhere uninvited.

It was Marty, in fact, who had angrily pointed this out, though Lex had been uncomprehending at first, and rather defensive. It was mid-December, three or four years ago, when Lex had called Marty "for no reason," mentioning that it had been a while since their last visit. Although Marty was the most emotional man he had ever known, Lex hadn't been prepared for his reaction: he became suddenly furious, insisting that if Lex had nothing planned for the holidays he didn't need to "fish" for an invitation. Why the hell was Lex so fearful, so held back, as if they were mere acquaintances?—as if they hadn't been close friends for nearly two decades? It was really a kind of insult, wasn't it, Lex's refusal to ask outright for anything? A way of disclaiming the friendship?

Alarmed, Lex had changed the phone to his other ear, casting his eyes about the room; but he said nothing. He pictured Marty

—short, swarthy, powerfully built; his dark eyes quick-moving, guileless. Lex imagined him performing a familiar gesture, running a hand through his curly black hair, exasperated. Lex wanted to speak, but in addition to remorse he felt a twinge of his own anger, for how could Marty dare to criticize him? What had happened to their humorous rapport, that longstanding mutual tolerance that had sustained them for so many years? Lex waited, feeling an unfamiliar stubbornness, and of course Marty had apologized, describing the stress he'd been suffering due to Priscilla's condition, not to mention Diane's growing depression, her frightening unpredictability—but still there was no excuse, Marty said, he'd never spoken to Lex that way before, had he, in all these years had they exchanged a genuinely harsh word? No, Lex had replied, but it's all right—really. I completely understand.

And Marty had taken a deep breath. His anxiety had been nearly palpable through the wires. Then you'll come for the holidays? he asked. Why not plan a long visit, stay right through New Year's . . . ?

Of course, Lex had said, relieved. I'll be glad to come.

When he reached Philadelphia, Lex remembered another friend. A girl he'd known in Boulder, Suzie Clegg, but hadn't really dated: she'd been a sophomore, lived in Lex's building with two roommates, had stayed only a semester. Yet she gave him an address when she moved, and sent him a postcard once or twice a year. Nineteen, honey-blond hair, a quick and somehow boyish laugh: even at the time he admitted that she frightened him. He'd recently turned thirty and had felt certain, with comical but genuinely painful despair, that his life was winding down. Now he had a sensation of panic, again, to think that after all this time she would still be in her twenties, and probably had not lost her infectious gaiety, her athletic, bouncing walk. She'd reminded him of a tennis star, he recalled now: Tracy Austin. But taller, with that graceful slope to her shoulders. More womanly.

He found himself in a corner phone booth in Center City, somewhere on Twelfth Street; it turned out that she lived only a few blocks away. He thought of calling Marty in New York, but then glanced at his watch—it was past midnight—and pictured his friend in the waiting room outside Intensive Care, slumped inside a vinyl chair, eyelids fallen shut. Lex was exhausted, himself; he'd spent last night in a scrubby motel, somewhere outside St. Louis, and was on the road again by seven this morning. And he wondered at his own audacity, calling Suzie Clegg out of the blue after seven years, past twelve o'clock on a weeknight. He came out of the phone booth with the collar of his leather jacket turned up, clutching the paper where he'd scribbled the directions she gave him.

Inside the apartment, she had to chide him out of the jacket. "Come on, it's chilly out," she laughed. "But not *that* cold."

It was true: this was only October, the temperature in the fifties.

He grinned. "Sorry," he said, hoping his awkwardness didn't show and knowing it didn't. Often, arriving anywhere, he felt himself a stationary object around which his friends busied themselves, as if acknowledging his wandering soul, his need for respite. Suzie took the jacket, hung it in a small but impeccably ordered closet, and handed him a glass of dark beer, talking all the while. She seemed absurdly happy.

He'd explained on the phone, but he said again, "I've got these friends in New York, Marty and Diane Krieger. Their little girl..."

"Yes, that's really awful," Suzie Clegg said, clicking her tongue. Her round blue eyes were pained, wondering as a child's.

Then he remembered. "You were going to work with kids, weren't you? A psychologist, something like that?"

"Physical therapy," she said, with a shrug of those lovely shoulders. She wore a wide-necked blouse that all but revealed them, and did reveal her taut collarbone and the tops of her pale breasts. A peasant blouse, he thought they were called, loosely fitted but alluring. She wore no bra; her jeans were tighter than his own.

"But I didn't make it," she said, pointing to her temple. "Didn't have it up here."

"I don't believe that."

They were standing near a small, battered sofa covered in brown corduroy; she had lost her hostessy good cheer and now seemed stalled, distracted. Why hadn't she suggested they sit down? Lex put his beer on a low table beside them. Suddenly everything pleased him: her confusion, the shabbiness of this cramped apartment, the sharpened image of himself her rather alarmed gaze gave back to him.

He stepped forward and they kissed, first gingerly, then with such fierce absorption that he lost himself again but it hardly mattered. Lying with her on the bedraggled sofa, he felt that within her orderly, chastened existence she had set herself adrift, had continued through the years with steadily diminished expectations. He had associated her with an affluent background, recalled a family on the Main Line, but when he asked her about it she smirked, her first hint of irony. "They don't approve of my life, the way I live," she murmured. She'd taken his hand, spreading his capable strong fingers as if preparing to suck them, like a child. "They only agreed to my going to Boulder because they hoped I'd meet someone there, get married, and when I flunked out Daddy got me a job in a bank, right here in Philly. But that lasted all of three days." She laughed, letting the irony slip away. She kissed each of his fingertips on one hand. "Anyway, I've been pretty much on my own since then. I'm not unhappy, though. I have friends, usually I have a good time. . . .

"What do you do?" he said, hoarsely as if rising from sleep. "For money, I mean."

"Right now I'm waiting tables," she said, again with her inconsequent laugh. "I really like it, though."

"No reason you shouldn't," he said.

"Of course, I have no idea where I'm going," and this time when she laughed Lex resisted the impulse to lay his palm across her mouth.

"Who does?" he said at last, softly.

She asked him to stay the night, and his only regret came the next morning when he stood, naked, before her peeling bathroom mirror with his face half shaved. The steam from his shower had begun melting off the mirror; the strokes of his razor slowly revealed his long, bony face, a face that might be twenty-five, or forty-five. His eyes were a pale blue, with only a few thin lines raying out from their corners; his wet hair was sand-colored, cut in a youthful, anonymous style. He had known so many people in his life, he thought, yet none of them knew where he was at this moment. Nor did he know, himself; before leaving he'd need to get more directions. Then, just as he noticed how his skin had paled beneath the stark-white remains of the lather, she came up behind him, smiling. She wore the same blouse as last night, but her hair was disheveled, as if pushed back carelessly with a single sweep of both hands. In the bleak light from the room's small, high window her hair appeared the same color as his own.

"Morning," she said, circling his waist.

He tried to smile; it was absurd, but his nakedness embarrassed him. Had she glimpsed his fear, his panic? No.

"I'll need to be leaving in a while," he said, politely. "I've got—"

"I know," she said, with something of the old, cheerful Suzie in her voice. She pressed her cheek against his warm, damp shoulder. "You've got friends in New York."

After breakfast, she gave him directions. He asked her to keep sending the postcards.

In the past decade, Lex had visited the Kriegers more than anyone else. They were the nearest he had to a "family," allowing him to return now and then, a beloved prodigal, and to depart just as abruptly. The Kriegers were not offended when he stayed at his favorite fleabag hotel in the Village instead of using the spare room of their brownstone. Marty had recently joined a prestigious accounting firm as full partner and Diane owned a thriving art gallery, but they never talked about their money and Lex never apologized for his. He and Marty had sustained their boisterous, pretended antagonisms through the years, while Lex and Diane had developed a camaraderie like a brother and sister's, tinged with erotic attraction. She was a small, slender-boned woman with luxuriant dark hair—a princess out of the Old Testament, Lex had once thought, a regal and mystical quiet beneath her abundant energy, charm, and good cheer. Lex had always thought her the perfect complement to Marty, who tended to brood and who took everything so seriously. Lex loved both the Kriegers, and normally visited in both the spring and fall. Last April he'd had to decline their invitation because of some repairs he had undertaken for the boarding house, but the previous year their visit had gone well, Priscilla having recovered from a serious bout with a lung infection, both Marty and Diane seeming invigorated by their latest triumph over fate.

This trip, Lex stopped at the hotel only long enough to drop off his bags and have his car parked in a garage before taking a taxi to the hospital.

He asked directions at the front desk, and when he reached Intensive Care half-expected to find Diane just as Marty had described her. As it happened, the folding chair was there but Diane was not. He found her in a windowless beige waiting room halfway down the corridor, huddled in a small chair of sculpted blue plastic with a blanket over her knees. He stopped at the doorway, lips parted in shock.

"Yes, it's me." She smiled wanly.

The smile both reassured and terrified him. Her face was creased and pale, the lines cutting most severely at the sides of her mouth. He felt an absurd reflex of anger, that she wore no makeup and had let her hair fall limp and bedraggled to her shoulders. Why hadn't he known it would be this bad? He'd heard the pleading, the terror in Marty's voice.

"Diane," he said gently. He came forward, pulling a chair next to hers. She sat with her arms and knees drawn inward, toward her womb; there was a sweet, helpless resignation in her posture that he'd never have connected with Diane. He tried to remember the feisty art dealer, the competent mother and wise friend.

"You took a long while," she murmured, idly. "Marty said—"

A nurse had appeared in the doorway.

"Yes?" Diane said, leaning forward with such urgency that Lex's arms came open to catch her fall. But she didn't notice; her eyes were glassy, opened wide so that the white showed above the sable iris.

"Has Mr. Krieger come back?" the nurse asked, politely. She

ignored Diane's alarm, in that "professional" way of hospital staff that Lex found so maddening: bad things aren't happening here, the rhetoric implied; you're childish to think so. The nurse was a pleasantly smiling blonde in her twenties, several months pregnant, but even so Lex wanted to slap her.

"No, not yet," Diane said, "he had to get some rest. Why do you need him? Couldn't I—"

The nurse shook her head. "That's all right, we can call him at home," she said, and now Lex had an inkling about the way she was handling Diane: the child's mother could not take any more stress, deal strictly with the father. Perhaps Marty himself had seen to this.

The nurse glanced at Lex, her eyes alert but unreadable; he felt she had assessed and dismissed him. Then she vanished. Diane sank back in her chair, eyes closed.

"That's the way they treat me," she said. "Like a child. A moron."

"They're trying to spare you," Lex said. "When Pete was in the hospital, I remember—" but he stopped. She didn't need to hear about that.

She kept her eyes closed, saying nothing.

"I would have gotten here sooner," he said, "but at the last minute I decided to drive. I spent last night in Philly."

He did not know what to say to her; like the nurse, he wanted to protect her, talk lightly of inconsequential things. But that would be insulting, and he had always believed in Diane. He decided to plunge in.

"Diane, how is she? How do things stand?"

She raised her head, and the look she gave him told more than her words: "Last night was the worst night. We almost lost her, Lex. Twice. They had a—what do you call it, Code 99. It's her breathing. She can't breathe."

She sucked in her own breath; Lex's gaze fell to the floor. He took her hand as she wept, but he still felt he'd never been more useless than from the moment he'd entered this room.

"It's—it's pneumonia," she choked out. "I guess Marty told you."

"Yes," Lex said.

"They're giving her as much oxygen as they can. They're doing what they can."

"Yes," he said.

They were silent for a while, and then Diane moved from the chair to the small vinyl sofa; a pillow in one corner already bore the mark of her small head. "Try to rest," Lex told her and she nodded, murmured something unintelligible.

He went out immediately and found the nurse.

No, she said, it wasn't a good idea for him to see Priscilla; in any case, she was comatose. When Mr. Krieger returned, perhaps he would authorize it, but she didn't want to disturb him again. To Lex's surprise the nurse reached out, touching his forearm, and he understood that his sore heart showed in his eyes. "We're glad you're here," the nurse said. "They'd been talking about you, saying you were coming." "I'd have been here sooner—" Lex began. "Most of their friends seem to just pop in," the nurse said, "leave some flowers and then disappear. It's understandable, of course. We see that all the time. This is a tough situation, no one knows what to say or how they can help." Lex nodded, dazed by her quick understanding, her clarity. He felt groggy. He asked, in a voice that must have sounded timid, "Will she make it? Is there any chance?" And the nurse said, calmly, "No, I'm afraid not. That's why your being here is so helpful."

He wandered the hospital corridors, not feeling helpful. Every few minutes he checked on Diane, who had slumped into one corner of the sofa; a discarded rag doll, he thought. He remembered that he had given Priscilla a rag doll on his previous visit; her birthday had been only the week before. Opening the package with her mother's help, she'd said nothing at first, but a slow and unforgettable smile had widened her mouth. Then she'd said "Tenk yuh" in her slurred speech, clumsily folding the doll in her arms, and Lex had understood, really for the first time, the passionate absorption of Marty and Diane in her every movement and gesture—the beatific calm of Diane when she helped feed Priscilla, or adjusted the neckline of her dress; the glittering tension in Marty's eyes as he watched them both. When he strained to remember his own early childhood, he didn't recall that his parents had been so protective or solicitous; after all, he'd been a healthy boy. Once, on a car trip through the Rockies, they'd encountered an obstruction in the road—a large dog of some kind—and his father braked abruptly and swerved onto the shoulder of the highway. Lex, four or five, had been standing on the front seat between his parents, and he'd felt both their arms shoot outward to keep him from crashing into the windshield. Afterward his mother had laughed, nervously. "Whoo, that was a close one!" she exclaimed. "Poor dog," his father said, craning his neck backward, his arm still out although they'd come to a stop. "Yes, poor thing," his mother agreed. His parents' voices came back to him gently intertwined, a duet; they seemed ghostly and distant as voices remembered from a dream.

Yet his memories, Lex thought, were no more dreamlike than the present—the hours, the moments he was living through. For several years an eerie sensation had plagued him that each day, each friend, each lover that held his earnest if mysteriously weak attention had no connection to anything else, and not much to him. He had no sense of unity, only of brief pockets of time, filled with numbness or elation, and a fleeting sense of relationship to this or that person. Islands of experience, he thought. Accidents. His life existed only as a product of his own "will," an idea that was laughable but somehow true. He could not will himself into a different life any more than his friends, Marty and Diane, could will their daughter back to health. He was himself, nothing more, and could not apologize. Lately, when he received the monthly estate check and would glance at his name, so neatly typed—*Alexander S. Stevens III*—his heart for a moment gave a shimmer of denial, as though emptying out his past and his disconnected love in a kind of visceral abandon. Then he would turn the check over and hastily scrawl the name. He would think how to spend it—repairs to the boarding house, gifts to faraway, impoverished relations, a gadget or two that might ease, but not clutter, the minimal flow of his life.

Whether the predictable dailiness or the little shocks of life depressed him more Lex couldn't have said, but when he returned to the waiting area and found Diane standing out in the hall, hugging herself and looking precarious—several nurses were gathered around her, brisk and talkative—he felt a familiar stab of dread. Everything had been so quiet, so unthreatening just moments before. When she saw him, Diane reached out one arm but then retracted it; the arm curled back around her abdomen, a desperate embrace. Lex singled out the blond nurse and drew her aside.

"Mr. Krieger is on his way," she told him. Her starched cap had come loose, and sat lopsided on her head. Lex's heart filled with terror.

The nurse added, in a lower voice, "The decision was made a while ago—you know, what to do when it came to this. That's why we phoned him."

"She's gone, then?" he said, in a wondering tone.

She nodded once. "You can go inside now, if you like."

He said quickly, "I can't," but as relief lightened him, guilt pulled him down. He could not move.

Again the nurse touched his forearm, smiling. He looked across the hall to Diane, who kept hugging herself with one arm and shredded a kleenex in her other hand. The nurses stayed near her, one of them keeping the flat of her hand, a prop, held between Diane's shoulder blades. The whites had expanded around the dark, roving points of Diane's eyes. For a moment they snagged on him, and his heart lurched; but they released him just as quickly. He felt that he watched her through a telescope, from an incalculable distance.

Then there was commotion behind them, an elevator door shuddering open and a man's loud, fast footsteps. Marty. He went immediately to Diane and held her, while Lex watched. Marty was crying. He murmured a few words into Diane's ear, and though she did not respond—she looked dazed, incapable of language—he left her, disappearing through the swinging doors of Intensive Care. Two of the nurses followed him, including the blond one. Lex wanted to cry out.

When Marty returned a moment later, however, he came directly toward Lex. Or rather, someone came toward Lex whom he half-recognized as Marty, his old friend. This man's face, tear-stained, seethed darkly with rage; he ran a hand through his curly dark hair as though reaching some final state of distraction, a point of no return. His eyes were pinpricks of darkness fixed upon Lex.

"Just look at you, look at you standing there," Marty said in a rough, trembling voice. His thick chest heaved beneath a wrinkled, wine-colored pullover. Lex pictured Marty's heart, beating fiercely in that big chest. "We don't need you *now*, do we?" Marty said, with vicious sarcasm. Lex remembered that his friend had a clever, wry sense of humor; he was never sarcastic. This was someone else. "It's a little late in the day, isn't it Lex? Your sorry presence isn't really required, is it? At this point?"

A nurse approached Marty but he waved her away.

"Marty, don't," Diane whimpered, and everyone looked at her in surprise. "He got held up, and anyway it's not his—"

"No, nothing is ever *his* fault," Marty said. "How could it be?" But his voice held a dying fall; he turned aside.

This had been, evidently, the final word, and in fact was a statement Lex pondered carefully once Marty had led Diane through the swinging doors and Lex had walked numbly to the elevators, where he illuminated the downward-pointing arrow with a single, unfelt touch of his finger.

Nothing is ever his fault, how could it be?

Downstairs, he sat at a small, sticky table in the coffee shop, then went to the doorway and stood there for a while, waiting. At the end of a long corridor were the elevators he had just used and he stood watching them, as though maintaining a vigil. He willed those doors to open. He willed his friend, Marty, to come hurtling out. Lex did not understand why this moment should be so important, and when the doors did open and Marty did come hurrying out, looking distracted and contrite, he did not understand the wild longing in his heart as he glanced to his left, to an automatic glass door that awaited only his footstep before admitting him into the wide, anonymous world outside.

He ignored his own emotion, of course, but later he would think that his sudden urge for flight, for distance, had shocked him as much as anything else that had happened.

ABOUT THE AUTHOR

Greg Johnson lives in Atlanta, Georgia, where he attended Emory University and earned a Ph.D. in American literature. The author of two volumes of literary criticism, he has also published fiction, poetry, and essays in a variety of magazines, including *The Southern Review*, *The Georgia Review*, *Ontario Review*, and *The Virginia Quarterly Review*. His stories have been reprinted in such anthologies as *Prize Stories: The O. Henry Awards* and *New Stories from the South: The Year's Best*. He has taught creative writing at Emory University and the University of Mississippi, and is now an associate professor of English at Kennesaw State College.